THE SLEEPER'S MOLE

ION ESIMAI

CIPARUM
PRESS

eISBN-978-1-63589-724-1
Paperback ISBN - 978-1-63589-725-8
Hardcover ISBN- 978-1-63589-726-5

Editing by Lee Caleca - Caleca Editing Services

Ciparum Press
270 Sparta Ave., Suite 104, PMB 152
Sparta, NJ 07871

GET THE NEWSLETTER
Sign up and receive a FREE copy of my book- There Are No Mountain Lions In New Jersey-and latest information on my upcoming novels! Click on Ion Esimai Newsletter to sign up.

Authors website:- www.ionesimai.com

PROLOGUE

Feodor

Feodor expected a crunch, but let out a heavy sigh when he caught sight of the squirrel in the side view mirror scurrying across the remaining half of the road tail raised high. He wasn't on a murdering spree, just had two simple rules when it came to animals dashing across the road right in front of his car. Never step on the brakes. Never swerve. You'll only end up losing control and killing yourself.

He rolled his tongue around his mouth. He was sore in some areas, a few loose teeth. The tangy metallic taste of blood coated his tongue. He must have taken one or two in the mouth. It had happened so fast.

A sadness he'd never felt since his days in the Baltic states enveloped him. Right now, he had crossed the point of no return. He knew this was the beginning of the end unless he acted real fast. He recalled the plan Yurik came with and wondered, why this time? It didn't make sense.

Inside the car was freezing; his fingers were almost frozen. Feodor turned the heater on and cranked it up. It bellowed like a hairdryer.

As the inside of the car got warmer, the smell of cheap cologne, body odor, and stale sweat engulfed Feodor. He glanced at his passenger, shook his head slowly, and then turned off the heater.

He pushed a button and the window lowered with a scraping hum. Cold air poured in, while hot air rushed out like a dog that needed to pee. Within a few seconds, the car was saturated with cold Sussex County air.

Feodor worked up a mouth full of sputum, stuck his head out of the window and spat. He wanted to remove the taste of death coating his tongue. It didn't go far. Some landed on the door frame, and some dripped down his lips. He wiped his mouth with the back of his hand. It was still sore and painful from the scrimmage.

Feodor's dry, calloused fingers made a rough grating sound as he ran his palms over the leather of the arc of the steering wheel. At his job, he came out of the booth each time a car pulled up, but he always wore gloves in cold weather. He wished he had on his glove from work.

The air roaring into the car reeked of burning wood, the smell of Christmas. That was three weeks ago. Santa and his reindeer were long gone.

Daylight was fading as Feodor continued along the windy rural road at a steady pace. The last thing he wanted was to be pulled over by a cop. Cops out here were known to be particularly snitty when they became bored sitting by the side of the road waiting for someone going two miles an hour over the posted speed limit. And in some areas, speed limits weren't even posted.

The terrain outside hadn't changed for miles—a parade of trees on both sides. Most had lost their leaves and looked like they were upturned, with their roots sticking up in the air. A striking resemblance to Medusa, the Greek maiden who was turned into a monster by Athena, the mythological goddess of war.

Feodor was in a war of his own. His thoughts drifted back to his passenger, and he looked at him. Yurik appeared to be sleeping, his body held in place by the seat belt, his head resting on his chest in an awkward position.

Feodor shook his head and sighed again. Assassinations had been easy business when it was his nine to five. Clean up was never part of the job. Now he had a mess on his hands, how to get rid of Yurik's body.

At sixty-three, five feet nine inches with a little body pain here and there, Feodor considered himself in good shape, but digging a hole was out of the question. The ground was frozen, and even if he tried, the best he could accomplish in a few hours would be a shallow grave. The smell would draw little critters to the location for a feast. He might as well dump the body on the ground and cover it with dried leaves.

If there had been snow on the ground maybe that would have been a good plan. Plant the body in the woods under snow and be long gone before some over-enthusiastic hiking nut or some animal discovered it.

Alternatively, he could buy a deep freezer and keep the body in his apartment until an opportune time to dispose of it. But that is the type of plan you make before, not after.

Thinking of a freezer made his stomach rumble. At home, he had a frozen meat lasagna TV dinner he was looking forward to after dropping off his august visitor. The smell of tomato sauce and sausages as it bubbled in the microwave and the taste after was vivid in his mind. Feodor was glad that a little violence still did not affect his appetite. Now his visitor had become permanent, and his dinner probably would remain frozen.

As if in answer to his predicament, a few snowflakes landed on his windshield. His excitement rose and fell almost immediately. It would take hours of heavy snowfall, a Nor'easter, to produce enough snow to bury a body. He had to come up with a solid plan like yesterday.

This patch of Route 181 was mostly deserted at this time of the night, dark and ominous. You wouldn't want to have your car break down here. The only advantage he had now was the approaching darkness.

Feodor looked into the woods at the procession of trees as he passed by. "Think, think," he said to himself. Now and then, he would return his gaze to the road. Light from the moon glistened off bodies of water scattered in the woods, some small, some large. He saw a large pond about the size of a football field, and an idea popped into his head. Tie the spare tire to Yurik and throw his body into the pond, then drive to the airport and vanish.

Now that was a credible plan. Pulse racing, Feodor stepped down on the gas. His eyes darted from the road to the woods, searching for a break in the foliage so he could drive up as close as possible to the pond and dump the body.

He returned his gaze to the road, and his breath caught in a sharp inhale. An animal stood in his path, the second time tonight.

"What is this!" The animal was larger, like a deer. One yellow reflection shined back at him. What animal was that? His grip on the wheel tightened. The animal wouldn't budge.

It looked more like a cat—a huge cat. But, there are no mountain lions in Jersey. Everyone knows that.

What happened next was pure reflex. Feodor hit the brakes—hard. The tires screeched, but the car continued moving. A body in motion stays in motion unless acted upon by an external force. Newton's first law of motion; he had learned that at the university in Moscow. He swerved, missing the animal. Within seconds he'd broken all his well thought out rules. And the next thing he knew, he was in a roller coaster, turning over and over. His life flashed before him. He felt a sharp pain on his head and then blackness.

1

Chelsea

Chelsea Piers set her plate down in front of her and stared at the TV. It seemed like everyone in XRCure had decided this was the best time to come to the cafeteria for lunch. She should have waited another five minutes before leaving her office. She would have had the place to herself.

At five feet eight inches tall with an athletic build, Chelsea was a confident woman. Dressed in blue scrubs and a white lab coat, with her blond hair in a ponytail, Chelsea could have been another medical practitioner walking the corridors of a hospital or clinic attending to patients. But she preferred the behind the scene part of medicine, and most of all, situations where she worked by herself. Research suited her best. She didn't dislike people, but being introverted, it was draining for her whenever she had to be out there with others.

An only child, and with both parents being physicians, one could say Chelsea was strategically placed for a lifetime of service in healthcare. Her father always joked that if it weren't for research, Chelsea would have hated ever following in their footsteps.

She had always had a curious mind. Computers had been her first love. Soon, she was learning about writing codes from books and watching videos online.

When she turned eight, she'd asked her parents for a computer and microscope as a birthday present. She could transfer images from her microscope to her laptop and see them in greater detail. She marveled at the different designs out there in nature.

Her fascination with microbes from a young age influenced her decision to study microbiology in college. Chelsea knew firsthand about microorganisms, and the damage they could do. After graduating from Harvard Medical School, she did a residency in internal medicine and a fellowship in infectious diseases. Chelsea's other love was coding. She was self-taught; even before she fell in love with microbes, she'd been coding, and the concept of AI, Artificial Intelligence fascinated her.

The smell of fries, spices, and coffee hung in the air of the cafeteria, reminding Chelsea of the food court at Rockaway Mall. Maybe she should have just gotten coffee instead of the Caesar salad that sat on her plate.

The sound of the TV became loud as if a ghost had gone by and hushed everyone. Chelsea looked around. All eyes were glued to the television.

The director for the Center for Disease Control, CDC, was talking about the current virus ravaging Wuhan, China.

. . .

"CORONAVIRUS DISEASE *2019 (COVID-19)* IS MAKING ITS WAY *across the globe. Its spread is remarkably like that of the ancient medieval plague that history books tell us also started in China, and moved west.*

"But unlike the ancient plague, it is advancing in leaps and bounds. With the world now a global village, an individual exposed in one end of the world could, within hours, land at the opposite end of the world, and being asymptomatic would spread the virus unbeknownst to them. Right now, it is not a matter of if, but when it becomes a pandemic."

APART FROM THE SMELL OF FOOD AND COFFEE, ANOTHER odor hung in the air, the scent of fear. Chelsea's pulse picked up a notch. Would she and the other researchers trying to tackle this be able to find a solution before it was too late? To her, it was a personal challenge, like playing hide and seek, looking for answers. And most of all, the surprise of finding them where you least expected.

There were already pockets of infected people, but when it reached epidemic proportions in the US as in China, people would freak out. Panic was never good for anything. She pulled her eyes away from the TV and let out a breath. She glanced at Lisa, sitting opposite her and pushed her plate to the side.

Lisa looked at her. "Lost your appetite, Chelsea? I don't blame you." She took a big bite off her cheeseburger and nodded at the TV. "That will stop anyone from eating."

Chelsea chuckled and pulled her plate back. She picked up her fork and shuffled the veggies in her Caesar salad around as if dribbling in a soccer match. She looked at Lisa.

"You're not worried?"

Lisa raised a finger, the universal sign for just a moment.

But, she still spoke anyway through a mouth full of half-chewed food. "I am. But with-" She squinted her eyes and focused on Chelsea's name badge on her Lab coat. "With people like Chelsea Piers, MD, Chief Researcher, working tirelessly to find us a cure, I'm confident we'll find a way out sooner than later. With the amount of time we've...you've put into this, a breakthrough is coming."

Chelsea pushed her plate away a second time. Lisa was right. They had been focused on another virus, but with the numbers coming out of China and Europe, they decided to revisit the coronavirus treatment they'd been working on previously to see if they could make it effective against the present outbreak.

The debacle with the 2016 Ebola outbreak had taught everyone a lesson. We don't have to wait for a disease outbreak before we start looking for cures. Some of these diseases were discovered a long time ago. But, because the demographic ravaged by the disease didn't have the financial capacity to pay for the treatment, most research labs, especially the bigger ones, would rather spend their millions where they would make huge profits from their investment.

Then, there's the general public's attitude—as long as it's not happening in my backyard, it's not my concern. But, since Ebola, most of the more prominent labs are rethinking their strategy. As the CDC director said, outbreaks could become pandemics within days.

"Busy mind, eh?" asked Lisa. "You seem far away."

Chelsea smiled. "No, I'm right here. I was just thinking of another approach to this madness. I wish I had as much faith in myself as you have in me."

"Are you scared?" asked Lisa.

"Of course. COVID-19 could become a pandemic. It would be like asking a policeman about to storm a building filled with armed men if he were afraid. Of course he would be afraid, but he would still rush in, despite his fears."

Lisa took another big bite out of her meal and nodded. "You can do it, doc."

Chelsea eyed the forty-something-year-old lab assistant who she had worked with the two years she'd been at XRCure. She wanted to tell her to cut down but decided not to. Lisa was beginning to add credence to the adage 'you are what you eat'. Twice divorced, Lisa always said she was no longer in the market for a husband, but any decent guy with a deep pocket could check if she wanted to play. She got up abruptly, placed her cup on her tray, and with her napkin, wiped the water rings her cup had made on the table.

Chelsea raised an eyebrow. "Where're you going?"

"See you at the lab. Here comes your admirer." She turned away to leave. "Hello, Bob."

"Hey, Lisa," said Bob, sliding into the chair Lisa had just vacated. "I hope you're not leaving on my behalf."

"No," said Lisa with a growl to her voice. "Of course not."

Bob put down his plate and grabbed his burger with both hands. "Hi, Chelsea." He took a big bite and started to chew.

Chelsea leaned forward. "Did you see the CDC director on TV?"

Bob nodded, swallowed, and took another bite. He chewed fast as his eyes roamed the cafeteria as if he were expecting someone to jump him and snatch his food.

"We have to find that cure. This is scary. Imagine an epidemic here in the States," said Chelsea. "We have to unleash my AI to find the right combination of molecules already out there to find a credible treatment. Get me those computers. The answers are out there already."

Bob swallowed. "I know Chelsea. We're already doing great work testing and eliminating them one by one."

Chelsea pursed her lips. "One by one is not good enough. It will take forever. Didn't you hear the guy? It's only a matter of when." She sat back in her chair. "What are you scared of? You think the cure would be stolen from us when we find it?"

"Well, maybe," said Bob with a shrug. "Especially if we're using the same programs and software as other labs. You never know what those guys put in their software. What information they're harvesting from the user as their programs run in your system."

"No. That won't happen to us. We'll use a program I wrote myself based on the parameters I wrote into the code. And those parameters are based on findings from our research so far with the virus." Chelsea paused. "Time is of the essence here. You know that."

Chelsea looked at Bob. He'd wolfed down the burger, and he fixed his gaze in his glass of orange juice, which he twirled clockwise and then anti-clockwise.

Bob was practical. Like Chelsea, he was also a physician and a researcher, plus he had a Master's in Business Administration; an MBA from Harvard Business School. Entrepreneurship was his passion. Everything else was just icing on the cake. He and Chelsea had been at Harvard at the same time, but their paths never really crossed.

Six feet tall, bald head, and built like a quarterback, Robert Brown was living the life he had imagined for himself. Divorced with six-year-old twins, a boy and a girl, and running a successful lab that straddled his passions, medicine and business, was a win-win for him. He was always on the lookout for ways to grow the company.

Bob took a long drink from his glass. "I'll think about it."

Chelsea got up from the table. "You do that and do it fast." She pushed the chair into the table. She knew what would get him excited. "There's money to be made without being greedy. Imagine if each country buys a dose for each of her citizens, and XRCure makes a profit of one dollar, just to be on the conservative side. We're talking about three hundred and twenty-eight million dollars just in the US alone. And remember, Uncle Sam never buys just one of anything."

Bob sat up straight, and unconsciously started to rub his hands together.

"I'll be in the Lab. I'm doing my best. You do the same."

"I've contacted some financiers from Europe and should be talking to them soon. It's just that I don't want to dilute the equity too much. We're already on the right track, and it's only a matter of time before somebody will bite."

"Okay." Chelsea had gotten company stock when she started. Maybe it was time she asked for more equity too. She believed her approach would work.

2

Rip

Sometimes, Rip felt he was in a dream he would soon wake from and find himself in his real job in a covert operation in Pakistan, Syria, Iraq, or Afghanistan.

But here he was at thirty-three, his six feet four-inch frame cramped behind a desk as Chief of Hendonville Police in New Jersey. Rip was all muscle. His hue floated in ambiguity because of his mixed parentage, but in his mind, there was no confusion. Sometimes people mistook him for a wrestler in a police uniform Halloween costume—until he gave them a ticket. He still couldn't believe he'd taken a desk job. Right now, he was bored out of his mind staring at the computer screen. Not that he didn't like the peace, he did. But, he always compared his old job to the new one.

He ran his palm over his bald head, then down his stubble. It felt rough and sounded like the coffee maker in the break room. Maybe he should make coffee just to kill time.

He went over to the break room and emptied the overheated black liquid that smelled like burned tires into the sink. He rinsed the glass jar and added a new pouch to the coffee maker.

In a small town like Hendonville, the only excitement at his job was when he issued speeding tickets, broke up unruly teenagers, or patrolled the highway that passed through the town apprehending drivers who broke one traffic law or the other, or those under the influence. Then there those who wanted to take advantage of the friendly people of Hendonville and engage in shoplifting or petty burglary.

At his old job, the only peace and quiet he got was when they trained, and live bullets were not flying around. His work involved jumping out of airplanes into enemy territory, blowing up terrorist camps, and neutralizing individuals who posed a threat to the United States and its allies.

The smell of coffee wafted up to Rip, and he almost jumped up to pour himself a mug. The people he pulled over on the highway had their alcohol, pot, and other illegal substances as their drug of choice; his was just hot black coffee. Sometimes he wondered why anyone would put stuff in their body that made them lose control.

A news notification flashed on his screen about SARS-COVID-19, a flu-like illness that was making its way out of China. Let's hope it's a slow progression. Or better still, *what happens in China, stays in China*, he thought. Rip's stomach rumbled. Talking of China made him think of Chinese food. He could taste Mr. Lee's spring rolls and spicy Szechuan chicken with mixed vegetables.

His mind drifted to how he ended up here. As it often does when he's bored. His teenage years were spent at Lake Placid after his parents perished in a boating accident, and his grandparents had raised him. He'd joined the military at seventeen, following his grandfather's footsteps. After West Point, he did a stint with military police. Rip smiled. It was that exposure that made it possible for him to qualify for this job without going back to school. His commanding officer saw something in him and recommended he apply to Special Forces. It was a lot of hard work, but Rip was not one to shy away from getting his hands dirty.

Serving as a Special Ops put him in almost all the hot spots Uncle Sam was involved with and exposed him to people who became great friends of his. People who say *I'll take a bullet for you* and go out and do it.

About three years ago, something happened, and he and some other colleagues quit. Some of his Special Ops friends became contractors for the military, and others joined the CIA, while he opted to spend a year trying to find himself.

Rip's reminiscing was interrupted by the outside phone line ringing. Cathy didn't get it at the first or second ring, so Rip decided to answer the phone and get some coffee.

Cathy was not at her desk when he got there.

"Don't touch it!"

Rip turned and saw Cathy dash from the bathroom, drying her hands with a paper towel and tossing it into the wastepaper basket. At sixty, Cathy was by far the oldest member of the Hendonville police station and the longest-serving staff. She'd seen several chiefs come and go in this small town of eleven thousand.

Married with no children, Cathy was born right here, in a house not too far from the station. The house had since been torn down, "thank God", she would say to anyone that cared to listen.

Cathy snatched up the phone after the second ring. "Hello, Hendonville police station. How can I help you?" She covered the mouthpiece as she inhaled and exhaled, catching her breath. She listened, asked some leading questions, and took down a few notes.

"Do we have to wait twenty-four hours? No. You did the right thing, Mrs. Morrison. Once you realize you have a case of a missing person, it's better to contact the police as soon as possible. The sooner, the better. We'll send someone over to your place right away."

Rip stared at Cathy as the implications of her words hit him, tying his stomach in knots. He wished he'd heard wrong. "Mrs. Morrison's son is missing?"

"Yea, Jude Morrison," said Cathy in her high-pitched voice. "He must have gone to one of his friend's houses to play Forthright, or whatever the kids play these days. Who in their right minds would name a game Forthright?"

"Fortnite!" said John, the deputy.

Cathy glared at John. "Whatever! Mr. I know it all!" She turned to Rip. "According to Mrs. Morrison, usually Jude would get off the school bus at the library and come in to meet her. He would do his homework as he waited for her to finish by five. Then they would leave together for home. Mrs. Morrison didn't realize he was missing until it was time to go, and she couldn't find him. She thought maybe he'd gone home. But she gets home, and he's not there."

Rip drained his coffee, walked back to his office, and placed the empty mug on his desk. "John, come with me. Bring your cruiser. We'll probably split off from her home." He headed toward the exit then stopped. "Cathy, please call the school bus company, ask them to check the buses. He could have fallen asleep and missed his stop."

Cathy gave him a weary look.

"It's happened before, maybe not in this town," said Rip.

Rip put on his cruiser's strobe lights, but not the sirens, as he drove out of the police station adhering to every protocol of emergency driving. He made a left and eased into the traffic onto Main Street. It was early in the evening, and his lights were bright. Cars gave way as his cruiser made its way up the gentle slope towards the top of the hill. He drove past the bank, the coffee shop, the cemetery with the Unknown Union Soldier statue, the dentist's office, and the post office. He stopped briefly at the light, then continued towards the valley, then past the library, the elementary school, and then up the hill towards the part of town were Mrs. Morrison lived.

Hendonville, New Jersey was a small town in Sussex County, like the one where he grew up in New York. A small town where everybody knew each other. Where they had more deer and black bears than people.

Rip hoped the boy had only wandered off, gone exploring, or gone home with one of his classmates. He hoped that by the time they got back to Mrs. Morrison's home, the boy would be back safe in his mother's arms.

Rip looked in the rear-view mirror. John's cruiser was right behind him. By the time the two cars drove up to Mrs. Morrison's home, most of her neighbors already had their lights on. Rip knew they could only see the houses because it was still winter, and the trees had shed all their leaves. In summer, when the trees are in full bloom, it would be impossible to see the homes inside those woods. The only evidence that there were houses inside those woods would be the letterbox and the long dirt driveway that wound its way until it disappeared inside the bushes.

Mrs. Morrison was standing outside her porch when the sheriff and his deputy drove up. The boy hadn't come home as he'd hoped.

"Sheriff, thank God you're here," said Mrs. Morrison as she hastily approached the car.

"We'll do all we can to find him, Mrs. Morrison," said

Rip as he got out of the car. "You've called all his friends? Do you know if they saw him get on the bus after school?"

"The ones I called cannot remember if they saw him get on the bus. And the ones who think they remember seeing him get on are not sure if it was today or yesterday."

That remark gave Rip hope. "What are the names of his friends you've already talked to about him missing? We'll have to go see them."

"Good evening Mrs. Morrison," said John walking up from his car. "We'll leave no stone unturned in looking for Jude."

"Mrs. Morrison nodded. Her eyes were far away, out of focus. As if she was there only in body.

"What are the names of his friend that you spoke with?" asked Rip.

Mrs. Morrison rubbed her hands together. "Peter. Peter Sloan." She gave him some other names and John wrote them down.

"What was Jude wearing when he left for school this morning?"

"He had on blue jeans, a red sweater, and a yellowish camouflage jacket."

Rip looked up. "Like army fatigues?"

Mrs. Morrison nodded.

"Does he like the outdoors? Like going into the woods to hunt or enjoy nature?"

"Yes, he could stay in the woods for days if I let him. But he would have asked me. Will…will you find him before it gets dark?" Her voice was shaky. She shuddered. "The temperature is going to drop overnight."

"Apart from the few storms we've had, it's been mild, snow-wise," said John looking around. "Good thing there's none on the ground right now."

Rip knew there was no Mr. Morrison. In the two years he'd been in Hendonville, it had always been Mrs. Morrison and Jude. "Do you have any family or friends who can keep you company?"

"My neighbor. He'll be around in ten minutes."

Rip nodded, then his cell phone started to ring. He looked at the phone. "Excuse me." He walked away from Mrs. Morrison. "Hi, Cathy, any news?"

"The buses are parked for the night, and all have been checked for stragglers. They were all empty."

Rip knew he forgot something. Yes! Cell phones. The phone company can find out his location based on the cell towers the signal pinged on.

"Rip?"

"Hold on Cathy." Rip turned to Mrs. Morrison. "Did Jude have his cell phone with him?"

She looked away and lowered her head. "He doesn't have one. I was…I was saving up to get him a phone when he turns eleven in two months."

They all turned to the sound of footsteps. A man walked up the driveway towards them.

"That's my neighbor," said Mrs. Morrison.

"Okay, we'll have to go. John, did you get the names of Jude's friends that said they were not sure when they saw him?"

John nodded.

Just then, Rip saw a snowflake float in the air. Then another, and another. Mrs. Morrison saw them too and a wail escaped her lips.

"Oh God…it's snowing. Jude…Jude, where are you?"

3

Chelsea

Chelsea sat down in her chair in front of her computer and was now feeding into her program some facts she'd just confirmed on the protein coating of the virus and ion channels in the membrane of SARS-CoV-2, the virus that causes COVID-19. Her office was small, what she liked to call a glorified closet, but she liked it like that. The closeness of her walls as if they were trying to close in on her kept her alert. Apart from the chair she sat on, she had one more chair in her office, which she used as a shelf to discourage people from hanging around.

Her desk was one of those with a one-level hutch which she filled with medical journals and reference books. The space between the table surface and bookcase, she used as a notice board. She pinned a calendar with her schedule and anything that interested her there.

The phone on her desk only served to startle her each time

it rang. If someone wanted to see her, they were better off coming to the office unless they didn't mind enduring the phone going to voice mail and then calling back several times until they got her. People who needed to talk to her always poked their heads through her door. Sometimes they would be there for something, and she would only notice their presence when she inhaled and smelled them or stretched and became aware of their presence.

Touching her while she was working facing the monitor could elicit one of two reactions: "Hold on, just one second while I type this out." (Which could take ten minutes). Or she wouldn't even acknowledge the touch, no matter how rough the visitor was.

Chelsea took a break from attacking her keyboard. Time to taste something sweet. She pulled out the top drawer of her table, reached in, and took just one wrapped confectionery from a bunch. In it was one whole almond and shredded coconut covered in milk chocolate. She unwrapped it and popped it in her mouth, ready to resume where she left off with her coding.

"I thought you were getting ready to leave?" said Lisa, peeping into her office.

"Not yet. There's something I need to take care of before I leave."

Lisa rolled her eyes. "That's what you always say. We come back in the morning and see that you never left."

Chelsea sat back on her chair. "It only happened once. I always go home. Remember, I have my parents at home to look after?"

"Yes, but you also have a nurse that comes in all day, and your mother is there too." Lisa exhaled and held her hands up. "Okay, how did you get here two days ago?"

Chelsea pursed her lips, twisted it, looked at the ceiling, and then back at Lisa. "I drove."

"No, I placed my hand on your car's hood in the parking lot, and it was dead cold." Lisa drew in a sharp breath. "Unless you went home with Bob."

"Oh, come on," said Chelsea sitting up and getting ready to start typing. "He's a married man, and he's not my type."

"Divorced. What's your type?"

Chelsea cocked her head. "Hmm, I don't know." She turned to face Lisa and said in a tone that suggested *we've taken this as far as it should go. I need to work.* "Perhaps, an available type. Single, no kids."

"Oh, come on, you shoot down everybody that as much as glances in your direction. Anyway, I don't want to take up all your time." She paused. "I don't want you to work yourself to death either. Don't be too hard on yourself. Sleeping in the office is not cool." She waved. "See you tomorrow."

"Bye Lisa." She waited until she could no longer hear her footsteps down the corridor and rolled her eyes. Her eyes went back to the screen. What does she know? They were only work friends. For the two years Chelsea had been there, Lisa had been trying to become her buddy, but Chelsea didn't have time for that. She had bigger fish to fry. If she could get her software to do what she wanted, she would be the one that saved the world from a pandemic. A Nobel Prize might even be in the works after that. She wondered where Bob was. He better line up the funding he was talking about and make things happen.

4

Rip

The headlights to Rips car had already come on, and he was apprehensive of what the darkness could bring. This time they drove to the Sloan's house without strobe lights. It was similar to the other homes around but had a shorter driveway. Rip startled a buck and a doe that were taking a leisurely walk across the driveway. They bolted into the woods.

He hoped Peter Sloan would be able to give them something they could work with to find Jude. If any of the Sloan's looked out of the window, they would be startled seeing two police cars coming up their driveway. Rip parked, got out of the car, and took a deep breath. The air was cold, dry, and smelled of wood smoke. He hoped it was just wood burning in someone's fireplace and not a house going up in flames. They already had their hands full. He saw smoke curling out of Sloan's chimney. He could even taste it. It kind of reminded him of December. John walked up to him, and they headed towards the main entrance.

"What do you think, Chief? The elements are not working in our favor here."

Rip glanced up and nodded. "There was no snow in the forecast. Whatever that was, I'm glad it has blown past. We don't need any freak weather pattern compounding an already delicate situation."

Rip walked with John beside him towards the main door to the house. He knew just like him, John was also thinking of a bad outcome but didn't want to voice it out.

"I heard his mother say he loves the outdoors," said John. "He must have picked up some survival skills."

They stopped at the front door and Rip rang the bell. Moments later, footsteps approached from inside, and a face appeared in the windowpane on the door. On seeing them, the eyes widened. There was a flurry of sounds as the door was unlocked, the chain attached to the door latch removed, and the door opened.

"Chief Chord! Deputy! Is everything okay?"

"Good evening Mrs. Sloane," said Rip. "Everything could be better. We just need your help…your son's help in finding Jude Morrison."

Mrs. Sloan's hand flew to her mouth. "Jude is missing?"

"Emm, we hope he just wandered off," said Rip. "Maybe he's at another friend's house. We just wanted to ask Peter a few questions if you don't mind."

Her eyes darted from Rip to John. "Is Peter in trouble?"

"No, no. We understand he and Jude are good friends. We just wanted to ask a few questions in case Jude told him of his plans."

"Plans?" asked Mrs. Sloan in a squeaky voice.

"Well, like if Jude told him anything about where he would be going after school."

Mrs. Sloan opened the door wider. "Yes, yes, come in. Mrs. Morrison called earlier on, but Peter said he didn't know anything. We were just finishing dinner."

Rip and John walked in.

"Peter! Come over here!"

Peter came through the living room door and froze when he saw the police. He swallowed.

"Hello, Peter," said Rip. "I'm Chief Chord." He pointed at John. "My deputy, John Reid. We're sorry for interrupting your dinner. We won't take up much of your time. We need your help in finding Jude Morrison. His mother reported him missing." Rip paused. He needed to get some yeses from the kid. "You know Jude, right?"

Peter nodded.

"Does he own a camouflage jacket?"

Peter nodded again.

So far, so good, thought Rip. "Was he wearing it today?"

Another nod.

"Did he tell you anything? Do you have any idea where he might be?" Rip held his breath and looked at Peter. He had earlier told Jude's mom that he wasn't sure if it was today or the day before that he saw him on the bus.

"Yes," said Peter.

Rip, and his deputy exchanged glances.

"Did you see him with the camo jacket after school?" asked Rip.

Peter swallowed and glanced at his mom, then back at Rip. "No, sir. I got off before him. He…he said he was going to get a picture of a mountain lion."

"What?" asked his mother. Her eyes widened. "From where? The zoo? There are no mountain lions in this area."

"Jude said he saw one dash across the road and go into the woods. He and his mom had been coming home from morning mass, and a lion just crossed the road right in front of them as it chased a deer. We had planned to go together, but-" Peter looked down. "At the last minute, I got scared." His voice faded into almost nothing. "I felt sick, so I went home."

From the corner of his eyes, Rip saw Mrs. Sloan nod her head. The worry lines on her face disappearing.

"A mountain lion? Here, in Sussex County?" asked John. "Don't they live in the Western United States? Maybe it was a Bobcat?"

"I don't know," said Peter, shrugging. "Jude likes stuff like that. He was convinced he saw one, and I believe him. He doesn't make up stuff."

"What was he going to shoot it with?" asked Rip.

"Oh, his iPad. He only wanted a picture. He said mountain lions only attack people walking alone. That's why we were supposed to go together." Peter's voice dropped again.

"Oh, God," muttered Rip under his breath. "Peter, do you know where he planned to stake out the animal?"

Peter shook his head. "Not the exact place. But somewhere on Route 181. We were going to get off the school bus on Wilson Street and walk."

Rip looked at John and jerked his head towards the exit. "Thank you, Peter. Mrs. Sloan."

"Do you believe his story about Jude seeing the lion?" asked John once they were outside.

"I don't know, but one thing we know for sure is that Jude believes it and he's putting himself in harm's way. He could get lost in the woods. And if there's really a mountain lion out there, that would put him at tremendous risk." Rip headed towards the parked cars. "We have to find out from his mother where exactly they saw this animal cross the road. He's probably headed in that direction."

"Must be there by now," said John. "Maybe I should head out and start driving around."

Rip pulled out his cell phone. He hit a number and spoke as he waited. "Let's find out exactly where Jude and his mom saw the lion. At least that would help limit our search area."

"Hello," a female voice sounded from the cell phone.

Rip raised a finger. "Cathy, this is Rip. I don't have Mrs. Morrison's number, can you three-way me, please? But before you do that, I have a quick question. Have we gotten any calls of mountain lion sightings?" There was a pause. "Cathy?"

"Chief," said Cathy in a low whisper.

Rips stomach hardened. He gripped the phone tighter and braced himself for the worst. "Yes."

"They found him."

5

Feodor

Feodor opened his eyes, gasping for air. Something sticky and slippery pushed against his face, trying to suffocate him. He turned his head to the side and filled his lungs. He sputtered and coughed, the sudden movement igniting the mother of all pain in his head. He felt like he'd been hit over the head with a metal pipe. It was dark all around him, and he was upside down. Why? He tried to move his hands and couldn't. He shivered. It was cold.

"What was that animal!" he muttered. His voice sounded distant to him. He then realized the balloon-like thing in his face was the deployed airbag. It had come at him like a grenade shot from a grenade launcher, straight and direct. Feodor remembered Yurik. He'd gotten into an accident and had a dead body with him. His troubles just doubled.

Stupid! Stupid! He took all the time to create a rule and then broke his own rule when he needed it the most. On the brighter side of things, he had been vindicated. When you hit the brakes and swerve, the animal always wins.

His eyes had gotten accustomed to the darkness. The windshield had cracked in a few places but was intact. There was no glass by his side window. It was just open. Maybe something had pushed down on the window control during the accident and opened it. He heard a fading whistling sound, like something turning at high speed and then gently slowing down. Probably the tires were still rotating. Feodor heard something else. Was the engine still on? He listened. Yes, it was. And…and he could smell petrol in the air. He had to get out of the car. In movies, cars always blew up after they rolled over. He hoped this was the time the movies were wrong.

The seat belt pulled taut against his chest was rather uncomfortable. It was a safety mechanism that kicks in when the seat belt is yanked, it locks to stop your body from moving. It is supposed to save you, but now it was killing him. He saw Yurik's body and jerked in surprise. His eyes had somehow sprung open and stared at him, as if saying *now what, wise guy*. A big gash on his head wasn't bleeding.

Feodor struggled again to free himself, but the seat belt was unrelenting. "Calm down," he said to himself in Russian. His voice sounded funny to him. He tasted blood. He shut his eyes as another wave of pain crashed through his head. He must get out of the vehicle. He could hear the voice of his old KGB trainer drilling instructions into him. Your mind is the best tool you have when you don't have a physical weapon.

Feodor shut his eyes. He'd decided not to do this job and had also killed the agent sent to help him. He had broken his oath. His oath was to carry out whatever the state demanded of him. Would he have killed his mother if the state demanded of it? Feodor chuckled to himself. Thank God his mother and father were already dead. But he would have done it if the state required that of him. He was that loyal. Until this.

He could think of worse things he had done in his career. But this…this he wouldn't do. Maybe age was finally catching up with him. He still needed to do one more thing, but trapped the way he was he would either freeze to death or die from whatever injuries he had. And that was if the police didn't turn up first.

At least at this time of the year, bears were hibernating. Was he located where a passerby could find him? The irony of life. Before the accident, he didn't want to be found. Now he was entertaining the thought. *Focus.*

The airbag pushed against his face, and his head hurt when he turned towards Yurik and groped with his left hand, trying to feel the release for the seat belt. He could see the red shape in his mind's eye, and he could see Yurik's eyes. He shut his eyes and continued to search for the knob. Yuri's eyes seemed to burn right through him. His hands were slippery from blood, and the cold was beginning to numb his fingers. Feodor wasn't sure what he was touching anymore. He knew in a few moments his finger dexterity would be gone entirely and even pushing down on the knob to release him would be tough.

Feodor had gotten used to the petrol smell, but a new odor hit him. It smelled like a dirty dog, mixed with the scent of decay. What could it be? A deep rumbling sound like an idling powerful Harley Davidson came from outside the passenger window. The sound intensified, and suddenly, Yurik's body jerked and moved towards the passenger window as if being pulled

Feodor's heart pounded like the drums that played at the

Red Square during the Victory Parade. It must be a bear, he thought. No, the animal he nearly hit.

The pounding of his heart coincided with the throbbing pain in his head. He felt around frantically. Now his fingers could not feel, but he pushed down on everything he could touch. He heard a click. He was rewarded.

Right away, he felt a sharp pain on his shoulder. At first, he thought it was the released belt touching an injury as it rolled back. Then his shoulder was yanked towards the window. The smell of decay was overpowering. Must be the animal he avoided hitting.

Feodor's head smashed against the door frame, again and again, as the animal tried to pull him out. His head already felt like an over-inflated basketball, but the air kept on coming. His ears rang, and the moonlight started to fade like someone was turning the light down, like one of those fade switches. The pain in his shoulder, sharp and intense a few seconds earlier, subsided. But the pressure was still there, uncomfortable with yanking and tugging.

The sound of ringing in his ears appeared to fade, then was replaced by a sudden whoosh. His vision was cloudy, like a flashlight in fog. The pain and pressure on his shoulder had disappeared but his head continued to throb as if his head had been used as a punching bag by Wladimir Klitschko and Tyson Fury.

Feodor felt the heat on his skin.

All that rocking has finally connected the petrol with the exhaust pipe, he thought. The car was on fire. They say that when you're about to die, your life flashes before you. Happy moments flashed through his mind, his childhood, when he met his wife… They were right. The last thing Feodor felt was the heat… then blackness.

6

Chelsea

Chelsea sat in her office, fingers on the keyboard, eyes glued to the screen. There was just a lot of data to crunch, and the AI was having a hard time going through it. Not having a hard time exactly, only the sheer amount of time it would take to go through it and check it all against the codes she'd written.

A banner that said 'done' flashed on the screen. Chelsea looked at the data, and there was nothing new in the result. She typed in another round of commands and hit enter. Now the waiting started again. This might take thirty minutes to an hour to conclude. She hoped it would move faster so she could take into consideration the results before she wrote new codes.

The building was quiet. Chelsea knew the different sounds made by any group in the building without leaving her office. Like the sound when it was 5 pm and the building started to empty, and the noise made by the cleanup crew when they arrived. And the different sounds depending on the activity they engaged in like vacuuming or emptying the garbage cans. That was about an hour ago. Now, it had another type of noise, the quietness of an empty building.

Probably just the security guard, Obua, left in the building. He was an immigrant from Nigeria and was studying for the medical boards. Nice guy. He studied in between his hourly rounds. The first time she saw him studying, she was impressed. He was already a doctor, but there he was in a guard's uniform. Whatever it takes, she'd thought at that time, and told him to feel free to ask her any questions. Chelsea was sure he had questions, but he never asked. He wanted to get into a residency in Family Medicine so he could attend to more people back in his native Accra. The computer beeped, pulling Chelsea out of her reverie.

She looked at the screen and sighed. The indicator showed it was only halfway done. Nothing was as draining as the waiting. Chelsea decided to get some coffee from the cafeteria while she waited for the computer to crunch the data. Lisa's last words about her spending the night in her office flashed through her mind. Spending the night at the office was never something she decided to do. It was where the work took her. If she worked and worked and suddenly it was sunrise, then that was it.

In the kitchen, the coffee stand was already cleaned and ready for a new day, courtesy of the cleaning crew. The sugar sachets and milk containers all stocked up. Chelsea didn't want to make everything untidy for just a cup of coffee so she opted to use the vending machine. She placed a paper cup under the spout, pressed the button for espresso, and waited as the device gaggled, sucking in water, and then started to make her strong coffee. It finished with a flourish of gaggles and hisses.

Then she heard another sound behind her, like something being dragged on the floor. It wasn't Obua. He never made that much noise. Somebody else was in the building? A lump formed in her throat. Chelsea whirled around.

Bob raised both hands. "Darn it!"

Chelsea placed hers on her chest. "You scared the bejesus out of me."

Bob walked toward her dragging his messenger bag on the floor. "Sorry. I thought I was here alone."

Chelsea pointed at his bag. "Isn't that supposed to go over your shoulder?"

"I'm too tired. "What are you doing here?"

"Working. I came up with another parameter. So I wrote the code, and now I have the AI looking through available data to see if we can find any mention of weaknesses in the wall of the virus, and which chemicals can take advantage of those weaknesses. And if it finds one, let us know if they exist in forms that can be used by humans safely."

"Wow, that's a tall order," said Bob.

Chelsea took a sip of her coffee and smacked her lips. "Not so tall that we can't reach. That is, if we get those computers. Then the process will be faster."

Bob nodded and grabbed a cup. "I shouldn't be drinking coffee. I should be preparing myself to sleep." He shrugged and placed his cup under the spout, and hit the espresso button. "It's on my radar Chelsea. Like I told you, I'm working on bringing in new money. Once they come on board, then we can get your computers." Bob looked at his watch. "Have you had dinner? We can continue the discussion over some food."

Since she'd started working for the lab, Bob had been

trying to schedule one type or another non-work-related hangout with her. He didn't hide where he'd like to take their relationship if she gave the go-ahead, from the boardroom to the bedroom. That was not her thing. She was not even in a relationship and a complicated one with a married guy? No way. Okay, his divorce just came through, but that was not in the works for her. She'd always said no to him. If you always say no to people, they will default to saying no to you too, the old tit for tat. She thought of the computers she needed for her job. "Okay, I'll come in my car, and go home from there. Where do you plan to eat?"

Chelsea went back to her office, she left her computer on to continue to crunch data, then straightened out her desk. She retrieved her car, a red BMW, from the car park, and tailed Bob to Applebee's.

Even that late at night, the eating place had good patronage. A waiter ushered them to a booth, and Chelsea could hear conversations mixed in with the clanging of forks and knives. She admired the framed photos of local sports teams, famous people, and regular Joes hanging on the wood-paneled walls.

Men and women sat around the sports bar, paying homage to the gods on the sports channels on TVs suspended over the bar. Wine glasses hung upside down like bats in a cave, waiting to pounce on the unwary. Was Bob waiting to pounce on her too?

Chelsea had eaten here before, but for the first time, she noticed the red curtains on the windows. They'd been pulled aside and held in place by clips. The bright light from the parking lot showed little particles of dust floating aimlessly in the air. Well, unlike them, she had a purpose for being there— keeping Bob motivated, even though he might have other things in mind.

It was only after Chelsea shoveled some fettuccine tossed with broccoli and rich Alfredo sauce into her mouth that she realized just how hungry she was. It tasted like a little piece of heaven.

Bob speared some potatoes on his sirloin steak dish. "What exactly do you need?" He put the food in his mouth and started to chew.

"Faster computers that can crunch data. And more time to write codes."

Bob chewed and swallowed. "I don't know much about code writing, but I've heard that for something like what you're doing, a whole team of coders is dedicated to the job."

Chelsea nodded. "That way, it moves faster. A team writes the code, another interprets the results and comes up with recommendations.

"So, what you might need in addition to powerful computers is workforce," said Bob, nodding. "I think now I understand better what you're doing. You need a team of coders."

Chelsea felt like a boulder had been lifted off her shoulders. At least Bob had paid attention."

"How are your parents doing?" asked Bob as he attacked the steak.

Chelsea was surprised by the change of topic. "They're hanging in there." She loaded food into her mouth while she thought of how much information to give him. It was no secret that her seventy-one-year-old father, retired Doctor of Obstetrics and Gynecology, had Alzheimer's. And her mother, a retired psychiatrist, had debilitating arthritis. She decided to come clean.

"Dad is just there. He goes through the routine of daily living. At least he still recognizes Mom and me, and can feed and dress himself. Every now and then he has a lucid interval and tells stories from the past. About his younger days as a doctor, about vacations, in such detail. Sometimes it is tough to watch when he can't remember. How one's mind could go just like that." Her voice drifted off a bit.

Bob nodded and let out a sigh. "I know what you're going through. My dad went through the same thing, but his was faster. I can't even imagine how you do it. At least I had my two sisters to help. It's just you."

"I have my mom too."

Bob chewed his food then swallowed. "Yea, but she needs help too. At a point, my dad would just wander off, and we wouldn't know where he was. It was gut-wrenching. Even with the three of us, rotating the time we spent with him to make sure one of us was always there, keeping an eye on him could be challenging. We didn't want to put him in a home, but we were close to doing that right before..." Bob's voice trailed off. "We should have done that."

Chelsea shuddered. The reason why Bob didn't put his father in a home was that one day, while wandering, he got hit by a car and died. Her father had started to wander off too.

Chelsea knew she was done with coding for tonight. Then her phone buzzed in her pocket. She looked at the screen and sighed. She placed the phone to her ear.

"Mother, how are you?"

"Isn't it dark where you are? Does it need to get darker before you come home?"

"Sorry, Mom. I should have called to let you know I was running late. I had a few things to take care of at the office. I'm leaving soon. How's Dad?"

"He's asleep. Come home soon." She hung up.

Bob chuckled. "Parents. No matter how old you are. You're always a kid in their eyes."

"I have to go, Bob." Chelsea opened her purse and peeled out some twenties.

Bob raised his hand. "Don't worry. I'll take care of it."

Chelsea dropped a twenty on the table. "Tip." She turned to walk away, then stopped. "Don't forget the computers-"

"Chelsea." Bob cut her off.

What now, she wondered.

Bob stared ahead of him. "I might be able to bring in new investors. With this angle on artificial intelligence, would you be okay sharing what you know?"

Chelsea let out a deep breath. "Maybe. We'll deal with it when we get to that bridge. Goodnight, Bob."

7

Rip

Rip listened as Cathy elaborated about how Jude showed up and was glad it was over. With a little luck on his side, he might get to relax this evening.

"So," continued Cathy. "According to Mrs. Morrison, she was standing outside with the neighbor after you left, they saw a figure rolling a bicycle up the driveway, and it was Jude.

Rip and John had raced back to the Morrison's house. The inside was like most homes in the area. The living room, dining room, and kitchen were one continuous space. Rip felt the change in the atmosphere from the last time they visited. It was happier. The TV was now on, with Steve Harvey asking a question on *Family Feud*. The tension Rip had felt earlier when Jude was still missing, that could be sliced with a knife, was not there anymore, and Rip could smell food. His head shifted following the smell, and there was the youngster, sitting at the dining table with a big plate of food before him.

Mrs. Morrison walked up to Rip and clasped his hand in hers. "Chief, thank you so much for all that you did." Tears rolled down her eyes.

"We'd only started looking. You have a good boy in your hands."

Mrs. Morrison wiped her tears with the back of her hand. "He's over there eating. He worked up a big appetite."

"Okay, I'll talk to him." Rip walked over to Jude, who sat at the dining table digging into a plate of spaghetti with meat-balls. He appeared tired with a surprised look that seemed to say, *why all the commotion*?

Jude stopped eating when he saw Rip coming towards him.

"How are you Jude?"

"Hi…hi Chief, sir," said Jude with a stammer.

Rip smiled. "You gave us quite a scare."

Jude looked down at his plate. "I'm…I'm sorry sir. I didn't mean to."

"What happened?"

"At school, I'd asked Peter to come with me. He agreed, but at the last minute, he got sick, so I went on my own."

"So, you left the library, went home, took your bike and left?" asked Rip.

"No, I didn't get off the bus at the library. I got off at my regular stop, close to home. I went to the house, got my bike and BB gun, and left."

Rip raised his eyebrows. "BB gun?"

Jude lowered his head. "Yes."

Rip had enjoyed one as a kid too. "Okay, where exactly did you ride to?"

"Route 181."

Rip raised an eyebrow. He knew that stretch of road was well forested and lonely. "What made you come back?"

"I didn't realize how fast cars moved. And it was lonely."

Rip grinned. "Did you see the mountain lion?"

Jude thought for a moment. "I...I think I felt it."

Rip smiled. Boys will be boys. He remembered his childhood in the woods at Lake Placid, New York. He would spend hours in the woods, raiding bird nests, eating wild berries, and then swimming in one of the many ponds. Jude's spirit of adventure resonated with him. But he still had to reprimand the boy.

"Jude, you had your mother–and the rest of the community–worried sick. Nobody knew where you were."

Jude looked down at his plate again. "I'm so sorry. I wasn't thinking."

"A few years ago, in Split Rock Reservoir in the Morris County community, not too far from here, a Boy Scout leader took some scouts with him to explore the woods. They got to a cave which he knew was 'safe'." Rip made air quotes with his fingers. "He woke up a hibernating bear and was lucky to escape with non-life-threatening injuries. I say he was lucky because he wasn't alone. The other boys called for help. Just wandering off into the woods, especially at this time of the year, wasn't the best idea."

"I won't do it again, sir."

Rip nodded. He knew he would do it again. "Always let your mother know whenever you go out, okay?" Rip saw the gun leaning against the wall and picked it up. It was a Crosman air rifle. "Any good with this?"

Jude smiled. "I hit a bull's eye every time."

"All right, you take care now, okay." Rip put the gun down and walked back to the living room and approached Mrs. Morrison.

She chewed the inside of her cheek, nostrils flared, her eyes fixed on Rip.

"I spoke with Jude. I told him always to let you know whenever he's going anywhere." He watched as the tension left her face. Maybe she thought he was going to detain him or something worse. "He's a good kid. See you around, Mrs. Morrison. He turned to head to the door, then stopped. "Mrs. Morrison, did you see a mountain lion on Route 181?"

She starred at him for a moment, then exhaled. "We were coming back from mass in the morning, and I saw something dash across the road. I can't for sure tell you what it was. But Jude was so excited." She nodded her head. "It wasn't one of the usual suspects. You know, a dog, deer, fox, and definitely not a bear."

"Okay, enjoy the rest of your evening."

"Thank you Chief."

Rip and his deputy left. Rip headed back to the police station, while John needed to follow up on something before doing the same.

Most of the staff were still around because of the missing kid. They'd been getting organized to ask for volunteers to search the woods.

"Thank God he came back," said Cathy as soon as Rip walked into the station. "It would have been risky having all those people crawling around in the woods."

"Yes, Cathy. Has there been any reports of sightings of mountain lions or any strange animals in the vicinity?"

"Not here in Hendonville, but there were two reports in Sparta Township and Newton."

"There must be something out there then," said Rip in a low voice. "There's never smoke without fire." He continued towards his office.

"I'm heading home," said Cathy. She got up and grabbed

her handbag. "That's enough excitement for one night. You better get some sleep too. You can't save the world. Sometimes you need to abandon things and pick them up later."

"Bye, Cathy. Are the night duty officers in yet?"

"Yep, they already have their duties. See you tomorrow Rip."

Rip sat down and powered his computer. He went into the county website and logged into the restricted area. He saw the report about the sightings Cathy mentioned, and read through quickly, then went to Google. From what he read online, Bobcats could be mistaken for mountain lions. *I'll just drive through there on my way home.*

Rip's cell phone buzzed. He fished it out of his pocket. One look at the screen, and a big smile spread across his face.

8

Feodor Konstantin
Latvia 1988

L atvia broke away from the Russian Empire at the end of World War I, and on 18 November 1918 The Republic of Latvia came into existence. With the outbreak of World War II, Latvia was forcibly re-occupied by the Soviet Union following a secret pact with Nazi Germany. However, that pact broke down when Nazi Germany invaded and occupied Latvia. In 1941, the Soviets drove the Germans out, and for the next forty-five years Latvia was a republic of the Soviet Union.

In 1987, the Singing Revolution started. The name coined by the Estonian artist and activist, Heinz Valk, would see the Baltic States of Latvia, Lithuania, and Estonia regain their independence by 1991. But, before the revolution succeeded, the Kremlin had tried to squelch it, and that was how Feodor

Konstantin found himself sitting at a café in old Riga, Latvia, gazing at the most beautiful girl he had ever seen.

He had arrived from Russia the day before with a lot of plans and a suitcase full of Lats, the local Latvian currency. He went straight to the house his boss had rented for their stay before he went back to Moscow. Feodor settled in, put away the bag of operational money given to him by the agency for the operation, and the next day took a taxi around town sightseeing.

Thirsty, Feodor stopped at an open-air café sipping coffee not too far from where he was told that the opposition gathered. He was proactive and gave himself the task of watching people around the area. Deep down, he had a gut feeling that the budding uprising would eventually gather enough steam and challenge the governance of the republic. But Feodor was committed to doing his best, and to be as ruthless as needed. He'd wanted to prove himself with this new position. He hatched a plan on his way to Riga that he believed would impress his boss.

Before his boss returned to Riga, he would have familiarized himself with the city and its people and make sure his plan was ready for execution. Identify the influencers in the budding uprising and, if given the go-ahead, assassinate them himself.

Of course, all the credit and glory would go to his boss. One thing he learned at the Academy of Foreign Intelligence, also known as the SVR Academy, was never to make your boss look bad or outshine him. In the long run, he would take care of you. It was a nugget most of the leading performers at this top-secret KGB institution, where Russian spies honed their deadly skills, took to heart.

Feodor Konstantin was just another engineering student at the university. Being a ward of the state, he learned from a young age to fend for himself and ensured that he was among the four percent of orphans from Russian institutions that got a higher education.

He did whatever he needed to do to stand out and make his way. He lied, stole, gave himself to men or women, as long as he got something in return.

At the university, he was good at math and physics and hoped to become an important scientist one day. Then he was approached by some men who told him his talents could be developed and channeled to serve a higher, more fulfilling purpose. A very ambitious young man, Feodor was amendable to being convinced. He joined the Academy, the number one training school for spies, which would boast of producing the likes of Vladimir Putin.

Each time Feodor reached a milestone at the Academy, he aspired for something more and was always challenging himself. Then he learned about the department that got things done and would 'let you see the world'. They'll teach you foreign languages and different ways to kill. It was called Department V and was responsible for "Wet affairs" (*mokrie dela*). Their job was straight forward: kidnappings, sabotage, and assassinations abroad.

A clatter of footsteps had brought Feodor back to the present. He took a sip of coffee, then turned to see what the commotion was all about. He froze. He watched the girl saunter past him. Blonde, full lipped, with enormous oval blue eyes and heavy eyelashes that shadowed her lovely face, she was the most beautiful thing he had ever seen. She carried a handbag with books sticking out the top. She had on a tight print dress that clung to her like a second skin, creating an innocent lustful appeal.

Feodor Konstantin did not remember getting to his feet. His heart sounded like galloping horses as it pumped blood all over his body. His head throbbed. He felt tingling in his toes and fingers. His eyes followed the girl as she went down a cobblestone alley, out of sight.

A waiter came by to refill Feodor's mug and gave him a knowing smile. "Beautiful, eh?" he said in Latvian.

"A beauty made in heaven," said Feodor in Latvian, still stunned by what he saw. If the man noticed his slight accent, he didn't react. Latvian was one of the half dozen languages Feodor could speak.

As he contemplated whether to pursue the girl or not, three young men, probably in their early twenties, walked down the same alley. They talked and laughed, pointing ahead. Feodor knew they were up to no good. A dark cloud descended over him. He took a big sip of coffee, dropped some money on the table, and followed the men.

At first, they kept a safe distance from the girl, but once they got to an area where Feodor was the sole figure following at a distance, they rushed the girl. One of them pulled at her books, another at her dress. It seemed to be a playful familiarity. *Maybe they were classmates*, thought Feodor, but the girl wasn't finding it funny; neither was he. One slapped her behind, and Feodor saw red. This was bullying. He walked faster, coming up with a plan on how to take down the three men.

"Hey, get your hands off her," said Feodor in Russian.

"Are you lost?" asked the tallest of the men in a red tee-shirt. "Why don't you mind your business?"

Feodor didn't break his stride; he continued towards them. The motormouth turned and faced him. Feodor kicked him in the groin. As the man doubled over, he punched the next one on the chest, knocking the wind out of him. The third man raised his hand, made a first, and backed away, shaking like a leaf.

"Take your friends and move away from here."

"Russian pig," said Mr. red tee-shirt, his hands covering his crown jewels.

The men huddled together and ran off.

"If I catch you bothering the lady again, I won't be as nice next time!" Feodor called after them. He turned to the girl. Close up, she was even prettier. "Are you all right?"

Eyes wide, she backed away.

"Are you okay?" he asked in Latvian. I hope they won't bother you again. Where are you going? I can walk with you."

The girl got up, gathered her books, and walked away briskly. Feodor walked faster, caught up with her, and grabbed her hand. "Hey, I just want to know you."

"Leave me alone," she said sharply. "I don't talk to strangers."

"Nice meeting you too," said Feodor and slowed to a stride.

Feodor's boss didn't show up until a week later, and Feodor had time. Every day, he would sit by the café, and when the girl walked past, he would stroll beside her asking her about school and what her name was. She never spoke, just continued walking.

On the fifth day, he walked beside her as usual, telling her about himself, and not getting any response from her. When they got to her house, she stopped and smiled shyly, batting her long eyelashes.

"Anna, Anna Karena."

Feodor fell in love.

9

Rip

The first and last time Rip fell in love was back in New York almost two decades ago. The end of that relationship had left him confused, angry, and with a death-wish on himself. Luckily, his grandfather had redirected that energy to the military. Since that incident, Rip had grown older and wiser, and gotten involved with other women, but he'd left his heart behind in the woods of New York. The little that was left had been hardened by his first-hand accounts of man's wickedness against his fellow man—atrocities he'd seen on the battlefields of Iran, Afghanistan, and Libya. And covert duties around the world and here in the US of A.

Rip reread the text from Melissa and typed his response, his body tingling with anticipation.

. . .

MELISSA: CAN YOU SWING BY. I NEED YOU.
   Me: Sure

MELISSA GRANT WAS A THIRTY-YEAR-OLD ELEMENTARY school teacher Rip had met when one snowy morning he had responded to a weather-related traffic accident at Hendonville Elementary School.

They had exchanged glances when she drove into the schoolyard, and later when he came back just before noon the same day to find out how the school was adjusting to the morning incident. He saw her herding her first graders on some type of excursion on the school grounds. Their eyes had lingered. She looked like the girl next door, tall and with a good figure. She wore glasses and had that nerdy look he liked.

Later that same afternoon, she'd called the police station and asked to speak with the officer that was at the elementary school that morning. "Do you have an emergency?" Cathy had asked. "Because the officer on call will respond right away." No, she did not have one, just wanted to speak to the policeman. Cathy transferred the call to Rip.

She didn't beat about the bush. Her name was Melissa Grant, and she wanted to know if he was available for drinks. Intrigued, Rip had gone along. Over drinks, she'd confessed that she borrowed a leaf from what she taught her students. Say what's on your mind. She didn't want to be a hypocrite. As a recent divorcee, she was done with any form of traditional relationship. After she found out he was unattached too, they'd ended up in her bed.

Later Melissa made him an offer he couldn't refuse. She liked him, and he wanted her, and they could have a no strings attached relationship, friends-with-benefits.

Initially, Rip thought she was joking, but once he found out she was serious, he thought he'd died and gone to heaven.

"Are you always this direct?" Rip had asked.

Melissa chuckled. "If I see what I like."

And so, their relationship started. Over time Rip figured out it was better when she invited him over, rather than him inviting himself.

He would stop and pick up a bottle of wine on his way. Then his stomach rumbled. He might as well order some food from the Chinese restaurant in the same mini-mart.

Covid-19 crossed his mind and he groaned. People were starting to boycott Chinese restaurants. He knew Mr. Lee, who owned and worked Dragon House, the Chinese restaurant in Hendonville, with his family. They were as American as apple pie. He was born and raised in San Francisco and moved out to the Northeast many years ago, and from all indication was doing pretty well.

Rip wanted Chinese food, but he leaned towards Italian. He didn't want Melissa sending him out to pick up food late at night.

"Sorry Lee," muttered Rip and pulled out his smartphone, then ordered takeaways from Applebee's.

Thirty minutes later, he exited the police station. It was about 9 pm when he got into his car and headed to the mini-mart. Rip waited for a red BMW to turn off before he turned into the parking lot. All that was on his mind was how lucky and thankful he was that Jude came back on his own, and they didn't have to use the people they were mobilizing for a night search.

What lay in store for him at Melissa's place flashed through his mind. He could see her come to the door dressed in a satin housecoat, which she somehow always managed to tie loosely. She would put away the food, or maybe not.

She would serve wine and by his second glass and her third, while they caught up on any highlights of the week so far, her robe would suddenly start getting undone, and then she would attack him. Jump him and have her way fast like a starved animal. Then they would eat—or not.

Rip remembered he had the police cruiser, so he parked at the restaurant and walked over to the liquor store just two doors down.. The department policy was to change into or out of your uniform at the station. Rip was relaxed about it, but he knew it wouldn't paint a good picture, him going into a liquor store in full uniform. He put on a jacket over his uniform. It wouldn't fool those that knew him. *Just this time*, he said to himself. He bought two bottles of wine, placed them in his car, and then went to the restaurant to pick up the food. Melissa's image was etched in his mind, and he wanted to get to her as fast as possible.

"When did you order, sir?" asked the receptionist.

She couldn't be older than twenty-one. There was no recognition in her face. *Probably lives in the next town*, thought Rip. "About forty-five minutes ago."

"Hold on a second." She went to the back.

Rip smiled. He tapped his fingers on the counter and looked outside. Is he ever going to get to Melissa's house today? His phone buzzed—incoming text.

MELISSA: WHERE ARE YOU? YOUR CHOW IS WAITING.

RIP GRUNTED. MAYBE HE SHOULD LEAVE THE FOOD. BUT HE'D already ordered. *I'm bringing the other type of food* he typed into his phone. The receptionist walked back. He looked up expectantly.

"Sorry sir. It will be ready in ten minutes."

Rip took a deep breath and nodded. He flashed her a smile and sat in a booth close to the bar.

Twelve minutes later, Rip drove out of the restaurant's parking lot. He contemplated using strobe lights and sirens for good measure. That would shave off some time for him. In the end, his integrity got the best of him and he decided not to. *That's what dirty cops do*, he thought. *Use their position for personal gain.*

He took Route 181, probably less busy at this time of the night. He could increase speed without any eyes watching and judging. But, even if they did see, they would think he was responding to an emergency. Rip chuckled. "Women and chow is an emergency." He floored the pedal, and the powerful cruiser lunged forward.

Something about Route 181 was on his mind but he couldn't remember why. His mind was already with Melissa. *What was it?* Rip replayed the events of the past few hours and then it came to him—the mountain lion.

Rip did not slow down. He gripped the wheel tighter as he navigated the turns, at the same time glancing into the woods. The way he was driving was a recipe for disaster, an accident waiting to happen, but he kept going.

He admired the bare woods. Column after column of leafless trees, with a misty shadow in the background. *It would make an excellent place to shoot a scary movie*, thought Rip.

The road curved and Rip knew he wasn't doing a good job—keeping his eyes on the woods when he should have been focusing on the road. He would have to forget about the lion for the moment otherwise, he was bound to lose control.

That was when he saw it. A beam of light shot from the forest floor to the top of the trees. As if someone was pointing out what the trees looked like without leaves.

Rip shook his head and muttered sarcastically under his breath. "Oh God, a copycat Morrison kid. That's all I need." He had a good mind not to stop. Then he saw smoke. He parked by the shoulder of the road and turned on his strobe lights. Then he saw the car resting upside down and flames rising at the rear. Rip touched the radio clipped onto his belt.

"Officer needs assistance; Route 181 just north of mile marker 24. Car on fire. Casualties probable." He dashed into the woods.

10

Chelsea

Chelsea headed home. She felt good about herself. It looked like Bob was finally going to do something about the computers. Hopefully, she would get to her bed on that high note without having to engage in an argument with her mother, which would keep her up the rest of the night.

Chelsea sighed. Old age does creep up on you and affects everybody around you, one way or the other. Maybe if her mother could still work instead of staying home, she would be in a better mood and not complain all the time.

She reduced her speed. It was foggy. At this rate, it was anyone's guess when she would get home. The time on the car's dashboard was ten-thirty. She pushed the radio button on her steering wheel and caught the end of the news. It wasn't good news. More countries in Europe were having incidents of the disease. Even though the incidents were few,

Chelsea was sure more people were already infected, which were presently unreported; the disease was still incubating.

She turned off the highway at her exit and entered the local roads. A few minutes later, at five after eleven, she drove into their driveway.

The light was still on in her parents' bedroom in their sprawling five-bedroom house with a swimming pool in the backyard. Her mother was probably awake, or she fell asleep with a book open on her lap. They had moved into this house after they left New York. Both her parents had worked in New York City hospitals and had kept an apartment in Manhattan, which they used when they worked late or had a late function. The apartment was still there, well maintained, but rarely used.

Chelsea contemplated parking outside and going in through the main entrance. That way she would avoid waking the whole house by the garage door opening and closing. But, walking to the front of the house in the dark wasn't something she wanted to deal with now. Bears, foxes, and whatever else was out there...

Her parents' room was at the opposite end of the house. They might not even hear the garage as it lifted, but sound traveled farther at night. She clicked the garage door opener clipped onto her car's sun visor, and it started to open with a deep humming noise.

Once inside and with the garage shut, Chelsea entered the house as quietly as possible. She climbed the stairs and made it to her bedroom door a few away from her parents' room. So far, so good. Holding her breath, she turned her door handle. Then her phone buzzed. Chelsea jumped, then sighed. It was a text from her mom asking if she was back.

Her mother was a light sleeper and must have heard the garage door after all. Chelsea had inherited her height and blond hair. Her mother had also tried to imbibe in Chelsea the habit of looking down on people. Luckily, it was not in Chelsea's DNA and never took root. But God knows her mother tried.

Mary Piers, née Barrow, was the only child of a doctor and homemaker. Like Chelsea, she lived a sheltered life, and her relatives were kept away by her parents. Young Mary went to college and medical school in the northeast, and did her postgraduate studies there as well. As a resident doctor, she met and fell in love with Paul Piers, an OBGYN in the same institution she was doing her psychiatry residency.

In their old age, Mary put her parents in one of the homes for the elderly, and after their deaths a few years apart, she was the sole beneficiary of their estate. She liquidated their various properties and put the money in stocks. She never went back to her home state of Georgia.

Chelsea stopped in front of her parent's door. She knocked softly and pushed it open, and immediately the smell of baby powder, Bengay, and flowery night cream drifted up to her nostrils. The yellow glow of a table lamp came from her mother's side of the king-sized bed. Her father lay covered with a blanket up to his chest, snoring gently, while her mother sat propped up with pillows and a book on her lap.

Chelsea smiled. "Hello, Mother." Her voice was low. She hoped her mother would take the cue.

"You're late, Chels, what happened?" said her mother in her normal voice—a voice that always sounded like she was making a demand.

"I worked late. We're working on finding a cure for COVID-19."

"Ah, that's interesting." Mother shook her head. "Children suffer the most. I saw the CDC director on TV earlier. The spread of the disease could be managed if people would do the basics. Stop digging their fingers into their noses as if they're mining for gold. Wash their hands thoroughly after, keep their secretions to themselves, and, most of all, stay home."

"That's true, Mother, but people have to work to earn a living. Not everybody has a nest egg sitting somewhere and can afford to stay home." Immediately Chelsea regretted her choice of words.

"We worked hard for our money and saved up for our golden years."

"That's true, Mother," said Chelsea trying to deflate an eruption. "I was just pointing out that everyone is not as fortunate as you to have thought ahead like that."

Her mother nodded in agreement. "So, what else happened?"

Chelsea knew she would approve of this. "Before coming home, I had dinner with the CEO of the lab. We discussed ways to speed up research using the computer."

Mother nodded. "Good. At least you're spending time with people of the same pay grade as you. Not those riffraff's you hung out with when you were a kid in New York."

Those were my true friends, Mother. You basically ruined my life back then and nearly turned me into a snob with no social life. But Chelsea didn't say that.

"All right, Mother, I need to get some sleep so I can function tomorrow. What about the nurse that comes in to help, is everything working fine?"

"Yes, she's okay. Goodnight, Chels."

"Good night, Mother." Chelsea went back to her room, turned on the shower to get it hot, and stripped off her clothes. Taking a bath with all those soothing salts would have helped, but she didn't have the time. She took a tablet of Diphenhydramine for her allergies and opted for a shower.

Once she finished, Chelsea dried herself, put on her night-gown and slipped in between the sheets. She knew sleep would eventually come, so she just waited.

Chelsea was in the forest lost and surrounded by darkness. She whirled from side to side, to the sound of running footsteps running towards her. Her whole body trembled. "Hello? Anyone there?" She asked in a shaky voice. In reply, something dashed out of the bushes towards her. Chelsea screamed.

She woke up, covered in sweat. Through a slit in the curtains, the golden rays of sunrise crept into her room.

11

Rip

Rip unclipped his police-issue flashlight from his belt and ran down the embankment. The air was thick with the smell of gasoline. The flames burned with a whoosh as they licked the leaking fuel. He knew that soon, probably within the next few seconds, the air would become thick with black smoke as the dry leaves on the forest floor ignited, and the car would probably explode.

He raised his flashlight above his shoulders and illuminated the inside of the car. A knot tightened in his stomach, and he directed his flashlight to the back seat, hoping there was nobody else in the car. It was empty. Just the two unconscious guys in the front to deal with, but it would be a lot of work. His mind raced. He tried the driver's side door but it was jammed; it only opened a couple inches. He had seen people burned alive in Iraq, trapped in the vehicle after an improvised exploding device, IED, had gone off.

The heat from the flames reminded him he had to hurry. He didn't have time to debate who he should get out first. The fire would eventually find its way to the fuel tank, and he was sure it would be only a matter of seconds.

Rip flashed his light on the driver's face. Older grey-haired Caucasian male. "Are you hurt, sir!" Rip was not expecting a speech from the man, just a moan, anything to help him decide. He placed several fingers between the man's jaw and neck to feel his carotid. Rip felt a pulse, but it also corresponded with the beating of his own heart. Non-conclusive. He flashed the light at the passenger. His head was twisted in an unnatural angle.

"This baby's going to blow," Rip muttered to himself. "Decide!" Precious seconds had already passed. He flashed the light again on the driver's blood-soaked right shoulder. The spread was getting wider. It was an active bleed.

Rip grabbed the folded serrated four-inch blade he always carried in his belt next to the flashlight. He pulled out the knife and, holding the flashlight between his teeth, clumsily steadied the taut seatbelt with his left hand and started to cut. The man's body jerked, then slid down when Rip sliced through the belt. He folded the blade, slipped it into his pocket, and reached for the man's shoulders. They were sticky and cold. The smoke got thicker, which meant the foliage was now beginning to smolder and would soon ignite. Rip was on borrowed time.

It all reminded Rip of roasting marshmallows as a kid; feeling the heat but still wanting to get closer and closer to the fire. This was a hundred times more intense. One part of his mind told Rip to abandon the man and run for it. The fuel tank was sure to explode anytime now. He maneuvered the man's shoulder to the window and started to pull him out. Rip hoped he would slide out easily, that his feet would not get stuck on anything. Rips muscles screamed as he pulled. The man's shoulders came out of the car.

Panting, he continued to pull, and slowly the man emerged through the window. Rip hooked his forearms under the man's armpits and dragged him back, pulling him away from the burning car. Rips back hurt with the effort. He heard sirens in the distance, giving him the badly needed second wind. He lay the driver down a safe distance and began toward the car again for the second victim.

The car did not explode, throwing debris all over. Instead, the flames got bigger and brighter. He backed away shielding his face with his arm. There was no way he could get the second guy from the car.

Panting and sweating from the heat and his own exertion, his jacket smeared with the man's blood, Rip watched the vehicle become wholly engulfed as the air became thick with black some, the smell of burning plastic and the unmistakable odor of burning flesh.

The sound of sirens grew louder. Rip could distinguish between the police and the fire service. He watched the burning car and shook his head.

"Are you okay, sir?"

A hand touched his shoulder and he nodded, pointed at the man, and struggled to his feet with the help of the fireman. The EMS guys arrived with a stretcher and started to assess the man's injury and administer first aid.

Rip walked toward his cruiser, leaving the EMS to their protocol. The firemen were already set up and doused the burning car and surrounding foliage with water. The smell of smoke and burning flesh persistently hung in the air.

First responders strapped the man onto a stretcher and rushed towards the waiting ambulance. He was alive. Rip drew in a deep breath filling his lungs. The fresh oxygen seemed to do him a lot of good. He put on his thinking cap. How did that car end up in the dish? Then he saw his deputy coming toward him.

"Chief, are you okay?"

Rip nodded. "Yes." He shivered and started to rub his hands together. They felt like eggs had dried on his palms and he stopped, noticing the dried blood for the first time.

John looked at him quizzically.

"Not mine," said Rip, shaking his head. "I dragged the driver out of the car. Unconscious, but alive." He paused and swallowed. "The passenger—I couldn't get to him…" Rips voice trailed off. He suddenly felt deathly cold and shivered again. The adrenaline rush was wearing off. He opened the door to his cruiser, and the smell of food rushed up to meet him.

Rips stomach heaved. He swallowed hard.

"I think you should get checked out," said his deputy. "Adrenalin high might mask any injuries you sustained."

Rip flipped his palms over as if examining them. "I'm fine. Just cuts and scrapes." He zipped up his jacket. "Have you had a chance to look at the scene?"

John pointed. "Yea, there are tread marks on the road over there. I think something caused the driver to brake hard. Like a deer, raccoon, or one of those funny-looking rodents…pussies."

Rip chuckled. "Possum."

"Yes, possum. Or he was distracted and wasn't looking, and when he saw it, he hit the brakes, swerved, and lost control."

Rip nodded. "Makes sense. We have to follow up with the hospital and talk to the driver once he's stable and can talk, then identify the other guy." He walked towards the skid marks.

Beyond them, a police cruiser was parked across the road with its lights on. *It's going to be a long night and probably a shitty morning, too,* thought Rip.

John walked up to him. "Chief, why don't you go home and get some sleep."

Rip gestured with his hands. "We still have all this."

"It's a straightforward road traffic accident. We don't both need to be sleep deprived in the morning working like zombies.

Rip looked at him and nodded. "Thanks. See you in the morning."

12

Feodor Konstantin
Latvia 1988

S ome of the best assassins belong to one of two camps or both. Those who didn't have any living close family members, and therefore couldn't be compromised in the usual ways. And those who are so selfish that they would sell their family members for a chance to advance. Feodor's superior, Dimitri Chicherin, fell into both categories.

Rumor had it that he used his niece to entrap a high-ranking member of the politico bureau with whom, shall we say, he did not see eye to eye. His niece, a rising ballet dancer, had caught the eye of a high-ranking minister. Following a tip-off, the police stormed the minister's hotel room, and in his coat was found an envelope with state secrets which he shouldn't have had. Both the minster and

Dimitri's niece got new addresses in Siberia, and Dimitri, a spot in the corridor of power.

Dimitri Chicherin left Riga just before Feodor arrived, and was supposed to be back a few days after Feodor got there. With ad-hoc meetings springing up all the time in Moscow, he got held up.

Feodor was at the safe house they'd rented, getting ready for the day. Since the day Anna divulged her name to him, something shifted in her, and she became more open. Anna was at the university studying computer science, and the men he had dealt with were just local bullies.

"They didn't mean me any harm, just boys being boys," said Anna.

Feodor smiled. "Until it gets out of hand."

They would meet at the park and go for long walks. At twenty-one, Anna was the baby of the house with two older twin sisters who have been teasing her to bring her new friend home to meet them.

"Not yet. They won't understand," she'd said to Feodor when he pressed her. "You are Russian."

Feodor told her he was a language researcher and was sent to Latvia to study the culture and language firsthand.

Anna teased him. "Hmm, you must know somebody in the employment office to get sent on an extended vacation," said Anna.

To prove to her he really was a language specialist, he asked her to quiz him in any foreign language she knew. Anna knew a few words in English and French. She asked him what they meant, and he responded.

Feodor had no role models when it came to love. Nobody ever loved him, and he never cared for anyone. When it came to sex, he lost his virginity at fourteen to one of the older girls in the orphanage who helped in the kitchen. After she turned seventeen and it was time to leave with a job lined up for her in one of the restaurants in a backwater town, she'd asked him to help her put away gallons of kerosene and firewood in the kitchen store. Once he arrived, she shut the door, led him to a corner with sacks of rice and potatoes, and reached for his pants. It was over before it started. Embarrassed, she told him it was okay, that he would be ready again soon. True to her words, he was. They did it atop the sacks of rice and potatoes. That was the last time he ever saw her.

He had a few girlfriends at the university, course partners in the academy, and a few prostitutes in almost every city he'd ever visited. But Anna was different, and it wasn't just lust. He wanted to possess her. The more time he spent with Anna, the deeper in love he fell. He wasn't sure she felt the same, but he knew he would win her over eventually. He kept on trying with flowers and walks in the park, and he focused attention as if she were the only thing that mattered in the world to him. That was the easiest part because she was.

Since meeting Anna, Feodor's elaborate plan of finding the opposition took a back seat, but he continued to learn the town and people. It didn't take him long to figure out Anna's political leaning. He tried to keep politics out of their relationship, but at the same time, wondered if he could use her to learn more. Anna's father, a university professor, was fed up with Moscow and was vocal about it. He would meet with other likeminded people and have rallys now and then even though they were banned.

About a week after he got to Riga, Feodor was just about to leave the rented house when he heard the fax machine ring, and soon the peculiar sound of electronic date transfer filled the air. The fax machine was locked up in a cabinet. Feodor retrieved the cabinet key from his suitcase, where he hid it.

By the time he came back to the cabinet, the transmission was over.

He opened the cheap wood doors and picked up the two curled papers which had fallen to the bottom of the cabinet. He unrolled the first glossy paper. It was just the transmission data–a cover sheet documenting the duration of the fax, originating fax number, and destination. He tossed it aside. Then he opened the second paper and felt like a huge weight had dropped through his stomach and into his shoes.

13

Feodor

He had drifted in and out of consciousness. For how long he couldn't say. The place must be a hospital. Foggy images of men and women in white coats walked in, studied charts, scratched their heads, and moved on. He heard sounds around him. Different beeping sounds, and sometimes people were going around him. Then he drifted off again into blackness.

This time he opened his eyes, and a bright light blinded him. He closed them tight and reopened them slowly. A dark-skinned woman wearing blue pajamas smiled at him. Who was she? Why was she smiling so much?

"Hello. You're awake." I'm Nurse Julie."

She paused as if to give him a chance to respond to that. "Eh…and you're at Hendonville Medical Center."

Feodor moved his mouth. It was dry and tasted like a cat took a dump in it. He tried to sit up, and a pain like a clap of thunder crisscrossed through his head. His head felt like an axe had split it in two like a piece of wood. Feodor grabbed his head, and that was when he felt the soft fabric wound around it. *Was his head bandaged?* In addition to pain, his head felt as heavy as a truck.

The nurse must have noticed the shocked look on his face because she started to speak.

"You hurt your head, honey." She walked towards the bed. "You were in a car accident last night. Do you want to sit up?"

Feodor followed her with his eyes.

She smiled, then picked up something beside him on the bed and pressed one of the buttons on it.

He jerked, causing pain to shoot across his shoulder as the back of the bed lifted, putting him in a sitting position.

Julie raised an eyebrow. "Is that okay?"

He didn't answer.

"This is the remote control for the bed, and also the call button." This is up, and this is down." She pointed at the buttons. "If you need help, you press the big round button with the white silhouette of a nurse."

"Ладно."

Nurse Julie's eyebrows shot up. "What was that? You speak a foreign language. Let me get your doctor. If you need anything while I'm gone, press the button." She pantomimed pressing a button.

The man nodded. *"Ладно."*

Nurse Julie giggled and left the room.

Feodor looked around and noticed the IV line in his arm. A plastic band with some numbers was on his left wrist. He could read the letters written in English: John Doe.

The door opened and two men wearing white coats hurried in with the nurse..

"My name is Dr. Jules. You've already met Nurse Julie."
He pointed at Julie. She waved. Then at the other man in a
white coat. "Dr. Bell. My resident."

The man nodded.

Dr. Jules looked at a chart. "You came in last night,
unconscious with a gash on your head, and bite marks on
your shoulder. We did an MRI. There was no visible struc-
tural damage, but based on the symptoms and signs you
presented with, we think you have a concussion. You must
have hit your head. But no major damage. You also have bite
marks on your shoulders." He paused. "Can you remember
what happened? Before we start, what's your name?"

Feodor could not remember his name. He could only
remember all that happened since he woke up. He paused and
thought, then spoke. *"Я не знаю."*

Nurse Julie smiled and exchanged glances with the
doctor. "I told you he spoke a foreign language."

"That sounds like Russian!" said Dr. Jules. "I had some
Russian doctors in my residency program, and they had a
similar accent to you." He brought out his smartphone,
scrolled, and raised it. "It's an app that can detect language
and translate it into English. Can you repeat what you said?"

Feodor did.

A female mechanical voice spoke. "Language Russian.
English translation, I don't know."

"He can understand English, then, and replies in Russian," said Dr. Jules. Excitedly, he fished out a notebook from
his pocket and scribbled on it. He raised it to Feodor. "Can
you read this out loud?"

Feodor looked at the note, then at the doctor. "I am in the
hospital."

Dr. Jules was all smiles. "You are bilingual. Can I ask you
a few more questions?"

Feodor didn't say anything. Dr. Jules took it as a yes. "What happened last night?"

"I don't know. I woke up and found myself here."

"We'll get a psychiatric consult for you as soon as possible." The doctor paused. "The police are also interested in talking to you."

The man did not show any emotion for or against the notion of meeting with the police.

14

Rip

The smell of blood, smoke, and burning flesh, and the unpredictable risk of the fuel tank blowing up as he pulled the man out of the vehicle, were stressors that resulted in an endorphin surge. A natural high enjoyed by runners that Rip missed since quitting special ops and the military.

His mind drifted back to a few years ago before he left the military. They had gone in for a quick grab and snatch in Pakistan and their escape helicopter-. Rip caught himself. Not only had he become a civilian, but he was also thinking like one.

He corrected himself out loud. "*Helo*, not helicopter." What if any of his guys like Max Brandon had heard him? That thought brought a smile to his face, then it quickly faded. Their escape *helo* had taken a hit, and he had lost friends. Just like tonight, he had gone back to retrieve wounded screaming soldiers and bring them to safety.

While going back a third time, the chopper had exploded. Rip was knocked unconscious and woke up in a field hospital. Emergency surgery and months of therapy healed his body, but his mind was never the same. He'd blamed himself. To him, he'd abandoned the rest of his team, despite having saved the lives of some, telling himself he had been foolhardy to go get them and he should be thankful he hadn't gone up with the chopper.

And last night he did it again, he had abandoned the man in the passenger seat. Rip knew the man was already dead, but his mind wouldn't accept that he did his best. Maybe, if he'd worked faster to free the first man, then the other man last night wouldn't have burned to a crisp. Rip knew he was being unreasonable and hard on himself. But that was the nature of the illness in his mind.

After traveling through the US, dealing with a few hot heads here and there, his attention was brought to the opening for Chief of Police at Hendonville, NJ. A small community, it was the type of place where most career police officers would only go as their career was winding down-maybe due to age, illness, or both. He'd applied and was surprised when they hired him.

"Good," Max Brandon had said. "At least that puts you within an arm's reach of the CIA. We need men like you to keep this country safe. Come join us, Rip."

Rip had politely declined, even though Max had used his office to facilitate things when Rip found himself up a creek without a canoe or paddle. Now he sat in his office and downed his cup of coffee. It was only five-thirty in the morning. John had given him an advantage by taking over last night, but he had not been able to capitalize on it. He walked to the break room, filled his cup, and went back to his office.

He thought of last night. Once he'd gotten into his cruiser, the smell of the takeaway food, which had initially made him gag, then reminded him of what his plan had been. "Shit," he'd muttered. He'd checked his phone. Melissa had sent him five text messages. And he could read the sentence progression from horny to angry by the fifth text. He had gone to her house anyway and let himself in with the spare key she'd given him. She was in bed, dressed in a sheer black lacy nightgown, with nothing else underneath and an empty wine glass on her bed stand. He could only look, not touch. Melissa enjoyed nothing else better than sleeping and would have gladly put a knife through him if he dared wake her up. Rip put the food in her fridge and drove back to his house.

Rip's home was a two-bedroom house he rented. He had a couch and a TV in the living room, functional laundry and kitchen, and a bed and reading table in the bedroom.

He showered and went to bed. But sleep wouldn't come. His mind kept drifting back to the older man and the burning vehicle. Finally, he'd had enough. He got up, dressed , and drove to the office. He came in as the digital clock on Cathy's table changed to five. He brought out the filter paper for the coffee machine, placed it in the receptacle, added a pouch of ground coffee to the device, hit the start button, and sat on his chair, resting comfortably while the coffee brewed.

"Chief! Wake up. The coffee is ready!" said a familiar voice.

Rip's eyes flew open, and he inhaled, filling his lungs with the smell of the fresh brew.

Cathy stood in front of his desk. "Did you sleep here?" She thrust a cup of steaming coffee in front of him.

Rip rubbed his eyes. "Good morning to you too. Yes…

No! I came in early. I must have dozed off." He took the coffee from her. "Thank you."

"That should wake you up. I see last night was busy. A rollover. One dead, one unconscious. Were they locals?"

"What time is it?"

Cathy turned and looked at the clock on her table. "Just after 7."

"I don't think they're locals." Rip got to his feet and drained his cup. "Good stuff." His stomach rumbled, reminding him his last meal was yesterday afternoon. "I'm going for some eggs and sausages on a bagel. Can I get you something?"

Cathy raised her lunch box. "I know you're just polite."

The local coffee shop was just across the road. The smell of fresh-baked donuts and coffee engulfed him as soon as he walked in. And people heading to work were coming in to get their caffeine fix or grab something to eat. Rip ordered another coffee even though he had one waiting on his desk. It never tasted the same anyway. Even when he bought known brands, it never tasted like it did when you got it in their stores.

Rip chatted briefly with the owner. Coffee was always on the house for cops, but Rip always left a generous tip.

He decided to stay and eat at the coffee shop. He found a seat. It was still early, and the customers coming in didn't linger. They were mostly folks commuting to work. They came in, took their food or drink, and left. Rip's bagel was soft and warm; just the way Rip liked it. He shoved the last piece of the bagel, with eggs and sausage, into his mouth, shutting his eyes to savor the taste. What he saw instead was the helicopter crash and the burning vehicle from last night.

He opened his eyes and pushed the thought away. He didn't want to start blaming himself this early in the morning.

He had an accident victim to question and a corpse to identify. The first thing would be to head down to the medical center and talk to the survivor.

The station was buzzing with activity when he walked back. The other staff members were all in.

"Long breakfast, eh?" asked Cathy.

Rip gave her a smug look and headed for his office.

"Just kidding." Cathy flashed him a smile. "Hold on Chief. I just got a call from the hospital. John Doe is awake."

Rip stopped in his tracks, and turned to face Cathy, eyebrows raised. "John Doe?"

"They said he couldn't remember last night or who he is."

Rip pulled up the image of the man in his mind again. He had blood on his head and shoulders. Probably hit his head. "Is John in yet?"

"Yes, he should be eating breakfast somewhere," said Cathy as her eyes darted around the office.

"When he's done, send him over to the medical center to get the man's fingerprints." Christ, what is he going to call the man? He hated not addressing people by their names. Rip grabbed his jacket and headed for the exit. He stopped by the door. "Call the police station in Newton, see if they have any cases of people reported missing. I'm heading over to HMC."

15

Chelsea

B y the time Chelsea hit the shower, it was nine in the morning, and she was definitely behind schedule. The lab would be calling any time soon. She adjusted the showerhead and felt the impact of the pinpoints on her skin, waking her up. Her mind drifted to last night with her mother and the dream that ensued. Why should events that happened so long ago still occur in the land of nightmares for her? She thought she'd gotten over them, but apparently not.

Sometimes, Chelsea loved her mother, and other times she hated her. No, hate was a strong word. She disliked her. Today, the latter was true. She consoled herself that most people had a similar relationship with their mothers. The events of that day when she was sixteen had faded in her mind, but she somehow felt her mother had played a pivotal role in the outcome.

Mother always had her wits together. She could be a charmer here, lean in there, cajole, deceive, intimidate—anything that got her what she wanted she would do. Other times, just the plain old bait and switch. The worst is when she's just mean for no reason at all, just for the sake of being mean. Chelsea believed she didn't need to talk about things that happened decades ago. She was just exercising her mean streak.

Chelsea got out of the shower, dressed, and went downstairs to grab a cup of coffee.

Her father sat in his favorite chair at the head of the dining table, his gray hair combed to the side and wearing a cardigan over a blue button-down shirt and slacks.

"Hello Chelsea. Come and hug your old father."

She smiled. "Good morning, Dad." She was glad today was one of those days he remembered her. It broke her heart each time she saw him struggling to remember people that he should know. She wrapped her hand over his shoulder and kissed him on the forehead. He smelled of his aftershave, Old Spice. She squeezed his shoulder.

Her father beamed. "Have you heard about the coronavirus epidemic in China?"

"A little," said Chelsea. She wanted to keep him talking. They'd discussed it many times.

He nodded. "I was reading an article online, and it said that meat for dinner in China is preferred fresh. That is, butchered just before it's cooked. So, in the markets, they have all sorts of live animals in cages around each other, and viruses that do not cause any disease in their host animal soon find their way into humans. And just like that, a new disease is born."

"But why China? A lot of other countries have markets

where livestock is butchered just before the customer buys it."

"Pigs can be infected with both human and bird flu viruses," said Chelsea's mother.

Chelsea and her father looked up to see her mother standing by the entrance to the dining room.

"Good morning," said Chelsea.

Her mother nodded and thrust her cane forward. "In the case of pigs, they become a Petri dish that allows genetic material from different viruses to mix and form basically new organisms.

Chelsea walked to the kitchen counter where the coffee machine was located, retrieved a mug from the cabinet above it, selected a hazelnut cup from the coffee selection, and popped it into the machine.

Her mother continued toward the table. "And because of the proximity between these animals and humans, the new and improved virus jumps into a new host. If the new host happens to be man, a new organism we've never encountered starts to spread, and soon an epidemic is born, and we have nothing yet to fight against it. It's like medicine is always playing catch-up."

"But as I said, there are markets like that all over the world," said her father in his slow deliberate tone as his wife walked over to the chair beside him and sat down. "Still, why China?"

Chelsea removed the mug from the machine and wondered if her mother saw what just happened. Her father just echoed her question, not remembering he was about to answer the same question asked by Chelsea before her mother walked in. She strolled to the table and pushed her mug towards her mother. "Coffee?"

Her mother nodded. "Well, because in these markets, they

have farm-raised animals and birds, kept in cages side by side with the wild variety, each with their exotic slew of viruses, just waiting for the right moment for the spark to happen. A new organism is formed, then host jumping occurs."

Chelsea nodded, seeing the point she was making. "I never thought of it that way." She knew she'd better make her escape before her mother turned the discussion to her personal life. Chelsea walked to the kitchen, opened a drawer, and retrieved a Styrofoam cup with a lid, and placed it under the coffee machine. When the cup was full, she said, "I'm running late. I have to go. See you later."

"Bye Chelsea," said her father.

Chelsea's mother cocked her head. "Don't stay too late."

Chelsea exhaled, and exaggerated a slumping of her shoulders. "It depends on the workload, but I'll try. Bye."

She entered the garage from the kitchen as her parents talked about viruses, and she wondered how long her father would be able to engage her mother before his mind abandoned him. Maybe that was what was frustrating her, watching the person she loved basically vanish right in front of her eyes.

As Chelsea drove away from the house, she passed the nurse and housekeeper who came in to watch her parents during the day heading towards the house. A cleaning crew came in twice a week. Initially, they were supervised by her mother, and now they mostly knew what to do.

Chelsea got out of the winding road that led to their home and joined Route 181. Her mind drifted to the conversation she just had with her parents and how she could use that information. Perhaps she could find out the different harmless viruses that live in these market animals without causing disease in them and write a program where these organisms interact with each other in many different variations.

Then she could take what the AI generated and analyze it to determine whether what they formed could cause disease in man and how to neutralize it.

The plan was becoming overly broad but looked like it had merit. The problem would be getting the manpower to handle it. There was no way they wouldn't need outside help to pull it off. The more Chelsea thought about it, the more she felt her approach could yield something useful.

She had another ten minutes to drive before she got to her office nestled in the forest on Black Hills. Named after black bears that live in the area, Chelsea was glad that in the years she'd worked there, she hadn't had the pleasure of seeing any of them.

She tapped her smartphone resting on a stand on the dash to activate the Bluetooth. Chelsea wanted to listen to the news, anything new with the virus, but didn't want to tune in to CNN or Fox.

"Play the news."

She returned her eyes to the road just in time to see a tawny colored animal leap from the shoulder about fifty meters ahead of her car. "What the…?"

16

Rip

Cathy had provided Rip with information on where to find John Doe at the hospital.

"Third floor. Stop at the nurse's station. They'll know who you are once they see you," Cathy had said.

On the drive over, Rip tried to prepare his mind on how to approach someone who can't remember his name. *Come on*, he thought. *Maybe the man's faking*. Deep down, for some reason Rip believed he would be able to prove that the man was faking. Rip laughed at himself. He sounded like a friend of his in high school who, after a workout, told Rip that he felt so flexible he believed he could dodge bullets.

Rip still hadn't gotten used to the surprise each time he walked into a hospital. The reception area always looked cozy, like someone's home. Today, HMC smelled of flowers. Then people started calling out to him. It was like a celebrity had walked in. *Hello, Chief. Hi Chief*, said people, mostly the older town residents he passed on the way to the elevator. He contemplated going to the receptionist's counter to ask for directions and make small talk. But since there was nobody there, he continued. A flat-screen TV hanging on the wall was showing data about COVID-19.

Inside the elevator were two women in scrubs, probably nurses, a man in civilian clothes, and a gray-haired doctor in a white coat.

Suddenly the doctor cowered and stared at Rip in horror. "Officer, I didn't do it! I didn't do it!"

Rip raised an eyebrow.

Then the gray-haired man burst out laughing, and the other people laughed with him.

Your idea of a sick joke? No pun intended. But Rip didn't say that. He kept a straight face looking at their reflection on the metallic door. They stopped laughing, and when the elevator opened on the next floor, they all got out shooting nervous looks at Rip.

Rip got off on the third floor, the encounter leaving a bitter taste in his mouth. He looked left, then right, and proceeded towards the nurses' station. Just then, his phone rang. It was Melissa. It would be quick, he knew, because she was in school. Even though they had signs all over, showing that cellphones where prohibited, Rip answered and moved towards the window.

"Hello Melissa."

"Hi Rip, I saw you finally made it last night. You should have woken me up."

"On my way to your place I ran into a rolled over car on fire. By the time we were done, it was late."

There was a sharp intake of air from the other end of the phone. "I hope there were no casualties."

"Unfortunately, there was. I'm at the hospital now just about to talk to the survivor. Can I call you back?"

"Yes, do that. I have to go, too. I have a parent-teacher meeting in a few minutes. Bye."

Rip decided to reschedule right away with a text. What about tonight? He hit send.

"Hello," said Rip to the nurse at the nurses' station. She was black, tall, and pretty.

The lady smiled, showing perfect teeth. "How can I help you?"

"I'm here to see the patient brought in last night following a road traffic accident."

"Oh, our John Doe." She looked Rip over. "I would have asked for some credentials, but your uniform gave you away." She batted her eyelashes flirtatiously and instinctively corrected her posture. "You must be Chief Chord. The psych team is giving him an evaluation right now. I'm sure they'll be done soon. His doctor is expecting you. If you can take a seat over there..." She pointed at a small waiting area with a table with magazines placed on it. "We have coffee if you're interested." Her eyes lingered on Rip's.

Rip smiled back. "Thank you." He took a seat and tapped his fingers to a beat on his thighs and waited. He looked at his phone. 9.30 am. The medical examiner must be in the office by now. Rip called his number but got a recording. He called Cathy.

"Chief, how can I help you?"

"I'm still at the hospital waiting to interview John Doe. I called the coroner but got his voice mail. Could you call them later to find out what they have on the burn victim?"

"Will do," said Cathy and hung up.

Rip looked around again, wondering how long the doctors would take with their evaluation. Then his phone rang. Cathy.

"I spoke with Dr. Aggrawal. He said they'll probably get to the autopsy after the weekend. But he mentioned that the belt buckle on the man's pants had a Russian inscription."

"Russian?"

"Yes, and that he's missing an ear and has puncture marks on his head and neck. He thinks an animal made them."

"Bite marks? Made by an animal?" *Fuck!* "Missing an ear?" *An animal got to them before I did.*

Rip looked up to the sound of a door opening and got distracted. Three men in white coats walked out of a room, just as the door adjacent to the room they were in opened, and a gray-haired older man with an eye patch stepped out.

"Hello, Dr. Jules," said Mr. Eye Patch. "You have a new patient! I see everything, you know."

Dr. Jules turned to him. "Yes, Mr. Pippin, and please don't bother the new patient; he's very sick."

Rip refocused on his conversation with Cathy. "What type of-"

The nurse called out to Rip. "Chief?" She pointed at the men.

Rip nodded. "Call you later Cathy. The doctors are ready." He hung up, jumped to his feet, and put his phone away.

"Chief Chord!" said the Doctor Jules. He was dressed in scrubs and a white coat, with a stethoscope hanging over his neck. The other two had on button-down shirts with ties under their white coats. One of them wore Malcolm X style glasses.

Rip nodded and smiled. "Yes."

"I'm Dr. Jules." He extended his hand. "The patient who came in last night unconscious is under my care. Preliminary toxicology screening ruled out any substances that could have impaired his memory or judgment, nor was any abnormality detected on MRI of the head. However, when the patient came to, he had no memory." Dr. Jules pointed at the other two doctors. "The psych team just did an evaluation, and they reached the conclusion he has PTA."

Parent Teachers Association thought a bemused Rip, but this was no time for laughs. "Some type of amnesia?"

"Post-traumatic amnesia," said Dr. Malcom X. "It's the term used to describe a state of confusion that occurs immediately after a traumatic injury to the brain. The injured person is disoriented in person, place, and time. They don't know who they are, where they are, or what time it is."

The other psychiatrist rubbed his chin. "PTA can present in two different ways. There's retrograde amnesia where the patient loses memories formed shortly before the injury, and then there's anterograde amnesia. This is a problem of forming new memories after the injury."

"So, which one does he have?" asked Rip.

"Unfortunately," continued the doctor, "based on the type of injury he has, it's more likely that he has both."

"Both?"

The doctor's fingers waved in the air as if he were pointing out directions to a fishing spot in the woods. "The patient might recall pockets or islands of memory if you will, which will only add to the confusion because he cannot make head or tail of them. They're completely out of context to anything and everything."

17

Feodor Konstantin
Latvia 1988

F eodor could not keep his hands steady as he read the
fax. He couldn't believe his eyes, but there it was.

SURVEILLANCE SUBJECT

DR. JANIS KARENA AND FAMILY
All Associates of Dr. Karena

FEODOR CHECKED THE FAX PHONE NUMBER THE MESSAGE HAD
come from, and it was from Moscow. He folded the fax

papers and took them to the kitchen. He struck a match and set fire to both and threw them into the sink. When all that was left was ashes, he turned on the tap and flushed the black remnant. Then he left the rented house his mind in complete turmoil.

The fact that Anna's father was active in the opposition wasn't news to Feodor. It was the fact that Moscow already had an idea of what was going on. *That* was news to him. He thought that was why he was sent there in the first place. Maybe Dimitri already knew before he left for Moscow and made the trip to Moscow to bring them up to speed.

Feodor arrived at the coffee shop where he usually waited for Anna on her way back from school. He ordered a breakfast of fried eggs, buttered toast and coffee. He had no appetite, but he forced himself to eat. Since he gotten the fax, he'd shifted into the battle mode. Feodor was trained never to pass up an opportunity to eat. He wondered how he'd gotten himself into this.

His last surveillance job was in Ukraine, and it ended with the assassination of the subject with members of his family and associates. It was a well-planned hit. Using a high powered telescopic sight, Feodor shot the man and his associates as they came out of a meeting. And later, the man's wife and children were eliminated as they came home from school.

If the opposition is crushed, the agitation for independence would only die down for a while, until someone else picked up the mantle. The same had happened in Ukraine after their activities there. Something was happening in all the Soviet-occupied states. Was communism failing? Or did it need reform? Feodor knew he was asking the type of questions that, if voiced out loud, could have him shipped off to Siberia.

Later that afternoon, he met Anna on her way back from school. She batted her eyelashes and smiled at him. One look at her face, and Feodor knew he would move mountains to have her for keeps.

18

Feodor

Feodor heard the knock and turned to the door. The three doctors had left not too long ago after asking him so many questions that his head started to hurt again. The two new doctors that came with Dr. Jules said they came to evaluate his memory. They did card sorting tests, language tests, and sometimes asked him the name of things he couldn't remember but knew what they were used for. For example, they showed him a pen. He knew it was used for writing but couldn't remember the name.

His head throbbed now and then. Dr. Jules said he'd hit his head during the accident. After the questions, they'd told him he had something called PTA, which they described as memory loss due to a head injury, but they would be back for more evaluation. Feodor ran his hand softly over the bandage on his head, and then there was the pain from the injury on his bandaged left shoulder. He could not remember how he got either of them.

The door opened and Dr. Jules walked in with another man wearing a uniform. Feodor, on seeing the uniformed man, stiffened but didn't know why.

"This is Rip Chord, Chief of Police in Hendonville," said Dr. Jules. "He's here to ask you a few more questions. We're all trying to help. Asking questions might uncover a clue that could lead to a breakthrough, and perhaps help you remember who you are."

"Hello," said Rip. "As Dr. Jules said, I'm the Chief of Police here. I was the one that pulled you out of the burning car. I was driving-"

"Burning car?" asked the man.

"Yes. Rip came closer to the bed. "I think you were driving. You must have lost control, and the car flipped over and crashed. Unfortunately, the man on the passenger side didn't make it."

Feodor was silent for a moment. "There was someone else in the car?" He paused. "Who? What does he look like?"

"We're still trying to find out who he was. I can't tell you what he looked like, the car went up in flames after I brought you out…with him trapped in it."

Feodor gazed at Rip, waiting for him to say more. But it seemed the police chief was waiting for him to react. Feodor felt trapped. He glanced around, suddenly feeling uncomfortable. He wanted to know who he was too. What was he doing here?

"So, do you remember what happened before the accident, or after?"

"*Я уже отвечал на этот вопрос раньше. Я не могу вспомнить!* I've answered that question before. I can't remember!"

Rip leaned back and cocked his head. "Don't be angry. Do you prefer to speak Russian?" asked Rip speaking Russian.

Feodor shrugged. "I've been asked the same questions over and over again." He replied in Russian again.

Dr. Jules looked at Rip wide-eyed. "It's Russian right? We had quite a few Russian doctors in my residency program. You speak the language?"

"Yes," said Rip. "I spent some time in the Navy. I have a thing for languages, and I honed those skills while I was in." Rip paused. "The coroner mentioned that a belt buckle salvaged from the other occupant of the car had an inscription in Russian."

"Perhaps he grew up in Russia then," said Dr. Jules. "His English has a little bit of an accent."

Feodor noticed that the doctor and police chief looked surprised and had a hurt look on their faces. He felt bad. "I'm sorry for yelling. I feel angry that I can't remember anything."

"It's okay," said Dr. Jules. "It's a normal response. I would feel the same if I were in his shoes." He turned to Rip. "Maybe you can question him some other time. You'll have the first shot at him before he gets tired, say like tomorrow morning. I guess all the questioning from the psychiatrists was a bit too much."

"Why don't we ask him first," said Rip. "This is possibly a vehicular manslaughter case, and there'll be a lot of questioning going forward. In fact, one of my officers will be coming around to get his fingerprints."

Dr. Jules looked at Feodor and smiled. "Is it okay for the chief to visit you tomorrow morning to ask more questions?"

Feodor said nothing but kept on watching and listening.

"That means fine," said Dr. Jules and walked toward the

door.

Rip followed. "What do you call him?"

The doctor shrugged. "I see a lot of patients. Most of the time, I go by room number when I can't remember the patient's name."

"What about Nicholas, after the last Czar?"

Something clicked in Feodor's head. Has he heard that name before? He watched the two men.

Dr. Jules adjusted his stethoscope. "We'll think of something."

"I nearly forgot," said Rip lowering his voice. "The medical examiner reported bite marks and a missing ear on the deceased passenger. Any such marks on him?"

"Really," said Dr. Jules. "Ivan here has bite marks on his head and neck." Dr. Jules paused and smiled, a smug look on his face. "Did I just say, Ivan?"

"Yes, you did," said Rip.

"Anyway, his shoulder was mauled by something," continued Dr. Jules. "He has deep bite marks as if an animal was trying to get a chunk out of him for dinner."

"Like a raccoon? Maybe a fox or skunk?" asked Rip.

Dr. Jules shook his head. "No, from the teeth marks, I would say something larger. Like a bear or wolf. I know we have bears around here but not wolves."

"Like a mountain lion?" asked Rip

Dr. Jules opened the door. "That too, but they're not found around here either." He fumbled for something in his coat pocket. "The nurse found this in his pants pocket." He gave Rip a clear sandwich zip lock bag with a piece of paper inside it.

Feodor watched Rip take the plastic bag from the doctor and slip it into his pocket as the doctor shut the door behind him.

19

Rip

The doctor assured Rip the patient would be in a better mood to work with tomorrow and bid him a good day. Rip took the elevator downstairs, thinking what a big waste of time it had been coming up to the hospital. But that was his job. Win some and lose some. Perhaps it wasn't a total loss, though. He did find out that both men had been bitten by a large animal. Something was out there for sure. And then there was the piece of paper in his pocket which might yield some clue.

He hoped to get back to the station as soon as possible and catch up with other things that needed to be done before this accident thing happened. The elevator didn't help his mood. It stopped on every floor, and each new person, once they saw Rip in his uniform, hesitated before getting on.

The elevator jerked to a stop, dinged, and the doors opened into the lobby. Rip was happy to be on the ground floor, and then he caught sight of his deputy, John. And his happiness of finally getting to the ground floor faded.

"Hi Chief. Cathy gave me your message," said his deputy.

"You still look fresh after staying awake all night, what's the secret?"

John shrugged. "Youth."

"Low blow."

"Good genes, then. Is the patient really…" He pointed a finger in the air, whistled three times while twirling his wrist around.

"No, he didn't lose his mind. He lost his memory. He can't recall who he is. The doctors called it post-traumatic amnesia." Rip noticed John's bag. He remembered why John was there and sighed.

"What?"

"I don't know if the man will let you take his fingerprints. He seemed agitated and confused from all the questioning." Rip thought it might be better to have John take his finger-prints tomorrow.

"Fingerprinting is the ace in the hole," said John. "The sooner we find out who he is, the better we get his family involved and help him regain his memory."

Rip nodded. "I guess you can try, but don't push him. Once he shows any sign of irritation, just let it go. We can do it tomorrow morning. He agreed to…" Rip remembered the man didn't agree to anything. "I'm supposed to see him tomorrow."

"Third floor, right?"

"Yes."

John headed towards the elevators.

"Hold on John. Hey, remember the Morrison kid that said he saw a mountain lion?"

"Aha, why?"

"The patient and the deceased both have bite marks from a large animal, as if something tried to eat them."

"Jesus. You think there is a lion out there?"

"I hope not, but you can't discard the evidence."

John exhaled, standing up to his full height. "What evidence?"

Rip told him what the medical examiner had said about the bite marks and missing ear.

John shook his head. "More work for us. We must take every reported sighting seriously then. People have been claiming to see mountain lions in Sussex County forever. I mean, with the beautiful scenery and mountains, mountain lions would fit in nicely with foxes, bobcats, black bears, coyotes, and what have you that roam about freely. And there's a healthy deer population for food too."

"But, the State Department of Environmental Protection has never confirmed it." Rip paused. "Anyway, let me not hold you up. See you later."

Rip drove back to the office. The thought of the likelihood of having to deal with a predator in their midst was overwhelming. Apart from the accident victims, nobody else had been attacked by an unidentified animal. But does he have to wait for someone else to get attacked before he let the public know? Then he thought about Jude Morrison. Didn't he say he thought the animal had touched him? Something like that.

Rip's phone rang, interrupting his thoughts. It was John. The last thing he needed now was a problem with the hospital. "Hey."

"Chief, we have a problem."

Rips heart sank. He braced himself. "What happened?"

"Ivan Doe was very receptive."

"Ivan Doe?"

John chuckled. "I had to go with a name. The skin of his palms is peeling off. I couldn't get a fingerprint."

"Peeling off? Like chemically removed?"

"I'm afraid so, Chief. Did you look at his palms while you were there?"

"I didn't get to it before he became agitated. You think someone is trying to stop us from identifying him?"

"His palms are red and peeling, so I think whatever agent was used was applied in the last twenty-four hours. And when I scanned them, it's just plain. I even tried ink and got the same result."

"Did you ask the nurses?"

"Yes," said John. "Apart from the doctors, then you, and the nurse taking his vitals, no one else has been there. And they do that every hour."

Rip shut his eyes and ran his hands through his hair. "You think he's faking the amnesia and did that to himself?"

"I don't know Rip. If you hadn't come along when you did, he would have perished in the fire, too, right?"

Rip nodded. That was true. Then he remembered he was on the phone. "That's right." He exhaled. "Come back to the station. Get a picture of Ivan's face. We'll figure out another way to ID him."

"All right, see you in a bit." John hung up.

Rip placed his phone on the desk. *What is going on? Could this be a homicide cover-up?* Then he remembered the zip lock bag Dr. Jules had given him. He pulled it out of his pocket. One side was blank, on the other side were two typed words in capital letters: CHELSEA PIERS.

A chill traveled down his spine as if an ice cube had been tossed into the back of his shirt. A dead body in a burned car with parts of the ear missing. *Torture?* A Russian, sixty something-year-old man in rural New Jersey with amnesia and destroyed fingerprints. The cold war was over. Rip had heard an excerpt of President Reagan's speech to the Russians in 1987 many times. 'Mr. Gorbachev, tear down this wall!' In November 1991, four years later, the Berlin Wall came down.

What was the attraction here? In Hendonville? There was nothing here but farmland, some industries, and beautiful mountains and woods. A suburban refuge for those who work in the big cities but want their dollars to go a lot further home purchasing-wise. Another thought hit him. Is it possible? Have they uncovered a terrorist plot?

Rip's gut tightened as if a giant fist had gripped and twisted it. Even with heavy traffic, the financial capital of the world, New York City, was only an hour away from Hendonville. He remembered in the news back then, after 9-11, some law enforcement agents had stopped some of the terrorists for one traffic infraction or the other, and let them go. Then, there were those training to be pilots. The warning flags were there but largely unrecognized. Was this another 9-11 in the making?

Something was up. He knew that much. He could smell it. People just don't get their fingerprints burned off. And there was no Russian community anywhere near here. The pieces just didn't fit. Not yet anyway.

Rip scooted over in his chair to face his computer. He saw his reflection on the screen, his forehead puckered with sweat. He moved the mouse, and the screen came alive. He Googled Chelsea Piers.

The first hit was www.chelseapiers.com. The website for a popular historic landmark in New York City. Some of the old piers were transformed into 28-acre waterfront sports and entertainment complex located between 17th and 23rd Streets along Manhattan's Hudson River.

Heart pounding, Rip read through the pages. A 2014

report showed that it got about four million visitors a year. Could it be a target? Any place where large numbers of people congregated for one activity or the other was a potential target for terrorists.

Rip returned to the Google search results page and scrolled down. The next hit was people, and perhaps because the Google bots took into consideration the location you're searching from, they showed results to your query as close to your location as possible.

Rip saw the name Chelsea Piers, MD, Chief Researcher at XRCure. He moved the cursor to an image and clicked on it to enlarge it. He looked at the image of the doctor, and his heart started to pound like galloping horses. "Jesus."

He would not be the one who left any stone unturned. The terrorist attack on 9-11 changed the world. America responded, and the world changed forever. Rip remembered his experiences in the Navy, things he had done and seen. Would he have had those experiences if it weren't for that attack on the World Trade Center, the Pentagon and the other unknown destination of the fourth hijacked plane?

He looked at the image on the screen again. It was most likely a dead end, but he would go down every mole hole if he had to. The world would not change again under his watch if he could help it. He did another search, this time he typed in XRCure Inc.

Rip was surprised that the company was tucked away in the wooded hills of Plainview Township and he'd never heard about them. He typed XRCure into the map app on his smartphone and hit search. Directions to their office came up. Estimated time distance from his location: twenty-nine minutes. What do you know?

20

Chelsea

C helsea didn't need to slam on her breaks. The animal crossed the road and ran off into the woods. It happened so fast that it could have been one of those situations where you wondered if you really saw what you think you saw. Was it a dog? It looked more like a cat, the size of a big dog. She was glad it hadn't been close enough to make her lose control.

By the time Chelsea drove into her parking spot at XRCure, she had forgotten all about the animal. What was on her mind now was how to write a code that would incorporate what her mother had described. The information must be out there somewhere. Find out all the viruses that could potentially cohabit with the farm animals and wild animals that are brought to market and simulate all the different ways their genetic materials could combine.

Chelsea fanned herself. It was suddenly too warm in the

car. Her idea could revolutionize medicine and go way beyond COVID. With this way of thinking, their research lab would be taking a proactive approach to fighting diseases instead of a reactionary one.

Excitement coursed through Chelsea. She wanted to get to her desk and start pounding away on her keyboard. The concept was so easy and straight forward that she wondered if perhaps she was missing something. She remembered a creative writing class she took in college as an elective so many years ago. The instructor was fond of saying, "Ideas are cheap. It's what you do with them that turns them into something people would pay you money for."

She got to her office without further incident. Some people had wanted her to stop and chat with them, but she gave them a quick smile and continued to her office, taking quick, purposeful steps as if she was late for an appointment.

Chelsea's computer had gone to sleep from last night. She tapped it back on, typed in her password, and was in. She scanned the results from last night's data-crunching- nothing new was uncovered. Okay, she let the program continue to run in the background, opened a page, and started writing her new ideas, saying a quiet prayer that no one would bother her again. Five minutes in, there was a knock on her door.

"Come in," said Chelsea. She glanced at who came in and continued to pound away at her keyboard. "Hi Lisa."

"Hey, good morning," said Lisa. "I was worried you didn't leave early enough last night and overslept."

Chelsea didn't answer. The only sound in her office was the sound of her fingers flying over the keyboard.

"Emm...I'll come back when you're less busy."

Chelsea spoke with her eyes still glued to the screen. "I left late last night," said Chelsea in a loud voice, still typing away. "But I made it here this morning. Actually, it was my mother that kept me awake last night." She worked some more. "Lisa, I just have to finish this. I'll talk to you later."

Chelsea continued to type. This was just to get the ideas down on paper. Next would be to arrange it into bite sizes and then write codes. To pull this off, she would really need help.

An hour later, her office phone rang. She knew it was an internal call from the sound, single and short. External call rings were always prolonged. Chelsea ignored it. She wanted to put all her thoughts on paper, so to speak, before attending to the day's workload.

Her office phone stopped ringing, and her cell phone took over as if it were a baton exchange in a relay race. Chelsea ignored that too. Her voice mail would get that.

"Wow. That is dedication!" said a familiar voice behind her.

She spun around. "Bob!" Chelsea placed a palm on her chest. "You scared me. Lisa didn't shut the door when she left. What's up?"

"Shut the door? You always leave it open." Bob jerked his head towards Chelsea's phone. "I've been calling."

"I was going to visit you later."

"Really, why?"

Chelsea felt her insides tingle. She wanted to share the new plans she had with Bob.

After hearing them, Bob hesitated. "But, you know, we're not a computer company. We'll have to incorporate that into what we do and fast. To get credibility in the industry."

Chelsea's heart sank. "How?"

"By buying a small medically focused technology company," said Bob as if he had been thinking about it too.

Chelsea chuckled. "XRCure doesn't have that type of money."

"Yes, but it can be part of the proposal we present to

investors moving forward." Bob became energized. "I know a few good companies we can acquire for cheap, who are already straddling this AI interface and can redirect their focus."

"But that would cost millions." Chelsea watched her dreams begin to evaporate before her eyes. She started to type again.

"What you've described is a game-changer. The technology and know-how are there. We find the right tech company to buy, we create a good business proposal, and we lay it out there. The technology is patentable. Our initial public offering, could be higher than those of Facebook, Amazon, and Google combined. Apart from going the way of the dinosaurs, a meteor hitting Earth, the only other thing that could wipe out humankind is a micro-organism. And we'll be right there waiting for it. We would become instant billionaires, and the planet saved."

The latter is what's driving him, thought Chelsea.

"Listen, I think I know where to get the money, but -"

Chelsea stopped typing. "Where?"

"Ever heard of Dimitri Masterkova?"

Chelsea spun around in her chair. "Russian? No way!"

Bob raised his hands, palms facing forward. "Hear me out first. Listen, the market is still reeling from the Theranos fallout, and most American financiers won't touch a Health Technology company with a ten feet pole."

"A health technology company?"

"If we want to look credible," said Bob. "No, not look. If we want to exude credibility, we must become a health technology company. We're already health-based. By adding a technology business to the mix, we'll get there. Instead of building a tech company, which will take years, we will buy one. Amazon does it all the time."

Bob paused and took a deep breath. His eyes shone with excitement as if he'd just realized the enormous potential.

Bob grinned. "To do that, we need someone with deep pockets." He nodded as he spoke. "As my grandmother would say, it doesn't matter how you get your money as long as you have enough for what's on sale."

Chelsea exhaled. She remembered the scandal. Theranos was a now-defunct health technology company that soared in valuation to $9 billion after the CEO claimed the company had revolutionized blood testing by developing methods that needed only small volumes of blood to run tests. *Forbes* named the CEO 'the youngest and wealthiest self-made female billionaire in America'. It later came to light that the technology claims were fraudulent, and *Forbes* revised the CEO's net worth to zero.

Chelsea stared off into the distance. "Is Masterkova an oligarch? Aren't all oligarchs under the control of the Soviet leadership somehow?"

"No, it's now Russia. The Soviet Union is defunct, remember?" said Bob with an exasperated look. "Oligarch comes from the ancient Greek words *oligos* — few, and *arkhes* — ruler, used to describe a handful of men who controlled much of the Soviet Union's natural resources more than two decades ago. Putin successfully put an end to that system. What they have now are successful, legitimate busi-nessmen. They've moved away from communism to capital-ism, just like the US."

"But still under Putin's control," said Chelsea. "Would we become a Russian company if we accept money from this Dimitri guy?"

Bob threw his hands down. "Chelsea, I'm only trying to breathe life into your idea. If you're friends with Bezos, Gates, or Zuckerberg, feel free to bring them on board. That is if they acknowledge your existence. I know for sure right now, Masterkova is looking for investments in the US. And he has greenbacks, billions of them."

She knew he was right. "Okay, but why do you need my approval? I'm more or less an employee."

"You're one of the first ten employees, and it's your idea. You know the medical part of it and the programming part and will be explaining it to the geek heads. You can't do that if we don't agree."

Chelsea nodded. Her phone buzzed, interrupting her thoughts. Another internal call. She grabbed the handle.

"Hello, Chelsea Piers."

"Dr. Piers, this is the receptionist downstairs. There is a gentleman from the Hendonville Police Department here to see you."

Chelsea's heart froze. "Are…are my parents okay?"

"One second."

Chelsea heard the receptionist talking to someone.

"He said he hopes they're okay too. He's here on a different matter and would only take five minutes of your time."

"Okay, I'll be down in a minute." Chelsea hung up and got to her feet

Bob frowned. "The police? You want me to come with you?"

"No, that's fine." Chelsea didn't know what it was about but didn't really want Bob knowing her business. "I'll let you know if I need you."

"I'll be in my office."

Chelsea took the elevator downstairs. With all these inter-ruptions, she'd never get her work done. She got off at the lobby, her heels clicking on the marble floor as she headed towards the reception area, wondering why the police were looking for her. She saw the policeman, his back to her, looking through the glass wall enjoying the scenery outside.

The receptionist smiled at Chelsea as she entered the square-shaped lobby area with three of its four walls plain glass.

Chelsea smiled back, then cleared her throat. "Excuse me. I'm Dr. Piers. You wanted to see me?"

The policeman whirled around, then smiled. "Hello Dr. Piers."

Chelsea's breath caught. She looked like a deer caught in a car's headlight. Last time she saw him, he was a skinny teenager, a far cry from the muscled and confident man standing in front of her. "Rip...Ripken Chord?"

"Yes, Ma'am."

21

Rip

Chelsea fixed her eyes on Rip's. "Rip. Rip? After all these years you call me Dr. Piers?" She stared at him, eyes wide, as if not believing what she saw.

"No, Dr. Piers…Chelsea. How are you?"

She spread out her hands and walked towards him for a hug. It was awkward, but they did it. Chelsea stepped back and looked him over.

"I'm fine. You look good. Chief of Police?"

Rip smiled, and his eyes found his feet. Get a hold of yourself. You cannot go back to being a love-smitten teenager. Rip took a deep breath, and his head snapped back up. He hoped she didn't notice. "Yes, for the past two years, I've been the police chief here in Hendonville."

"Two years? And I've been here about two years too, and our paths have never crossed."

Rip had no answer to that. He drew in a sharp breath.

"I'm sorry to bother you, but your name came up in a preliminary investigation we're carrying out. Is there a place we can talk in private?"

Chelsea's eyebrows narrowed. "My name came up?"

"It's probably nothing, but we just have to explore every lead."

Chelsea glanced toward the receptionist then back to Rip. "One second."

Rip watched her walk to the receptionist's counter. The receptionist looked up from his screen.

Chelsea smiled again. "Any free boardrooms I can use for ten minutes?"

The receptionist looked down at his console, forehead furrowed. "Boardroom 101 right here on the ground floor is not in use for the next twenty minutes."

"I'll take it, thanks." She walked back to Rip. "Come with me."

Rip walked behind her. The sound of her heels, the ding of the elevator, and muffled conversations accompanied them as they headed to the boardroom. His thoughts drifted again to the last time he saw her and what happened after that. He pushed the thought away, refocusing on the here and now. She wore a white coat, and he couldn't tell what she had underneath, but the years had been good to her. They say time heals all things, but things he thought he had buried away hit him like a thunderbolt. He looked at her left hand, no ring. He let out a deep breath he didn't even realize he was holding.

Chelsea opened a door. "Here we are." She stretched her hand to the side of the door and threw on the lights.

Oak paneled walls. A big oval-shaped table that could seat at least twelve people was at the center of the room. A star-shaped gadget, probably some type of phone system, was at the center of the table. Suspended from the ceiling like a black metallic spider on a thick web was a projector. On the wall opposite the projector was a white screen. Rip shut the door behind him and cut off all the office noise from the lobby.

"Nice, he muttered."

Chelsea pulled out a chair at the end of the table, and another at the side, which she took. "Please sit."

Rip sat and leaned forward. "I'll get straight to the point. Last night there was a car accident on route 181."

"Oh my God. I hope it wasn't bad."

Rip pursed his lips. "Two men were involved. One was found dead on the spot. The other survived."

"Sad."

Rip nodded. "But the man who survived has lost his memory. The doctors called it post-traumatic amnesia."

"Depending on how hard he hit his head, his memory should come back," said Chelsea.

"So they say. We have nothing on him. The car went up in flames after I pulled him out. He -"

Chelsea sat up in her chair, pointed at Rip, and swallowed. "You…pulled him out of a burning car?"

"Yea, that's my job. Anyway, he had no ID on him. We're still trying to trace the VIN and the plates. But, in his pocket, we found a piece of paper with Chelsea Piers written on it." Rip's eyes never left her face.

She kept her eyes on him, expecting more.

"I know it could be any Chelsea Piers, and there's a big facility in New York with that name too. We're just following leads at this time. I thought since you work in the area, I should see if there's any connection. Can I show you a picture in case you've seen him before?"

"Sure, where is he from? Oh, I forgot. You have nothing on him."

"So far nothing, but he speaks English with an accent, and speaks Russian like a native. We think he grew up in Russia." Rip could swear Chelsea's eyes widened when he mentioned Russia. He brought out his phone and scrolled to the photo he had taken of the man.

Chelsea leaned closer and looked at Rip's phone. "Let's see, a Caucasian male, looks healthy, vacant haunting eyes, about sixty-plus-" She shook her head. "I don't think I've ever seen him before."

Rip didn't know whether to mention her reaction when he mentioned Russia. He decided to go for it. "You reacted when I mentioned Russia."

Chelsea paused. "I was just in a meeting with the CEO, and we were talking about Russia on a business matter. It was just funny that you should mention it."

Rip got to his feet, tucking that last bit into the back of his mind. "I don't want to keep you away from your meeting. Thanks so much for your time."

Chelsea got up and walked with him back to the lobby.

Rip headed towards the door.

"Thanks again for agreeing to see me without an appointment," said Rip. "I knew this was nothing."

"This was happenstance, or you just wanted to see me?" said Chelsea. Her voice almost a whisper.

Rip felt the skin in the back of his neck tingle.

Chelsea smiled. "If I knew you were in the next town over as Chief of Police, I would have come to your town and caused some civil disobedience so that I would end up in your jail."

Rip laughed and looked around. He noticed a woman, middle-aged with a little extra meat on her bones staring at them. He looked away and reached for his breast pocket. He pulled out a business card. "This is my card. Call me if you remember anything."

Chelsea looked at the card, then sighed. She raised her head. "We have to talk Rip."

Rip smiled. "There's nothing to discuss. Seventeen years has wiped the slate clean. Thanks again for your time." He exited the building and walked along the bridge that led to the parking lot. His heart was pounding. He thought he had gotten over her, but he had been lying to himself. Seventeen years had layered scar tissue over his whole body, but not his heart.

22

Feodor Konstantin
Latvia 1988

Feodor didn't skimp on his job. Now, it was easier for him. He was already spending time with Anna. She was like a personal guide on a sightseeing tour. Inquiring about her father and his activities seemed normal as if he was getting to know her family, but Anna was no fool; she asked the right questions back.

"You always want to know where my father is going," asked Anna one evening. "Do you want to join the uprising, or do you want to bring it down?"

Feodor took his time before he answered. She must know, or at least have a high inkling that he was KGB. He didn't want to spook her. Even though she appeared nonchalant, this involved her father. It was no secret that KGB agents could become "friends of the cause" or *agents provocateur*. Infiltrate target groups on purpose. Disrupt the organization by sowing dissension and disinformation that would affect their politics.

"I'm neither here nor there. As a Russian, I would take a nationalistic approach. But, having been here in Riga, and seen firsthand how your lives are affected by policies made by people that don't have your interests at heart, makes me wonder if the way the system stands today is the right approach."

That answer seemed to satisfy Anna, and she didn't ask any questions like that again. Feodor still was troubled on how to proceed. His boss Dimitri kept on pushing back his return date to Latvia. It presented both a problem and an opportunity for Feodor. Feodor had been thinking of a solid plan to get Anna away from the bloodshed that he was sure was coming. If it were just Anna, he was sure he could get her out. But there was her father, mother, and two sisters. How would he convince them to come away with him from their homeland? The more he thought about it, the more impossible it looked.

How can you convince a nationalist that he has to move away from the motherland he's fighting for? He can lay down his life for what he believes in. That was the difference between the man who stays home and the man who defies the authorities and does what he thinks is right. But, with the threat of physical harm and death, most people would change their minds.

The other side of the coin was Feodor's life. Was he willing to sacrifice all that he had been through for Anna? Was she worth it?

23

Chelsea

C helsea strolled to the glass wall of the lobby and pretended to take in the scenery for a few seconds. She turned and searched out Rip's figure in the parking lot as he strolled towards a police car. That image looked familiar to her, but this time, the man exuded stoic confidence. From the corner of her eye, Chelsea noticed Lisa watching her. No, she was waiting for her.

Lisa looked Chelsea up and down as she approached. "What business do you have with the police?"

"I'm a suspect in a police investigation."

"Get out of here," said Lisa, then giggled nervously. "No, really?"

Chelsea smiled. "Yep, I'm a suspect, and they're leaving no stone unturned. I'm going back up."

"You? A suspect?" Lisa walked fast to keep up with Chelsea. "I ate an apple while shopping at the grocery store last week. That is stealing, right? That hunk should come and investigate me too. I have plenty of hiding places on my body he can probe."

Chelsea would have laughed at a remark like that from Lisa, but this time she felt a burning sensation cut through her chest. Lisa's words seemed to light a fuse inside her. She wanted to lash out as they stood in front of the elevator, waiting for the car to arrive. *Was she jealous?* But she had no right at all to be jealous.

Lisa stepped to the side and let the people out of the car, then held the door with one hand and ushered Chelsea in with the other. "Did you just meet for the first time, or did you know him before?"

Chelsea looked ahead, even though it was just the two of them in the car.

"I never liked chemistry, but the two of you standing side by side was like an acid-base reaction!" Lisa fanned herself with both hands. "Talk of heat!"

Chelsea knew what Lisa was talking about because her inside was vibrating too. After seventeen years. She thought she had forgotten this guy, but it didn't seem like that now.

"Chelsea? So how did you guys meet?"

"We grew up in the same town. Went to the same high school." Chelsea didn't want to talk about it, so she summarized it. "I haven't seen him since high school."

"Oh my God. That explains it. Your crush from high school. Most crushes look like slobs when you see them later in life, but I can say with confidence, this one even looks better than he did when you were in high school." Lisa winked at her. "Girlfriend, you are in trouble. Thank your stars you're not married or have a boyfriend because what I see in your future would be grounds for divorce or break up."

Chelsea turned and looked at Lisa sharply.

"Don't give me that look." Lisa shook her head and gave Chelsea a pitiful look, then said in a low voice, "You don't even know where you're headed." She leaned closer to Chelsea and grinned. "You're going to ride that guy. It's just a matter of when."

Chelsea made a face and drew back.

Lisa sniffed the air like a hound dog. "I can smell it. You're already giving off those pheromones or whatever they call them."

"Yeah, right Lisa. "You and your theories.

The elevator dinged, and the door opened.

Chelsea stepped out first. "I'm going back to my office. Need to get some work done."

"See you later," said Lisa. She stayed back in the elevator.

Now, where was I? Chelsea settled in her chair and read what she'd written on the screen before she was interrupted. "Okay." She started to type again, but her thoughts were no longer flowing as before. She found herself thinking about that night years ago. Her pulse started to race. She felt like she was suffocating. Like someone was sucking the air out of the room.

Chelsea got up and went to the window, breathing rapidly and telling herself to calm down. Moments later, it went away, just as quickly as it had started.

A panic attack. Chelsea thought she'd gotten over them. Where was he all these years? Had he been thinking about her? Chelsea remembered what she did to him, and a sob escaped her lips. Tears welled in her eyes, but she fought them, realizing that this was not all behind her as she had thought.

She whirled to the sound of knocking on her door.

Bob peeped in. "Hey, everything alright? I saw the -" He came in and shut the door behind him. "Chelsea, are you okay?" he asked in a low voice. "Are your parents, okay?"

Chelsea sniffed and forced a smile. "Don't mind me. That was an old friend from a long time ago. High school."

"I'm really sorry, who died? Were they sick?

"Sick? Died? No, no." She just realized the confusion. "The police chief is an old friend. I hadn't seen him in years."

"The cruiser said Hendonville police. That's the next town over. And you didn't know the police chief was someone you went to school with?" Bob shook his head in mock disbelief.

Chelsea pursed her lips and smiled. The embarrassed look on her face said it all. Was Bob snooping around.

"What did he want?"

Chelsea sat back at her desk. "Some guy was in a car accident and lost his memory. In his pocket, they found a piece of paper with my name on it. Well, not my name…you know like Chelsea Piers."

Bob's eyebrows shot up. "Chelsea Piers? That could mean anything."

"I think he just saw my name and then found out I worked here and decided to come and see me."

"Ah, lost love," said Bob. "Melanie and I were high school sweetheart. Now, we're at each other's throat. I'm glad the divorce came through." He shook his body like a dog shaking water off its coat. "Anyway, I'm going to change the story to business. I'm getting positive feedback. The Russian financier is showing some real interest. So, start working on a presentation."

"For you to present?"

Bob straightened. "Gosh no. You're the driver of the boat. It's your presentation."

"All right. I'll think about it over the weekend."

24

Rip

Rip could not believe that after all these years, Chelsea Piers was less than an hour away from him, and she'd been there for two years. What he couldn't fathom most of all was the effect she still had on him. He would need to wrap this case up fast so he could forget about Chelsea Piers. He could now check that particular lead off his list as a dead end. That should put an end to seeing her again for any reason. What if she calls with new information? Rip had no answer. He'd deal with that if and when something new came up.

With the dead body yielding the first plausible link to follow, the belt buckle with the Russian inscription, Rip thought maybe it would be a good idea to be present for the autopsy. He picked up his cell phone and called the medical examiner. It went straight to his voice mail. Maybe the secretary he'd seen a couple of times would be there. He called the office.

"Medical examiner's office, Beth speaking. How can I help you?"

"Hello Beth, this is Chief Rip Chord, Hendonville Police. Is Dr. Aggrawal there?"

"Hey, Chief. How are you?"

Rip let out a breath. At least she recognized his voice.

"He's currently doing an autopsy. Can I take a message?"

"I was wondering when he's scheduled the autopsy for the burn victim from last night."

"You want to come in and observe?"

"Yes," said Rip. "We're still gathering information on the case, and I'd like to be there to see first-hand."

"One second. Let me look it up."

The on-hold music came on. It sounded like static mixed with a party beat that faded in and out. It was bad.

"Chief, it's scheduled for 10 am Monday, assuming there are no emergencies."

"Thanks, so much Beth, I'll be there. Kindly let Dr. Aggrawal know."

Rip contemplated driving to New York and visiting the Piers. It wouldn't be wise if he just showed up at peak time and alarmed everybody. On the other hand, they might not take him seriously. He decided to think about it first. He headed back to the office.

Rip took Route 181. When he passed the spot where the accident happened the night before he slowed down and stared. You wouldn't notice the fire damage or the vegetation disturbances unless you were looking for it.

Back in the station, Rip went to his office and started typing up his report. Every lead so far had led nowhere. He wondered if it was time to involve the FBI. Terrorism was the number one federal crime but Rip knew that inviting the FBI now, when they had nothing to go with, would turn his police department into a laughingstock. He wouldn't call them yet. But he promised himself that once they found anything that remotely smelled like terrorism, he wouldn't hesitate.

Rip engaged himself in paperwork, and the hours flew bye. By late evening fatigue was setting in. It was one thing to stay awake when you had a pressing task at hand and another to try to keep your eyes open when there was no urgent need.

He was dozing off when his phone buzzed. It was a text from Melissa reminding him that he had suggested they meet up tonight. He sent her a text right back that he would be there.

Rip now had a task at hand, and sleep vanished from his eyes. When he was in Special Ops, and in enemy territory, he could keep awake for days, especially in situations where the luxury of sleep meant death.

Rip didn't bother getting more food. It was just Melissa at her home, and the food he brought in last night was probably still untouched. They would heat it and have a feast.

He left the cruiser at the police station and took his F150 truck. He drove home, took a shower, and changed into jeans and a long-sleeved tee-shirt. During the drive, his mind's eye traveled from Melissa's head to her toes, then back, his hands caressing every inch of her body. He could hear her moans.

It started to feel hot in his car. Rip stepped down on the gas pedal, and the vehicle lunged forward. Outside in the woods, the parade of trees became a blur as he sped along the road.

Melissa came to the door with the first ring of the door-bell. "Hi handsome," she said in her smoky voice and flashed him a smile.

Her eyes were glazed, like she was tipsy. She had an almost full wine glass in her hand and wore a black lacy mid-thigh nightgown and a sheer wrap. She was showing just enough skin to put his imagination to work. She was beautiful.

"Come on in," said Melissa and walked toward her dining room.

Rip followed, breathing in the flowery musk of her perfume and the smell of wine. Looking at her and what she had on did things to him and got his pulse racing.

Her living room floorplan was like the plan of most homes in the area, one big open space encompassing the living room, dining, and kitchen, with doors leading to the bedrooms and bathrooms. Rip removed his jacket and tossed it on the couch.

Melissa batted her thick eyelashes. "I couldn't wait anymore, and started on the wine without you."

"That's fine," said Rip. "Sorry about yesterday."

She drew in a deep breath, pushing out her chest. "You're here now."

"Can I have some?" Rip didn't wait for an answer. He took her wine glass and emptied the contents in one gulp.

She stared at him. "Wow, you've worked up an appetite. Do you want to eat first?"

"As long as you're the main course." Rip's hand snaked around her waist, and he drew her closer.

Melissa gasped. "Maybe not!" Breathless, she pushed her body against his.

Rip placed the glass on the table and took her lips. She tasted of wine. His mouth was glued to hers as they fumbled to get their clothes off. Moments later, panting, he had her hoisted up and pinned against the wall. It was Chelsea he was making love to.

25

Feodor Konstantin
Latvia 1988

The success of the 1987 campaign to stop the construction of a hydroelectric dam on the Daugava River through organized protests had motivated a lot of Latvians, including Anna's dad, Dr. Karena, to do the same. Trying to get him to abandon that fight and leave Riga would sound like the ranting of a madman to him. Then the other consideration was trying to explain who he was and why Dr. Karena should care about what he had to say.

In the Baltic states of Estonia and Lithuania, there were agitations with political undertones too. The Soviet leadership still believed that their approach, using small units like Dimitri's to divide and conquer the organizations, was the best approach. Infiltrate dissident groups and sow seeds of discord among the members, using money as an incentive. Or the outright removal of a leader—or leaders as they get replaced—and keep the campaigns in perpetual confusion and continuously undermined.

To Feodor, most people involved in such struggles were passionate about the course, and he had strong doubts that money would sway them. Maybe removal of the leaders was the only guaranteed solution, and that would not be good news for Anna's dad or other influencers.

Feodor weighed his options. Anna's mother stood firmly by her husband. Anna's twin sisters, who are two years older than her, have their boyfriends to consider. Plus, the excitement and promise of a better tomorrow they could help shape was at the front and center of their activities. Anna could be said to be of the same mindset as her sisters, so the onus would be on Feodor to convince her. He decided that he would plan to save only Anna.

Feodor knew that failure would mean death for him. Once he set his plan into motion, there wouldn't be any turning back. For now, he would keep it close to his heart, and keep the suitcase of rubles even closer. Money was the grease that lubricated all wheels.

26

Chelsea

Back in her office, Chelsea was surprised she was able to work. A smile danced on her lips as her fingers flew over the keyboard formulating commands. All these years, she'd pushed Rip to the back of her mind, occasionally wondering *what if.* And boom, he resurfaces.

Chelsea knew she'd wronged him all those years ago, and when he came, he still had a big smile on his lips. He was cheerful, did not harbor any malice. But behind those eyes was a hardness she'd only seen in people who have been through stuff. People who have seen things that they could not unsee.

A lot of water had gone under the bridge. Seventeen years was a long time. As much as Chelsea would have loved to believe they could just pick up from where they left off and make up for lost time, she knew it would never happen like that. They were two different people who had lived different lives for a long time. If not for sheer luck, they would never have met again.

Most professional women at her age were already married or had tried it, but she was still single. He wasn't wearing any ring. She'd checked. That doesn't mean he wasn't married. Some men just don't like wearing rings.

Chelsea believed that he only came over to her office just to see what she looked like. Had he been thinking about her all these years? And now that he'd seen her, what does he think? Questions like that crossed her mind as she worked.

When they were younger, Chelsea hoped she and Rip would spend the rest of their lives together, but so did a lot of teenagers. As Lisa said, it was a crush, puppy love. Praying for a lost love was almost always in vain, but hers had been answered. Even though a total surprise, she should not turn around now and screw it up.

Chelsea realized she'd been staring at the cursor, her fingers no longer moving. She'd successfully developed a problem that wasn't there two hours ago. Rip's reappearance just opened a part of her that she had put on the back burner for a long time.

Chelsea knew she had a choice to make, even though she would be working with a lot of hypothetical situations, she must decide. It wouldn't be fair to insert herself into his life, just like that. He probably didn't want her. She was sure police officers have a way of knowing where people live or work, and he must have used that. He probably knew where she was, but never bothered to make contact. Now he had to because her name literally popped up under his nose.

But Bob, on the other hand, never missed a chance to show he was interested in her even though he was married then. Maybe she should revisit his interest now that his marriage was over.

Chelsea had to act fast and not make a fool of herself, wanting someone that doesn't want her. The only way she could avoid thinking of Rip was distraction. She had to have something else consume her. Later that evening, as she was leaving the office for home, she stopped at Bob's office.

"You're still here." asked Chelsea poking her head into his office.

Bob blew out a breath and sat back in his chair. "Will be leaving soon. I've been talking to other potential investors to see who would be interested in investing. So far, I've been getting good vibes. People are interested, but Masterkova seems to be the only one ready to dive in. Just make sure you come up with a killer presentation."

"I will."

"The medical stuff is not my forte, but the business side I can handle and perhaps throw in one or two things to tie in with your presentation." Bob paused as if in deep thought. "Hey, how are your parents doing?"

A lump formed in Chelsea's throat, he always inquired about her parents even though he'd never met them. Before she could stop herself, it came out of her mouth. "Why don't you come over tomorrow and meet them?"

Bob's eyes widened. "Like, come over to your house, house?"

"Yes, for dinner. Then you can meet them."

Bob seemed to get over the shock fast. "That'll be lovely. I'll be there!" Bob replied quickly, as if he expected Chelsea to rescind the invitation. "What time?"

27

Rip

E ven though Rip and Melissa had an understanding, he couldn't wait for sunrise so that he could get out of her place. Chelsea had taken over his mind, and he felt he was cheating on Melissa.

As the fiery orange and pink colors of sunrise crept in through her window, he disentangled himself from her. He peed, kissed her, and left.

Melissa always slept late on weekends, trying to catch up from waking up early from Monday to Friday for school. Contrarily, Rip woke early and knew he had to be productive. He wouldn't just wait around until she woke up, and anyway, his job was done for now. He decided to head home. Since he was off today, he reckoned he would cross the border and do some exploring.

Since the incident with the burning car and the Morrison

kid's story about the mountain lion, Rip seemed to always find himself driving along Route 181. He hoped he would be as lucky as Jude and at least see the animal dash across the road. That would give him the conviction to call Fish and Wildlife.

Since seeing Chelsea yesterday, she had occupied his mind like an anchored ship. Undulating with the waves but rooted to a spot in his mind. She had grown from a skinny fresh-faced teenager to a beautiful woman. Again, Rip wondered if she was dating anyone. He quickly pushed the thought away. Chelsea's social life was not an onion he would like to peel. Moreover, he still had to unravel the mystery of the man with the lost memory. Right now that was top priority.

Rip considered calling Max to see if he could use their facial recognition software on the guy. He knew Max would start pitching him to come and join them, 'and you can use the facial recognition software to your heart's content'. Anyway, he didn't have much yet to go on. Maybe by Monday, after the autopsy, if there were nothing new, then he would consider reaching out to Max.

He showered and put on fresh clothes: jeans, button-down white shirt, and a blue sweater. Rip made himself a cup of coffee, and as he nursed the black brew, he turned on the TV. The coronavirus was eating its way through Wuhan, China in the town where the first case was reported. Rip hadn't paid much attention to this virus, but it seemed to be gathering steam. He thought it would go the way of other illnesses, and fizzle out after some time.

On the news, it seemed like China was being accused of somehow being the origin of the growing epidemic. The Chinese government was slow in letting the world know about the disease, but it seemed like they'd started to restrict movement to and from the epicenter in the town called Wuhan. Rip raised the volume to the TV.

"A GROUP OF RESEARCHERS PUBLISHED AN ARTICLE IN 2005 citing the Horseshoe bat as natural reservoirs of the SARS-like coronavirus. Further work led isolating over 300 coronavirus sequences after sampling thousands of bats across China. Fast forward to December of 2019, with the outbreak of cases of pneumonia associated with an unknown coronavirus, samples recovered from patients were found to have a 96% match to a sample the Wuhan Institute of Virology had collected from a Horseshoe bat in the South of China. Now, whether the virus ravaging the globe came from the lab or jumped hosts is still being investigated..."

RIP TURNED THE TV OFF. A FEW YEARS AGO, IT WAS SEVERE Acute Respiratory Syndrome (SARS). It, too, had come out of China and got the world accustomed to seeing people wearing surgical masks as if it were a clothing accessory. Now this.

He wondered if Chelsea's lab was doing any work on this virus. Chelsea was where she wanted to be, doctor and researcher. He was far from his teenage dreams. He had been impressed with her father when they were kids; with his calm and friendly demeanor, and the way he treated everybody with respect. He had influenced Rip's desire to become a doctor too, but that plan spectacularly derailed.

"Dr. Rip Chord," said Rip, and chuckled. He gulped down the rest of the coffee, used the bathroom, then got in his truck and hit the road.

The drive into New York was smooth. Traffic hadn't

started to build up yet, permitting a stress-free trip and time to reflect on all that was happening, a brief introspection. That was a question Rip had struggled with all his life. Who was he? He knew who he was. The better question would be, what was the purpose of his life? He had joined the Army to serve his country as that was his purpose at that time, but today he would settle for solving this case of amnesia. And right now, he had nothing.

The traffic slowed down as the vehicles approached the George Washington Bridge toll gates. Each time he drove over the bridge, he marveled at the engineering. Rip recalled what he knew about the GWB. It was a double-suspension bridge made of steel. Construction started in September 1927, and four years later, in October 1931, opened to the public. The bridge was of so much utility that upper and lower levels were added in later years. As of 2016, the bridge had daily traffic of approximately 289,000 vehicles.

Rip took the ramp off the bridge and got onto Hudson River Parkway. It was a leisurely drive. He passed people walking their dogs and a few people jogging, despite the cold, on the pedestrian trail along the Hudson River.

"Is that an Air Force carrier?" said Rip to himself. There was an Air Force carrier in all its glory parked by the river. A sign close to it read: The Intrepid Sea, Air & Space Museum. Rip stared at it until he had to get his eyes back on the road. The female electronic voice of his GPS alerted him he would be reaching his destination soon.

Rip parked in the designated parking area, and as he walked, a gentle breeze brought a waft of the earthy organic smell of the river to his nose. This was Rip's first time at Chelsea Piers, and he realized it was three piers connected at the head house. It was an entertainment complex. A golf course and driving range. Ice rinks, fitness centers, bowling alley, and a venue for events.

When in full occupancy, there could be a lot of people here. Rip didn't think it could have as many people as the Twin Towers, but even one person that fell to a terrorist attack was significant. An attack here would send a message: *We can get to you where you play*. But still, he didn't see the piers as a location for an attack. He reminded himself he was only following a lead. A name scribbled on a piece of paper found in a man's pocket.

A thought occurred to Rip as he stared at the turf of the golf course. He had not even bothered to get Ivan's handwriting and compare it with the writing of Chelsea Piers found in his pocket. It might narrow things down if it were his.

Rip walked from pier to pier, passing early morning risers that came in for one thing or the other. He concluded it was not necessary to involve the security detail at this time and cause unnecessary panic. Loss of business, too, if word ever got out that the venue was even remotely thought of in that way.

Rip spent less than a half-hour at the facility and decided to call it a day. He got back in his car, hit 'home' on his GPS, and began the reverse journey back to New Jersey. He was on the bridge when his phone rang. Melissa.

"Baby, where are you?" Her voice was groggy. "Don't answer that. Just bring me a Starbucks on your way back."

"Okay. It will take like an hour plus."

"An hour?" Her voice was a little high pitched. "Are you going there on your hands and knees?"

Rip laughed and told her he was on his way back.

"New York! Okay, I don't even want to know why; just bring coffee and hurry back. You still have work to do."

Rip smiled. She was inviting him back. Is their relationship entering a new phase? He hoped not. He was not the committing type. He stepped down on the gas.

Chelsea

C helsea went home early on Friday night. She was too excited to stay at work and continue to code. Nothing was making sense. She would stare at the screen for minutes and then realize she'd been daydreaming without doing anything. Then Bob showed up, and her mind went off on another tangent.

"Get a grip on yourself for Christ sakes," she muttered under her breath. "You're not a teenager." Even though she admonished herself, Chelsea's relationship well had been dry for a long time. And in one day, it suddenly filled up close to bursting. She'd reconnected with Rip and finally decided to take a chance with Bob.

"I invited Bob for dinner tomorrow evening," said Chelsea to her parents after she got home. They were relaxing in the living room. In a way, still living with her parents seemed like not much had changed in her life since she was a child. Of course, before they cared for her; now she looked after them.

"Who's Bob, Chels?" asked her father.

Chelsea knew her father didn't remember. Whenever his memory failed him, he would call the person 'dear' as a cover if female. If the person were male, he would say, 'young man', irrespective of the person's age. He'd met Bob before and should remember him thought Chelsea.

Her mother sighed. "Oh, come on Dave, you know, her colleague from work. The doctor turned businessman."

"Hmm, is he coming to sell us something? I'm not buying whatever he's selling!"

Chelsea laughed. "No, Dad. I invited him to dinner. He's always asking after you and Mother."

"About time Chelsea," said her mother. "You have finally pulled your head out of the weeds. "I hope this is the beginning of a happy ending. Lucky for you, my mother is no longer around; she would have married you off a long time ago. She wasn't successful with me. I married for love."

Chelsea's grandmother had wanted Chelsea's mother to marry from a family of her choosing, but she had gotten pregnant, and the rest, like they say, is history. Chelsea was not sure it was a good idea mentioning she met Rip. It would only succeed in sending mixed signals, which wouldn't be far from the truth.

On Saturday morning, Chelsea's mother woke up early and woke her up, reminding her of the dinner planned for the evening.

"Mother, it's only nine in the morning. He's not coming until five in the evening."

"But we have to get ready, cook dinner…" Mother's voice trailed off.

"Why don't we worry about breakfast; dinner is already taken care off."

Her mother's eyebrows shot up. "What do you mean, already taken care of?" She let out a puff of air, and her eyes narrowed. "Did you cancel?"

"No! I ordered the food online, and they should have it here early enough."

Chelsea's mother reluctantly left her room, but not after complaining that the food should have been home-cooked rather than bought. Chelsea kept her mouth shut. Even if they did cook at home, her mother could only stand for so long. The rest of her time would be spent giving instructions to Chelsea.

Since she was already awake, Chelsea got ready for the day and went downstairs, drawn by the smell of coffee.

"Good morning, Dad."

"Morning Chelsea, did you sleep well?"

"I did thank-"

The doorbell rang.

"Oh, that must be the cleaning lady," said Mother. "I called her to come in and do some touch-ups."

"But...but she was here two days ago," Chelsea stammered.

"Glad you said two days ago," her mother said with a nod. "I thought it was yesterday. "Now get the door."

Chelsea opened the door. "Hi Maria."

"Dr. Chelsea! I didn't know you were home." Maria turned and pointed at a girl behind her. "This is my daughter Isabella." She threw her hands up, as if exasperated. "Your mother said to bring help!"

"It's okay. Come on in." Chelsea smiled and opened the door wider. Chelsea leaned in conspiratorially. "We'll go through the motions to satisfy her."

"Okay," whispered Maria. "I was here just two days ago. It can't be that bad. Hello Dr. Piers."

Chelsea's father turned towards Maria. "Hi dear, good to see you."

Maria said she was fine, but the fact that he called her dear was not lost on Chelsea. If she hadn't been on the lookout for such a slip, she wouldn't have noticed it. Maria had been with them for more than a year, coming twice a week. If her father already forgot who she was, then he was deteriorating fast for sure.

Maria and her daughter spent about an hour cleaning and tidying. Just before they left, they helped set the table. Chelsea almost had a heart attack when her mother responded to a question from Maria.

"Are you expecting a lot of guests tonight, Madam?"

"No, just one. We hope to marry Chelsea off," said Chelsea's mom with confidence.

Chelsea opened her mouth to respond, thought the better of it and shut up. She thanked Maria and her daughter, and they headed for their car.

Sometime after two in the afternoon, Chelsea heard a car outside and looked through the window. It was a catering van delivering the food. Good timing. She unpacked the food and got rid of the boxes. Looking at the spread, it would look like she'd spent the whole day in the kitchen. She went upstairs, took a shower, and decided to keep it casual: jeans, and a tee-shirt. Chelsea felt nervous. Was she doing the right thing? This was not a joke. Thirty-two-year-old women are expected to put out eventually. Was she ready?

One look at the time on her phone and her heart started to race as if it would burst out of her chest. It was ten minutes to five, and Bob was a stickler to time. He should have been here already or probably just about to ring the bell. Chelsea's breath caught as she inhaled. *Calm down, Chelsea. This is just dinner. Your parents are here.* She opened her mouth, sucked in air, and let it out through her nose. She did it two more times. By the third time, she was calm. She headed to the stairs, and the doorbell chimed.

"I'll get it!" said her mom.

Chelsea heard the excitement in her mother's shaky voice.

"Who is it?" asked her father.

At the foot of the stairs, Chelsea caught a glimpse of Bob's bald head as her mother swung the door open.

"Hello there." said her mother and stepped aside.

Bob stepped in with a bouquet of roses. "Dr. Piers! Nice to see you again." He lowered his head and pecked her on each cheek, then gave her the roses..

Chelsea's mother almost passed out with all the attention. That was when Chelsea noticed Bob had a second bundle as he walked in.

Bob offered Chelsea the second bouquet. "Hi."

"Hello Bob. You brought roses, thanks very much."

"I'll put them in water," said Chelsea's mother collecting the flowers from Chelsea and wobbling to the kitchen.

"Dr. Piers," said Bob with a slight nod of his head as Chelsea's dad approached.

He stuck out his hand. "Hello young man."

They shook hands.

The young man remark was not lost on Chelsea.

Chelsea's mother came back from the kitchen, her flowers in a vase with water. Within minutes of Bob arriving, she had them at the dining table, sipping wine and about to dig into the spread.

Chicken noodle soup with warm French bread. An option of rotisserie chicken and/or beef ribs. Chicken, mushroom, and spinach lasagna, fresh steamed broccoli, and spinach. Desert was coffee and red velvet cake.

The conversation around the table was mostly medical, about the ongoing outbreak and a little talk about the lab. Father concentrated on his food and wine, while mother played matchmaker, trying to find out all she could about Bob.

"So, Bob, any plans for the spring?" she asked. "That's a good time for weddings."

Bob swallowed. "Yes, you're right. "I was thinking of taking the girls to The Algarve, Portugal."

"The…the girls?"

"My girls from my first marriage."

Mother fingered her necklace. "Oh." Her lips quivered. "We used to go there a lot until Chelsea stopped liking it. I mean Portugal."

"I loved The Algarve," said her father, joining the conversation for the first time.

Chelsea made a face. "I didn't like it there. I mean, I used to, but I guess we went there too often. What did you like about The Algarve, Dad?"

"Well, plenty of sun, the whitewashed fishing villages." Chelsea's father smiled as he seemed to reach into the deep recesses of his memory. "Fresh fish by the beach, and the sandy coves. It was always quiet and peaceful." Then he pointed at Chelsea. "You were born there, remember! And I delivered you myself."

Bob glanced from Chelsea to her dad. "What? Really? Most doctors would have another doctor do it." Bob chuckled. "I mean, it's okay, but it's like treating yourself."

"You're right young man. Professional objectivity and emotions could interfere, but it was an emergency. Chelsea came early."

Chelsea was happy her dad remembered, then glanced at her mother. Her lips were drawn thin. It was a sweet and sad experience for her. She wanted him to go on but knew it would make her mother miserable.

Bob turned to Chelsea with an amused look on his face. "Hmm, since you were born outside the states, you could never run for the highest office. You're not a natural-born citizen."

"Nonsense!" said her father.

Chelsea jumped.

Her mother sat up straight.

"McCann…no! McCain. John McCain wasn't born in the US, but he ran for President of the United States. He was born in-" He snapped his fingers to aid his recall, then shook his head and shoveled food into his mouth, chewing to hide his embarrassment.

Bob brought out his smartphone and tapped it a few times, then read from the screen. "You're right, sir. McCain was born in Panama, but because his parents were American citizens at the time of his birth, he's considered a natural-born citizen. It's indeed stated in a congressional act in 1790."

Father nodded. "Hmm."

The rest of the dinner continued with small talk between Bob and Chelsea, her parents each receding to their different thoughts while moving their food around on their plates. The mention of Portugal seemed to have snuffed the light out of the evening. After dinner, when Bob said goodnight, even he could feel the tension in the air.

"I think I laid an egg there," said Bob. "I'm really sorry."

Chelsea shrugged. "It's okay. You took them down memory lane."

"Yeah, memories they didn't want to revisit." Bob took

Chelsea's hands. "I'm sorry." There was an awkward silence, then Bob leaned closer and kissed her lips.

Chelsea fought the impulse to bolt. She drew back once their lips connected.

Bob raised an eyebrow. "Too soon?"

Chelsea nodded, not trusting herself to speak. The effects of things that happened to her in the past were still very present in her future.

Bob got into his car. "See you on Monday then."

Chelsea waved as he drove into the darkness.

29

Feodor Konstantin
Latvia 1988

O nce Feodor made the decision, he went to work. Secrecy would be of the utmost importance in carrying out the plan. Having a few hours head start before Anna's people or Dimitri discovered he was missing would go a long way in ensuring a successful getaway. His plan was straight forward: get a passport and travel documents for Anna, catch a flight from Riga and fly to Spain. From Spain, they'd vanish to South America. The Nazis did it and were quite successful. It wouldn't be that difficult for a KGB officer hiding from his country.

The second part of the plan would be to convince Anna to leave with him; that he was saving her. It could either work or blow up in his face. He would wait until everything was in place.

His next task would be getting Anna's travel documents.

But getting a passport picture without telling her of his plans would be tough. He didn't want her to know prematurely. The less she knew, the better for them.

On one of their walks in the park, Feodor saw a man taking pictures of ducks swimming in a pond. He would call on people passing by and ask them if they wanted their photos taken. Feodor saw an opportunity. So, he and Anna posed for pictures.

"Why don't you take one of yourself alone," said Feodor and tried to step away.

Anna grabbed his hand and pulled him closer.

Feodor's heart sounded like someone knocking on a door.

Anna smiled seductively and whispered. "I want you in the picture too."

Feodor thought fast. "No, just you, for my wallet."

"Why? What am I to you?"

Pulse racing, he pulled her even closer and kissed her on the lips. When he let her go, he was breathless. "You mean the world to me. One of these days, I'll make you my wife."

Anna drew back, her full lips sleek from the kiss. She looked genuinely surprised.

Feodor stepped away, and the photographer took several shots. From that day, Feodor noticed a shift in her affection for him. She would hold his hand while they walked. Give him a hug and a kiss for no reason.

Anna's gestures spurred Feodor into action. He could have easily gotten her travel documents through official channels, but that could put him on the radar of someone in the intelligence community. Instead, he used a third party in the black market. It was expensive; the funding was done with Dimitri's money from the briefcase.

Feodor was speechless when he walked into the rented

house and saw Dimitri talking on the phone with a glass of straw-colored liquid in his glass, whiskey to be precise.

It seemed like Dimitri was waiting for Feodor to spend some of the money entrusted in his care before he returned.

He'd smiled, talked a little more on the phone before he hung up, and walked to him.

Dimitri was a jovial man and in a back-slapping mode. "What have you been up to?" He said in his loud, deep voice, and whacked Feodor on the back. "Is everything all right with you? You look like a hostage. Your color is not good. Come, help yourself to a finger of whiskey. That should cheer you up!"

Feodor did not want to drink, but he couldn't say no. He poured himself some whiskey and tossed it down his throat. The liquid warmed him up as it traveled down to the pit of his stomach. Dimitri was right. It helped calm him, and he felt better. He hoped Dimitri wouldn't ask about the money.

"Sorry I didn't make it back sooner," said Dimitri. "You know how it is in Moscow, one meeting after the other. Before you know it, days are flying by. It doesn't help matters that all over, everybody is agitating for one thing or the other. Change is coming. We just must keep on moving to be on the good side of whatever comes. Anything new from the fax I sent you?"

Feodor didn't want it to look like he'd been idle. Despite Dimitri's friendly disposition, he knew the man's brain was working overtime. He must give him something. "Dr. Karena has been organizing a lot of rallies as if there was no law in place against such gatherings."

Dimitri laughed and beat both hands against his chest. "The professor must think he's made of Kevlar. Good, good, stay on it. The academic types are the dangerous ones."

Feodor felt sick to his stomach.

30

Rip

R ip went to the office early Monday morning, took care of the paperwork, and then headed to the hospital for his appointment with the medical examiner. His mind drifted to the past weekend. Despite their understanding of the relationship, Rip felt like a subtle shift was happening. The beginning of what could become a seismic disturbance in their relationship. Was Melissa becoming more like a girlfriend, or was he trying to give a dog a bad name so he could hang it? Since he saw Chelsea, she was always on his mind. Rip was glad when Melissa said she was going to hang out with some other teachers from her school on Sunday, so he went to his place.

When he arrived at the medical examiner's office at the HMC, Dr. Agrawal had already started the autopsy. The secretary gave him a temporary key pass, then Rip put on one of those paper overalls, grabbed shoe booties, a face mask, gloves, and a cap and headed for the morgue. It was underground, and as he walked the tunnel leading to the dissecting room, he passed doctors and allied medical personnel going about their business. The closer he got to the morgue, the stronger the smell. Rip stopped at the door with 'Pathology' written on a blinking keypad. He brought the white rectangular plastic close to it, and the light blinked green. He turned the handle and entered.

The pungent smell of formalin hit him like a blow. Despite the paper overall he had on, goosebumps appeared all over his skin. It was always cold in the morgue.

The first time Rip met Dr. Aggrawal, he'd wondered why anyone would want to hang out with the dead as a job, so he asked him why he chose pathology as a specialty.

"I didn't. It chose me," was Aggrawal's reply. He'd gone to medical school in India, and when he moved to the US decades ago, a pathology residency was easy to get into for a foreign-trained doctor. Back then, his American-trained counterparts wanted the more lucrative residencies like dermatology, orthopedic surgery, or radiology, so he applied to a program and got in.

"Today, pathology is now lucrative, and no longer easy to get into for foreign-trained doctors," continued Aggrawal.

At that same visit, as Rip watched Dr. Aggrawal work, a large beep sounded on one of the shelves filled with human parts in formalin. Rip ignored the sound, but every few minutes, another would go off. The doctor wasn't bothered, so Rip asked him about it.

Aggrawal had shrugged. "Oh, just pacemakers harvested from deceased patients at autopsy," he'd said in his melodious accent. "They give off those shrills when the batteries are weak. We're still waiting for the owners to come and change them." He laughed. "Sorry for the dark joke. I'm a bastard, yeah?"

Dr. Aggrawal sat, hunched over a black mass laid out on top of the silver metallic dissecting table. He looked up as Rip approached.

"Hey, you made it," said Aggrawal. "I thought you finally chickened out. Did you come across any of these during your tours?" He pointed at the burn victim.

Rip had attended a few autopsies with Dr. Aggrawal. As a young man, Dr. Aggrawal served in the US Army. Rip had been in the Army, then Special Ops, so service was something they had in common, and their discussions would often revolve around it.

"Yes. Sometimes I was there as it happened. Other times, soon after. The smell got to be. For a long time, I couldn't eat barbecue."

Dr. Aggrawal nodded. "Burn victims' autopsies can be challenging too, especially if there's suspected hanky panky. It's difficult to separate antemortem injuries from postmortem ones. Then there's the added problem of artifacts."

Rip associated artifacts with treasure hunters. Aggrawal must have seen the puzzled look on his face because he explained.

"Insignificant things that show up in the victim, that mean nothing, but could lead you astray."

Rip nodded.

"In India, I saw more than my share of dowry murders. The bride is murdered somewhere else, and her body brought into the kitchen, doused with kerosene and set on fire, burning the kitchen down, making it look like an accident."

Rip knew that dowries were gifts given by the bride's family to the groom at marriage. If given as a precondition for marriage, then it was illegal.

The India Dowry Prohibition Act of 1961 prohibits the request, payment, or acceptance of a dowry as a precondition for marriage. With money and property involved, misunderstandings might arise—and end in murder. Despite the law, dowry murders continue to take place unchecked.

Aggrawal's face mask that barely covered his salt and pepper beard puffed out as he exhaled noisily. "In most cases, family members would claim they saw the victim cooking. 'Suddenly she was on fire and burned to death.' If she had been alive as they claimed when this intense fire that consumed her and the hut started, we would expect to see soot staining the upper airway, due to inhalation of hot air. The tongue, pharynx, glottis, larynx, should be affected, with pulmonary edema in the lungs."

Rip nodded. "Dead people don't breathe. So, when soot staining is absent, it means the person was already dead before the fire started."

"Bingo!" The medical examiner pointed at the subject of the autopsy. "Your passenger here was already dead before the fire started."

Rip was mildly alarmed at this information. It put an entirely new angle on Mr. Ivan Doe and what he might have been up to that night.

"I can't tell for sure if these tissue changes are antemortem or postmortem," said Aggrawal as he pointed at some breaks on the skin surface.

"Before the fire or after," whispered Rip under his breath.

"He was well burned," continued the doctor. "Maybe he was somehow doused with petrol during the accident, and it acted as an accelerant. Or maybe the driver did him in somewhere else, like in the dowry murders, and staged an accident."

Rip shook his head. "Unless he wanted to kill himself too. I pulled the driver out of the burning car myself."

"Hmm, a challenge. But stranger things have happened before. The other problem is identification. There's been tissue slippage from the heat, and the fingerprint structure is gone. We took X-rays when the body was brought in. When we review the films, we'll see if we got good dental record shots you can use for identification purposes. Dental records could be a long shot since there are no databases of people's teeth unless he was in the military."

Rip spent about forty-five minutes with Aggrawal, and he found nothing significant. Aggrawal gave him the belt buckle and told him he'd let him know once the patient's dental films were ready.

"One more thing," said Rip. "Did you get anything from the bite marks? Any determination as to what the animal was? Can you tell by the size or shape of the bite?"

"Oh, yeah, sorry. This was definitely a cat. And by the size and depth of the marks, it was a big cat. Not domestic."

"How do you know it wasn't a coyote?"

"Upper canines are farther apart and considerably larger than a coyote's."

"But cats don't attack people, do they?"

"Some cats, like mountain lions, are opportunistic feeders. They usually go after whatever they can get their teeth into. But there are no mountain lions in Jersey."

'Okay, thanks."

"Don't be a stranger, drop by whenever you feel like," said Aggrawal as Rip left.

Rip got back in his car. He sat there and thought of what he had achieved so far, nothing yet. Instead, he had reopened an old wound. Rip started the car and drove out of the parking lot on his way back to the police station, then his phone rang. It was the medical center.

"Hello, Chief Chord."

"Good morning Chief, Dr. Jules speaking."

"Hi."

"Listen, the patient seems to be getting some of his memory back. You might want to swing over here."

"I'll be there in five."

31

Chelsea

C helsea was home most of Sunday writing codes. Bob had sent her a list of companies he was interested in approaching for a buyout and wanted her to look at them and find out the one that fitted most to the direction they wanted to take. Her mother had asked after Bob, wanting to know when he would be visiting again.

"I don't know, Mother."

"Well, start thinking of something, the two of you look good together." And as an afterthought, "And he brought me roses."

Chelsea let it slide. She didn't want to say something that would send her mom into one of her moods. Her father, on the other hand, was back to his old self, parked in front of the TV soaking in the news.

Monday morning came in earnest, and this time Chelsea was back to her usual schedule. She arrived early and went to the cafeteria for some coffee and breakfast. Coffee in one hand and a banana in the other, she stopped and listened, looking up to the TV like most people in the cafeteria.

NEWSCASTER: *"ITALY IS NOW ON TOTAL LOCKDOWN. FREE OF tourists, the gondoliers have finally rested their oars and gondolas in the City of Love, allowing the sediments in the lagoons and canals to settle. The water is so clear, and for the first time in a long time, dolphins and other fish can be seen swimming in the Venice canals. What a difference a week can make."*

"WHAT DIFFERENCE A WEEKEND CAN MAKE," SAID A FAMILIAR voice behind Chelsea.

Chelsea turned and smiled. "Hi Lisa. I hope you had a nice weekend too."

"I can tell yours was better. "You are glowing." She tapped a finger on her lips. "Hmm, who was it? The officer or the bodice ripper?"

"Oh my God, Lisa, you're depraved."

Lisa ignored Chelsea's remark. "I'll say the officer. For some reason, men in uniform make my legs turn to jelly, and I'm sure I can speak for other girls too."

"Okay, Lisa, next time I see him, I'll let him know you've fallen for him."

Lisa shook her head. "No, it won't work. You should have seen the way he looked at you. He wanted you. There was also longing in his eyes."

For a moment, Chelsea was lost for words. "All right, Dr. Phil, thanks for the free session. I have to get to my office."

At her office, Chelsea was glad for all the work she did on

Sunday. She couldn't concentrate. Inside, her head felt like a ping pong championship was going on.

Her mind drifted to her college days when she didn't know what was happening. A cute boy in her freshman class had taken it as his calling to date her. She liked him but didn't give him the time of day, shutting him down before he got a chance to ask her out. One day his persistence paid off, and before she knew it, they went to a party together. She enjoyed the evening, and after a dance, they'd gone out for fresh air.

"I've been waiting for a chance to have you all alone," the boy had said. "You're so lovely."

He took Chelsea's hands and resisted her every attempt to get away from him. He'd kissed her on the lips. Chelsea remembered it as if it were yesterday. A feeling of pure terror had seized her, and in a panic-filled frenzy, she'd punched the boy hard in the mouth and lashed out at him.

"Get your filthy hands off me! You beast!"

People saw and heard. The music literally came to a stop.

Chelsea lashed out at the anger, fear, and panic that still lingered after all those years, from that day in the woods. After that incident, she never dared go out with any other guy in college, earning her the nickname the Human Icicle.

She threw herself into her studies, graduating top of her class and earning an academic scholarship to Harvard Medical School, then residency, and a back to back fellowship. She'd hidden all that fear and panic behind her work, and now her facade was being threatened again. Chelsea heard her name called and it drew her out of her reverie.

Bob stood by her door. "Working on this virus has consumed your mind."

Chelsea sighed. "Sorry." She remembered the weekend, and heat rushed to her cheeks. She looked away.

Bob didn't seem to notice. "Listen, XRCure's board of

directors approved more shares for you." He smiled. "We have a few potential investors, but only one is extremely interested—the Russian. I heard he's connected with Putin, and that makes his pockets very deep indeed. Do you think you can have a presentation ready in two days?"

"I think so. I worked on it on Sunday." Chelsea frowned. "Isn't that too soon? Don't they have to book the flights and all that?"

Bob chuckled. "This guy has a fleet of private jets. His planes fly when and where he wants them to." Bob paused. "You think you can put something together by tomorrow?

32

Feodor Konstantin
Latvia 1988

The first few days Dimitri was back in town, he would sleep all morning and most of the day, then at night, they'd go to a restaurant, eat, and then drink until the early hours of the morning.

At thirty-four, bald headed, five feet eight inches tall, Dimitri was thick, built like a bulldog and with a neck to match. He loved drinking, eating, and womanizing. He would pick up a lady of the night, every night a different one. The only thing he loved more than all these was himself.

That wasn't Feodor's style, and he wondered how a man with all those vices got to become a colonel in the KGB in his late twenties. It could only mean there was more to the man than met the eye.

With Dimitri around, Feodor couldn't sit out at the café

and wait for Anna so he could walk her home every day after school. He didn't want his boss to think he was wasting time and he didn't want him to meet Anna either. She was so stunning that he would want to add her to his trophy list.

On the second day after Dimitri came back and after a night of excessive drinking, Feodor knew his boss would sleep into the afternoon, so he went to meet Anna. To let her know he was just busy, his boss had come in from Moscow, and there was a lot to translate.

"Ah, so your vacation is finally over, eh?" Anna had said. "Is that your way of saying goodbye."

Her remark startled Feodor. "No, not at all. It's just a lot of work, but I'll see you soon."

They'd left it at that. Within a few days of returning, Dimitri seemed to have tired of the fun. He started going to bed early, waking up in the morning, and spending time at the KGB office. After the first time Feodor went with him, Dimitri assured him it wasn't necessary to come again. He didn't have to compromise his cover as a translator. If he spent too much time at the office, locals would then confirm their suspicions.

On Friday, the fifth day after Dimitri came back, Feodor got word that the travel documents he requested were ready. He was to pick them up from a local bookstore. His excitement dampened when he thought of what could go wrong. The what-ifs. What if it was a trap, and Dimitri was there waiting for him?

When he went to pick it up at the bookstore that acted as a front for the forgers, he walked by the store three times and only went in the fourth time, after making sure no suspicious characters were lurking around.

A bell jingled as Feodor opened the door, and the

aromatic smell of old books hit him as soon as he stepped in, reminding him of the library at his university. Sunlight cutting through the window-shopping glass facing the street showed particles of dust floating around the air lazily.

Inside, he took his time browsing, and watched the two people in the store, a man and woman, shuffle around leisurely like the dust particles. Feodor monitored them from the corner of his eye. From all indications, they were regular shoppers. Satisfied, he went up to the store clerk and asked for a used copy of *War and Peace* by Leo Tolstoy as his contact had asked him to.

"Here you are," said the cashier. "It's already paid for." He handed Feodor the door stopper of a book which he pulled out from under the counter and gave him a brown bag, rough to the touch.

"Enjoy."

Feodor smiled. "Thank you." He walked away, crossed the road, and discreetly looked behind to make sure no one was following. He took a few steps, saw a bus on the other side of the road and dashed across again. He just made it to the bus before it departed. Nobody else came on board after him. About three blocks away, he got off the bus and walked into a coffee shop.

With the brown bag clutched underneath his armpit, Feodor stood in line for his turn to order. A sizzling sound behind the counter was followed by the smell of frying onions, tomatoes, and bacon. His stomach rumbled, and his mouth flooded with saliva. Feodor ordered a bowl of oatmeal, a buttered bagel, an omelet and bacon, and coffee to wash it down. He stood aside, and when his order was ready, they handed it to him on a tray, and he found a seat. While eating, he watched every one that came in after him. There were no familiar faces.

One man wearing a hat at an angle to hide his face came in and glanced around as if looking for someone. His eyes settled on the lady taking orders. Once she looked away to grab a bagel, the man rushed to the café's bulletin board, posted a poster, and walked away.

As he left the cafe, Feodor looked at the poster and was surprised to see that Dr. Janis Karena was having a rally at the village square later that evening. "That will be interesting."

Feodor didn't look at the book he bought until he was back in his room. He took the book out of the brown paper bag and opened it. The forgers had carved out pages inside the book to create a cavity and placed two passports in it. One was an internal passport, usually issued at sixteen to every Soviet citizen and used by Soviet citizens to travel within the Soviet Union, and the second was an abroad passport for leaving the USSR. Both were for Anna. Feodor didn't want to show his hand by asking Anna if she had one or not.

Excitement and fear crossed each other out as he stared at Anna's picture on the passport. He didn't know when, but he would need to start dropping hints soon.

Feodor saw the problem with the travel documents— where to hide them. Since it was just him and Dimitri, he decided to hide them in the most unlikely place Dimitri would search. He opened the briefcase of money, lifted some bundles, placed the passports, and covered them. He changed the lock combination just in case and left it in his closet. Dimitri would never think of searching his own briefcase.

Later that evening, Feodor took a shower, dressed, and left a note for Dimitri that he was attending a rally Dr. Karena was organizing to see what he could learn.

The taxi dropped Feodor by the entrance to the park, and he walked in. There were quite a substantial number of people there. *People are no longer afraid*, thought Feodor.

He listened to Anna's father speak, and he, too, was moved by the man's charisma and passion for the fate of their Latvia. He was so focused on the speech that he didn't notice movement behind him until a hand covered his face. Feodor's heart jumped into his throat.

33

Chelsea

C helsea didn't stay too late at work this time. What she would need was a good night's rest and was lucky she did most of the work for the presentation on Sunday. All she needed to do now was to arrange the facts in her mind and remain calm during the presentation tomorrow.

"I have a big presentation tomorrow morning," said Chelsea when she sat down for dinner with her parents.

Her mother scoffed. "You always have a big day. What makes tomorrow different from the others?"

Chelsea bit her tongue and took a deep breath. Her mother had always been adept at giving backhanded compliments.

"Sweetheart, what's happening tomorrow," asked her father, gazing at her and smiling.

Chelsea's hand stopped midair. She put down her fork

with mushroom, spinach, and broccoli speared on it, leftovers from Saturday night's catered dinner.

"Okay, what is it?" asked her mother.

"Well, we are looking for more investors so that we can expand and extend our approach to the way we work. We want to acquire a bioengineering company, so we can use both AI and computers to analyze data. You know, to augment medical research in finding cures more efficiently and quickly." Chelsea inhaled and exhaled noisily. "So, I'll be presenting to some investors tomorrow. I think my presentation holds the key to whether they bite or not.

"That's a lot of weight on your shoulders," said her dad.

Chelsea blew out air through her mouth. "I'm so nervous."

"That's always been you, Chels," he said. "You were usually a nervous wreck before and after every major exam you've ever taken, until the result comes out. Do you remember? You would call me up the night before, telling me how much you still had to cover, and how little you knew. And what you did know you couldn't recall. Then you'd go in and ace the exam." He smiled at her. "You haven't changed. I would have been worried if I knew you were going in for something major and you *didn't* panic about it."

Chelsea let out a sigh, stretched her arm, and touched her father's hand.

"Don't worry, you'll do great," he said.

"Thanks Dad. But this is something big. If we get the funding, then we can probably play a role in stopping this virus and responding to future diseases quicker."

Dad turned to her mother. "Jenny, you agree with me? You remember those years when she was in school? Always worrying."

Her mother's lips expanded in a rare smile. "Your father's

right. I'm surprised he remembered all that. Sometimes I wonder if he's just playing us or if he really forgets things."

"I do remember a lot of things, especially from when we were younger, even before Chelsea was born," said her father.

Chelsea knew little about her parent's lives before she was borne. Her mother was always tight-lipped, and her father too busy. But now that he had time, Alzheimer's had him gagged. Chelsea would take any stories he had to tell.

"That's great, Dad. Is there anything you want to share?"

He shook his head. "My mind is on vacation right now. When something interesting pops in, I'll let you know."

"Okay." She chuckled and looked at him with admiration.

They finished the rest of their dinner in silence. Chelsea told her parents to relax in the living room, and she would take care of clearing the table and loading the dishwasher. After that, she would retire to her room to polish her presentation. Deep down, she knew her father was right, and she wasn't the jaunty type. Maybe that was her superpower, over-preparing.

Back in her room, she opened her laptop and started to read through the files she created for the presentation. Talking to her father did instill some confidence in her. Tomorrow would take care of itself.

34

Rip

Rip's pulse raced as he waited for the elevator to arrive. Someone must have held it up on the last floor it was on. He considered taking the stairs when he heard the elevator arrive. He waited for the people to get out, and then got in with two other folks. One of them hit the second button and looked at Rip with raised eyebrows.

"Where to, Sir?" asked the young man.

"Third floor," said Rip with a nod. He hoped he would get answers from the man when he saw him. He needed to get the case going. The other passengers on the elevator got off on the second floor, and Rip continued to the third floor alone.

Rip nodded at the nurse in the nurses' station.

She smiled. "Excuse me Chief. Dr. Jules said he'll be up in a minute. You can wait for him or go in. Entirely up to you."

Rip nodded. "I'll go in. Do you know how much of his memory he got back? Does he remember his name? The accident?"

"Dr. Jules will tell you better."

Rip nodded. "Okay, thanks. I'll go see him."

He stopped at room 302, knocked, and waited. Silence. He knocked again. "This is Chief Chord of Hendonville Police. I'm coming in." He turned the handle and peeped in. The patient stood in front of a window, wearing a hospital gown and staring out of the window.

He turned around. "Hello." He spoke in English with a slight accent and waved Rip in. "Good to see you again, Chief. Do you now know who I am?"

Rip tried to hide his disappointment. "We're still working on it. What have you remembered?"

"I've had thoughts about a young man as if I knew him very well. I can't make out the face, but there's always someone running, and sometimes being chased. But the full picture flees from me."

"So, it could have been you? Does he have a name in your memory?"

"Yes, it's like on the tip of my tongue, but I can't get to it." The man rubbed his chin with his hands in a reflective mood, then looked at his palms, puzzled. "It's peeling."

Rip exhaled, not sure whether to tell him about what they suspected. He told him anyway. "We were going to run your fingerprints through the database. The officer that came earlier tried, but they seemed to have been removed."

The man stared at Rip. His eyebrows shut up in surprise.

"Removed?" He raised his palms again and looked at them. "How?"

Rip shrugged. "Do you remember doing that?"

"I don't know."

"Do you remember the accident?"

The man exhaled. "I remember flashes of something, never a full picture. I remember rolling in the darkness." His forehead wrinkled as if in pain. "My head hurts. I remember it was dark, and I can't say if I was alone, or if it was the accident that brought me here."

Rip walked closer to the man and peered out of the window to see what was keeping his interest. It was just cars in the parking lot. "A piece of paper with Chelsea Piers written on it was found in your pocket. Does it ring any bells?"

"Chelsea Piers?" the man asked with a rise in vocal pitch as if it meant something to him.

Rip's pulse picked up a notch. "Why would that be found in your pocket."

The man pursed his lips and shook his head. "I can't think of any reason. Maybe someone put it there. You said I was with someone in the car, right?" He shrugged. "I can't remember."

Rip smiled. They just called him back for nothing. The smile faded from Rip's face. A thought struck him like a bolt of lightning. What if he was here because he was looking for Dr. Chelsea Piers. She lived here in Sussex County. The accident occurred within a thirty-mile radius from her home and work.

"What is it? It seems like something is going through your mind."

Rip raised a finger. "Give me a minute. I'm still trying to process it." He lowered his head and walked away from the window. He'd showed the man's picture to Chelsea, and she said she'd never seen him before. Maybe he should show him a photo of her, or better, bring her to see him. He walked back to him. "Okay, are you open to receiving visitors?"

The man seemed to think for a moment. "Yes, but who?"

Just then, the door burst open and Dr. Jules walked in. "Hi Chief. Ivan has improved a lot, right?"

"Who is Ivan?" asked the man.

"Sorry, that's just a placeholder name. Instead of referring to you as the patient or that man. You can tell me what you prefer." Dr. Jules turned to Rip. "Did he tell you about the chasing and running?"

"Most likely it's him in the flashbacks if he grew up in Russia." Rip shook his head as one would do when trying to decide between two things. "Probably the Soviet Union, and then migrated to the States at a point."

The man held his head with both hands, his face contorted in pain. "My head."

Dr. Jules stepped forward. "Are you okay?"

"My head is hurting."

"How long have you been with him, Chief?"

"Ten minutes tops?" said Rip.

Dr. Jules walked over to the patient. "I think we'll give him a break for now." He took the patient by the hand and walked him toward the bed. "I'll tell the nurse to get you some Tylenol."

Rip thanked the man and Dr. Jules and left. He was walking across the lobby when he remembered he never got the consent to bring a visitor. He stopped, then thought of the poor man in pain and decided against going back up to ask him. Rip couldn't say if the man was faking it or not. *I'll just bring Chelsea if she agrees to come.* He made a mental note to ask her.

In the parking lot, Rip saw a woman walking her German

shepherd. It was a full breed, with a very thick coat. Right away, he remembered the mountain lion. He hadn't done anything yet. Alert the public? Would he be accused of causing panic if he reported it? He got into his cruiser and headed back to the office.

Chelsea

C helsea had barely slept two hours when her alarm went off, and she jumped out of bed. Two hours was enough for her to operate on for the day. She brought out her slides and went through them once more before getting ready. The meeting with the investors starts at nine in the same conference room she'd spoken to Rip in when he visited.

Dressed in a black pantsuit and an off-white blouse, Chelsea felt the tension in the air as she walked along the glass tunnel towards the main entrance of XRCure. She went in early so she could pour through the presentation once again, or in case someone had something to add.

She had her ID in hand, ready to place it against the sensor to unlock the door when she heard a click, the receptionist had unlocked it. She opened the door and stepped into the -ceilinged reception area.

"Good morning, Dr. Piers," said a voice with an accent.

"Good...morning," said Chelsea, more by reflex as she looked at the receptionist's counter. It was the guard, and she couldn't remember his name. "Oh, you're still here."

"Yes, Ma'am," he smiled and waved. "My shift is almost over. I leave in ten minutes."

Chelsea was the one not usually here by this time. She smiled and waved as she headed straight to the cafeteria. There was almost nobody around yet, but the aroma in the air at least meant coffee was ready. She poured herself a cup and grabbed a banana from the fruit basket. At the counter, the cashier yelled from the back that she was coming. Chelsea took out a five-dollar bill from her purse, placed it on the counter, and held it down with a bottle of ketchup from the closest table, then went to her office.

She remained in her office, looking at the references she was going to quote, making sure everything was in order. She ate the banana and sipped the coffee. At about 8:00 am, continuing to prep was now overkill. She was confident but was surprised she felt butterflies in her stomach. A few minutes later, Bob came to her office.

"Wow! You look like you just stepped out of Vogue magazine." Bob clasped his hand over his mouth. "Is that politically correct to say in an office?"

Chelsea laughed. "You look well put together yourself."

"It's just a suit and tie," said Bob.

"Same here, sans the tie."

Bob said he wanted them to test-run the technical part of it before the presentation started. So, Chelsea gathered her stuff and they went downstairs.

The machines were perfect, soon the guests started to arrive, and it was show time.

"The keywords here are replication and mutation," said

Chelsea. She'd been talking for about five minutes now after the introduction from Bob. "Replication is the process by which DNA makes a copy of itself. The DNA structure is made of two strands like a zipper and can unzip itself."

"What do you mean, unzip itself?" asked Mr. Nicolai Masterkova in deep, heavily accented English.

Chelsea picked up a jacket she'd brought along to explain this. Cell replication had been hard for her to understand in college and medical school, but once she understood it, it was like 'Open Sesame'.

"Mr. Masterkova, do-"

"Please, call me Nikolai. Do I...what?"

Chelsea smiled. "Nickolai." She walked over to where he sat. "Do you own a jacket with a zipper?"

He cocked his head. "Several."

Chelsea nodded. "When you unzip this jacket," Chelsea unzipped the jacket she brought with her, "you can see the two sides of the zipper." Chelsea took a deep breath. "During replication, DNA 'unzips' into its two strands and makes copies, using the original as a template. This way, mistakes are avoided." Chelsea put down the jacket.

Bob handed her a small bottle of water. She took a sip and continued.

"But the coronavirus is a single-stranded RNA virus and does not have the double helix, like its DNA counterpart. And because it's single-stranded, it lacks that zipper-like effect. During replication, it's not guided by the original strand as a template, and therefore has the propensity to make a lot of mistakes." Chelsea paused for effect. "In gene terms, copying mistakes are called mutations. RNA viruses mutate rapidly."

"Go on," said Nikolai nodding his head.

"So, what we propose at XRCure Labs is to create a system that would simulate cell division and generate the outcome of all the different ways the RNA replication could occur, and analyze those outcomes or mutations and determine if they could become a health risk. When the AI identifies a health risk, the system would go through all existing databases and come up with a response. It could be a management protocol, treatment, and or prophylaxis. We want to be ready for unfavorable outcomes from mutations. Remember, not all mutations are bad." Chelsea looked around at the people in the room. "One of us here has a very prominent mutation."

An uneasy laugh broke out among the audience.

"For example, the gene for eye color," said Chelsea. "A team at the University of Copenhagen tracked down a genetic mutation that took place six to ten thousand years ago that resulted in people having blue eyes." She fixed her gaze on Mr. Masterkova. "Some are beautiful."

Despite his buff macho exterior, a flush crept across Mr. Masterkova's cheeks. He smiled and blinked rapidly. "Continue, please."

For the next five seconds, everybody stole a glance at Masterkova as if realizing for the first time he had blue eyes.

"So, when bad mutations occur, we'll be ahead of the game. Our system will provide a proactive edge. Instead of scrambling during an outbreak or a pandemic, as COVID is threatening to become, we'll already know the different forms the virus can mutate into, and act accordingly. Be it Ebola, polio, Lassa, SARs, smallpox; we will be ahead of the game. When there's a new outbreak, we isolate the virus, cross-check its RNA or DNA against our database, get a match, and boom!" She clapped her hands together. "Right away, we know how to fight it. No second-guessing."

"That's like being lucky all the time," said a member of the billionaire's entourage.

"Better," said Chelsea. "The opposite of good luck is bad luck. Our system won't rely on luck, prayers, or faith. We will be looking at the molecular function of these mutations and predicting the future with facts generated by our medical and computer labs. Just like watching weather patterns and predicting the weather. But unlike weather predictions, we will be right all the time."

The silence was deafening, as Chelsea had cast a spell in the room.

Bob clapped his hands. "That's brilliant. I'm sold!"

Others joined in the clapping."

"Sounds like a page from the Ewald studies," said Bob out loud. "You know the Ewald studies?"

"Of course." Chelsea knew what Bob was trying to do. By letting the potential investor know that other well-meaning scientists had given this approach some severe thought, it authenticated their position.

Chelsea swiped her hair behind an ear. "Of course, I'm only standing on the shoulders of giants."

Paul Ewald of the University of Louisville once commented that failure to monitor how viruses are adapting to human hosts would continue to allow viral evolution to proceed haphazardly, favoring harmful strains in one setting and mild strains in another. Chelsea planned to take it a step further and use software to monitor and predict virus adaptation and come up with ways to counter or enhance their effects, by sieving through available data rapidly with the help of supercomputers.

"So, even with mutations," said a doctor on Nikolai's team, "your program will be able to adapt?"

"Exactly!" said Chelsea. "It's all about numbers. Our program will run through every feasible way the virus could mutate and cause disease, scour existing databases to find solutions, and if the mutation is novel, produce one for it and have a response on standby. It's all about speed, gentlemen. The human brain and supercomputers working in synergy is the future of medicine for humankind."

Chelsea knew she had the audience's attention. "So." She clapped her hands together as the light came on. "We need your participation to make this a reality. We need to attack this current outbreak and be ready for future outbreaks. It's only a matter of time before the incubation time for COVID-19 shortens, and virulence becomes more aggressive. Thank you!" Chelsea bowed.

There was silence, then the clapping started.

36

Rip

R ip was in deep thought after he left the hospital wondering if he had finally bitten off more than he could chew becoming the Chief of Police of a small town. Was he in the wrong profession? His friends in the CIA had warned him. Would clandestine activity with the CIA be better? He was tired of having to carry out orders whether he believed they were right or wrong.

Rip was a soldier, and soldiers obeyed orders, but sometimes, the civilians at the top had no idea of the implications of their decisions.

His thoughts drifted to Milgram's Research of 1962. Stanley Milgram, a Yale University psychologist, through a series of experiments, reached the conclusion that any human was capable of a heart of darkness. He tested whether "ordinary" men and women would inflict harm on another person after following orders from a figure of authority. His findings said given the right circumstances, they would.

Now, why was all this going through Rip's mind? He had a series of unresolved cases in his hands. A dead man, a man with amnesia, and missing fingerprints. A potential terrorist threat and a damned mountain lion on the loose.

He might have to call his friends at the CIA for a favor, and in their line of work, a favor was a promissory note. It would be like him enrolling in a Milgram research study, knowing down the line he would be asked to do things he probably wouldn't agree with.

"Cathy, you are sure no missing persons have been reported?" asked Rip from his office.

"Young man! I was already doing this job while you were still in Pampers trying to decide whether what you found in there was another type of Play-Doh. I've called all the police stations in Sussex County. From Vernon to Newton to Dover and every station in between. Nobody has reported any two old men missing."

There were a few snickers around the office.

"What about outside the county?" Rip braced himself and waited.

Cathy exhaled loudly. "Okay. You finally got me. I'll work on it."

Rip let out a sigh. "Okay, sorry I asked." Rip decided to get out of the office. Maybe he'd sleep on it. The subconscious does wonders while you are sleeping. As he passed the scene of the accident, he pulled over and got out of the car. The scene still looked as it had that night. It was also getting dark.

"Einstein, you chose the best time to forage for clues," said Rip to himself. Walking back to the car, he thought perhaps he was wasting time. He might as well call the C I A.

He knew it might cost him, but that would be chump change compared to living with himself if his inaction led to anybody else getting hurt. He walked back to his car and turned the engine on. With his phone in his hands, he took a deep breath and tapped Max Brandon's number and waited.

"Ripken Chord," said the deep voice on the other side of the line. "Surprise, surprise. Are you ready to take my offer? You couldn't have chosen a better time. Your country needs you."

"Hi Max, I need a favor."

Max laughed a deep-throated laugh. "You know we don't do favors."

A moment passed, and when Rip said nothing, Max continued.

"You are aware of the rules. Like Don Corleone would say, one day, I'll call on you. How can I be of service to you, Rip Chord?"

37

Feodor Konstantin
Latvia 1988

F eodor was at the park watching Anna's dad speak when a hand covered his face from behind him. He expected to feel the hard tip of a pistol jammed into his ribs. Or the sharp prick of a knife pressed against his neck. His stomach tightened. He fell back to his training. KISS. Keep it simple stupid. His response would be to inflict pain and cause them to lose balance. The first move, stop breathing if you can help it. Make a fist, with your thumb resting on your forefinger. Bend your elbow and jab your thumb where your attacker's face should be above your shoulder, then shove back into them. If your thumb jab gets them in the eye, they'll let you go at once. Leaning back into them would cause them to lose their balance. Then, take it from there. Flee or follow-up with a devastating punch or kick.

But Feodor didn't get a chance to do any of that. Instead,

he did what he wasn't supposed to and drew in air, filling his nostrils with a familiar smell. The hands were only covering his eyes. They were soft and gentle.

"Guess who," said a familiar voice behind him with a laugh.

Feodor smiled. "The most beautiful girl in all of Latvia."

The voice giggled. "Silly. You're too busy to see me, but you have time to watch my father rant and rave?"

Feodor turned around. "Hi Anna. I came here to see you." He stepped back and looked her over. She wore a red dress and a jeans jacket. Her blue eyes seemed to sparkle as they reflected light off the streetlamps. Her blond hair cascaded over the shoulder of her jeans jacket. "You're even more beautiful than the last time I saw you."

Anna stuck out her tongue. "Liar." She smiled and rushed into his open arms."

Feodor hugged her and shut his eyes. He felt complete as if life now had meaning. When Feodor opened his eyes, he caught a middle-aged woman watching him. She nodded and gave him a knowing smile that seemed to say, 'nice catch.' Feodor never knew his mother or father, but the approving look from that woman he felt was the closest he would ever come to experiencing his mother's love.

They continued to listen to her father, who was now talking about Latvia and how great the people were, and it was time they took matters into their own hands, and Latvians are put in charge of Latvian affairs.

"I've heard this speech a thousand times," said Anna. Let's go for a walk. I'll tell you about it." She tugged at his hand.

Feodor followed. "You know your father's speeches by heart?"

"Some of them. Not like I sat down and memorized them.

Father practices them on us all the time. You know, to gauge the tone and the delivery."

"Then you give him feedback?"

"No, that's my mother's job."

Hand in hand, they continued along the pathway in the park, moving away from the crowd.

The few vendors in the park had all moved closer to the rally. Rip felt that some people joining the crowd were just curious park-goers.

Rip and Anna moved in the opposite direction. The further away they strolled, the fewer people they encountered. Earlier in the day, Feodor did some shopping. He was checking off the things he had to do to get Anna away to safety. Her travel documents were in place. Next, he had to find out if she had any feelings for him. Feodor reached into his jacket and brought out a velvet box.

"Here," said Feodor and pushed the box to her."

"What is-" Anna's voice caught. "For me?" Her mouth dropped open. She snatched the box from him as if he would change his mind and take it back. She pulled open the box. "Wow. It's beautiful."

Rip watched Anna admire the silver pendant with the words 'I love you' printed on the other side of it. He saw the emotion that went through her.

Anna looked around. "I need to sit down." She noticed a park bench surrounded by a hedge, walked over, and sat down.

Feodor sat beside her. "I wasn't sure you'd like it."

Anna whirled to face him. Her eyes glistened with moisture. "None of my...my friends ever gave me gifts." She reached behind her head and gathered her long blond hair over her right shoulder so it fell over her chest. She gave the necklace to Feodor and lowered her head. "Please."

Feodor felt the breeze on his face when she swept her hair to one side. It smelled of wildflowers and coco-butter. He sat up and took the necklace. He unclipped the clasp, raised it over her head, and brought his hands closer behind her to clip it together again. Even under the moonlight and reflections from streetlamps far away, her skin was pale in contrast to his tanned hand. Feodor lowered his hand and kissed her shoulder and left a wet trail from her left shoulder to the right.

Anna giggled and playfully trapped his hand between her shoulder and cheek.

"I love you," said Feodor.

Anna raised her head as if stung by a wasp, her head straight forward. "Please, the necklace," she whispered.

Feodor tried to join the fish and hook while sitting on the bench in a dark corner of the park. Did he offend her? He missed connecting the necklace and tried again. His light source was the moon, and shadows thrown off by the lamps in the park made it difficult to see. He closed his eyes and relied on touch alone. Within a few seconds, the necklace was connected. He let out a breath. "It's done."

Anna traced her fingers over the necklace to the pendant. "Thank you."

"Are you mad with me? I didn't mean to-"

Anna whirled around and placed a finger on his lips. Her hands dropped to her sides. She looked at him, her chest rising and falling as she inhaled and exhaled.

To Feodor, it looked like she was trying to calm herself down. "I don't know what I did, but I'm-"

Again, Anna placed a finger across his lips. "Shh." She hitched her dress up and straddled him. "I think I've fallen in love with you." She grabbed him by the neck, and her lips found his. They became a tangle of lips, tongues and moans.

With her lips still locked on his, her fingers headed south. They stopped at his waist, then tugged and pulled at his belt.

Feodor's heartbeat sounded like a housefly buzzing against a glass window. The excitement he felt matched his first time in the kitchen store at the orphanage. No, it exceeded it. This was love. When she pulled him free, his heart felt like it would explode. Seconds later, a gasp escaped his lips when she mounted him.

A sound like a puppy flowed from Anna. She took the reins and rode him like a horse leaving Feodor gasping. It was not her second or third rodeo, but he didn't care. He was in love, and she loved him too. As Feodor felt the finishing line rushing to him, he could hear Anna's father's voice fading in and out in the distance, urging everyone to come for the next rally.

38

Rip

Driving to work on Tuesday morning, Rip wondered if he had done the right thing asking Max for help. He had a feeling it would come back and bite him. He shrugged it off. What was done was done. He had told Max about his dilemmas and asked for his help with their facial recognition software. Rip recalled the phone call with some amusement.

"I know you're one of the sharpest knives in the collection," Max had said. "But this beats me. Why don't you, you know, fingerprint the bastard!" Before Rip could reply, he added. "Prosthesis?"

"No, fingerprints wiped off. Both hands."

Max whistled. "That's intention right there. It could be something we might be interested in. I'll get back to you."

"One more thing!"

"Oh God," breathed Max. "It's not your birthday, you know."

"Emmm…ever heard of mountain lion sightings in North-west Jersey."

"Jesus Rip. We're the CIA, not the dog pound!"

The line went dead.

Rip exhaled as he headed to the station. Max's response last night that this might be serious got Rip thinking. He decided that since he was in the asking for help mood, he might as well ask Chelsea to visit Ivan to see if her presence sparked a memory. He would drop by her office later and ask her.

Rip was on Route 181, and as he approached the scene of the accident, he decided to stop again. Last night was a total disaster. It had already been almost dark. Maybe the other officers missed something. He parked, opened the glove compartment, and retrieved a pair of gloves and an evidence bag, then stepped out of the car.

With the morning light, he appreciated the scene a lot better. The signs of the fire were still there. Scorched leaves, grass, and tree branches. A big evergreen tree, with a consid-erable gash on the trunk, seemed to have taken the brunt of the impact. *Must have been what stopped the car from contin-uing its roll down into the valley*, thought Rip.

He walked up the hill back to the road to see if he could retrace the path the car took as the driver struggled with the controls. That's what he should have done in the first place. He was surprised cars were slowing as they passed, the driv-ers' eyes looking all over.

"Rubbernecking," muttered Rip. "Trying to see what gruesome accident he was investigating. He smiled and waved them on, the sound of their engines going deep as they stepped down on the gas. Milgram has a point there, people always obeyed authoritative figures. As the cars moved on, he noticed fading tire marks and hazarded a guess of Ivan's car trajectory as he fought for control. He glanced at the bushes around in case something was thrown out of the car as it rolled over. Nothing.

Nobody...well, no sane person drove around without an ID, thought Rip. What if you got pulled over? Unless he was already forgetful before the accident, it was likely Ivan had a money clip or wallet.

Rip walked up and down the path again and came up empty. He was about to head back to his cruiser when something caught his eye. He came closer. It was a wallet, lodged between the tree trunk and a rock. Rip slipped on the gloves, reached for the wallet, and pried it out.

Rip smiled. This gave a whole new meaning to being stuck between a rock and a hard place.

Rip's heart pounded as he turned the wallet over and over in his gloved hands, feeling the smoothness through the gloves. His lips twitched in a smile. Getting the leather that smooth from touching, was enough friction to rub someone's fingerprints off. The wallet was old and weathered with discoloration where the brown of the leather had been rubbed off and was almost white.

Looking at it reminded him of his old wallets the few times he'd emptied them to transfer the contents to a new one. Once he removed the credit cards, debit cards, driver's license, and business cards saved in them, they still looked puffed up, but you could sense the hollowness. The elation he found in finding the wallet quickly eroded to an empty feeling in his heart.

Hopefully, there was something in the wallet that would help him figure out who the man was. He raised the wallet to his nose and sniffed. It reeked of cigarette smoke and stale sweat. *The owner must have been one hell of a smoker*, thought Rip. And if he were a betting man, he would say the wallet was nothing less than five years old. He could see the rectangular outline of the cards that had been in it. He was still delaying in flipping it open because once he opened it, any hope he had that there was something in it would be gone.

Rip heard car engines and looked up. More cars were slowing, hoping to catch a glimpse of the accident the police were looking at. The sun was climbing, meaning the day was progressing. He had to get a move on. He opened the wallet. Empty. He'd expected it, but confirming it caused more disappointment. It had several pockets, and he poked a finger in and ran it through all of them, they were all empty. There was the outline of a key in one pocket, circular imprints left by coins in another and rectangular markings.

Rip sighed and tossed the wallet in a zip lock bag and sealed it. He walked back to his car, slipping the gloves off as he walked. Inside the car, he tossed the evidence on the seat, sat back, and took a deep breath. What now? He looked at the clock on the dash and was surprised he'd spent almost an hour at the scene.

With this avenue that had looked promising suddenly shutting down, Rip decided he would pay a visit to Chelsea Piers at her office. He looked at the wallet again and wondered if somehow the name or numbers on the cards became embossed on the leather and could be used. He remembered seeing a credit card reader from the '80s, where the card is put on a machine and rolled over, leaving its imprint on a paper.

Rip put on gloves again and opened the zip lock bag. He examined the wallet; there was no way he could get an imprint from it. But prolonged use had already left marks of numbers and alphabets on the leather. He could make out 'eodo' in the first name section, and a 'stati.' It was too short of making head or tail of it, but Rip wrote it down on a piece of paper then called Cathy.

"Hi Cathy, I found an empty wallet at the accident scene, and some letters embossed on it. Could you run it with DMV and see if it matches with anything?"

"Okay, Chief. Will do. I'll call if anything comes up."

39

Chelsea

"That was an excellent presentation," said Masterkova.

Chelsea beamed. "Thank you, Mr. Masterkova."

Nikolai adjusted his neck as if removing a kink, displaying his broad shoulders, and stretching himself out to his full probably six feet frame. "Please, Nikolai." He took Chelsea's hands.

"My apologies, Nikolai. Please, call me Chelsea."

"Chelsea, have you ever been to Moscow?"

Chelsea looked at him, and for a moment was lost in his sparkling blue eyes and bearded jaw that connected with his blond hair. He was beautiful up close, and with that accent, he exuded sexy. She shook her head.

"Ah, it is the most beautiful place in the world. The

people are friendly." He kissed her hand. "A beautiful, smart woman like you, they will treat like a queen."

He still had her hand in his. Chelsea felt like someone had put a tube down her throat and started to suck air from her. Heat cascaded down her body as a knot tightened in her stomach. She felt he was crowding her and wanted to break away and escape. From the corner of her eye, she saw Bob approaching.

Bob extended his hands. "Nikolai!"

Reluctantly, Nikolai let go of Chelsea's hands and shook Bob's hand.

Chelsea sucked in air.

"How did you like the presentation?" asked Bob.

"It was wonderful."

"Excuse us Chelsea," said Bob. "Come, Nikolai, I have some papers to show you." He led Nikolai away.

Chelsea let out a shaky breath and watched them walk away. She held her hands together to stop them from shaking and headed for the exit. She needed to calm her nerves and walked towards the door of the boardroom to head to the cafeteria. Coffee would calm her.

People patted her on the back, and she felt things crawling on her skin where they touched her. Some gave her a nod, others said 'good job'.

The smell of fried chicken dominated the aromas in the cafeteria, and Chelsea knew what the kitchen staff was preparing for lunch. Eating was the farthest thing from her mind. She poured coffee, took a sip, and fought the memories from her youth that had invaded her thoughts and were trying to cripple her.

Why did she react so to Nikolai? Bob and other men around her didn't make her overreact. He looked like the boy next door that blossomed as a young man. She and Nikolai could be age mates, but he'd achieved so much at such a young age. How did he become a billionaire at such a young age? They say behind every great wealth is a crime. Was that the part of him she was feeling? She didn't think he'd built a platform like Twitter, Facebook, or eBay that went public and gave him his billions.

Chelsea took another swallow of her coffee, and the warm liquid seemed to comfort her as it traveled down. She drank a little more, walked over to the sink, and dumped the rest. She tossed the Styrofoam cup in the trash bin and headed back for the boardroom. Then she saw Lisa approaching.

Lisa was all smiles. "Hey girlfriend! I heard you slew it!"

"Thanks."

The smile faded from Lisa's face. "I need a favor."

"What?" Chelsea's face mirrored Lisa's expression.

"Can you hook me up with this, Masterkova? How can one man be worth billions of dollars?"

"I know. I was just asking myself the same thing."

Lisa brought out her phone. "Look at this. She tapped and scrolled on the screen, then stopped. "Nikolai Nicholai Masterkova, 34, single, Russian billionaire, interests - oil and gas. His parents are university professors. He studied petroleum engineering in Russia, then earned an MBA from INSEAD France." Lisa scrolled down with her fingers. "It says here he has close ties to the Kremlin. Maybe he makes investments for the president of Russia?"

Chelsea shrugged. "Who knows?"

"Dr. Piers?"

Chelsea looked up.

The CEO's office admin walked toward them. "Sorry to interrupt, but Dr. Brown said I should call you. I think they're about to make an announcement in the board room."

Chelsea turned. "Excuse me, Lisa, I'll be right back." Her heart started to pound as she headed to the board room. She felt like a long-awaited result was about to be announced. Chelsea saw the bottles of champagne on the table and flutes and knew the investment had been made. Was Nikolai a front for the Russian president? Were they about to become a Russian company? She hoped Bob knew what he was doing.

Small champagne flutes were passed around, just enough that everybody in the room got one if they wanted. Bob beamed from ear to ear and made the announcement. Congratulations were exchanged, and champagne flutes clinked. The golden bubbly liquid splashed down people's throats forming the glue that cemented the contract signed by the concerned parties.

You must stand up to your fears, Chelsea said to herself as she walked over to Bob and Nikolai, smiling.

Bob beamed. "Chelsea, we couldn't have done it without you."

"Congratulations," she said to Bob, then turned to Nikolai. "Congratulations and welcome aboard."

Nikolai placed his palm on his chest. "Thank you. We all won today. My team believes in XRCure Lab's science and technology, and I believe in you." He cocked his head and raised his eyes as if searching for something. "How do they say this," He muttered to himself, then leaned closer to Chelsea. "We leave for the airport, and then on to Moscow in the next forty minutes. Do you want to come?"

Chelsea's mouth dropped open. She was so taken by surprise that she didn't, couldn't find the words.

Nikolai smiled sheepishly. "You know, visit Moscow as my guest."

Chelsea's jaw tightened, and she could hear herself inhaling and exhaling. Did he think by investing in the company he had also bought her? She turned and looked at Bob, her body shaking.

Bob shrugged and laughed nervously. "We'll hold the fort."

Nikolai, sensing he had overstepped, tapped a finger on his Rolex. "I have to run. Some other time, princess." He was already walking away before any of them could respond.

"Did…did you hear what he said?" stammered Chelsea realizing she still had her drink in her hand. "He propositioned me."

"Lower your voice," hissed Bob. "I remember someone saying he had beautiful eyes. A mutation that took ten thousand years in the making." A nervous laugh burst out of Bob. "Now, now, Chelsea. We have to keep our number one investor happy and the ink hasn't dried yet."

Chelsea mimicked Bob's voice. "Maybe, you should go to Moscow and rock his world. I'll keep the fort."

Bob scowled, exhaled loudly, and went after Nikolai.

As she watched him go, Chelsea knew at that moment that she and Bob would never succeed as a couple. It would be drama all the time, and she also had other issues to deal with. But she felt good inside. At least Nikolai found her attractive. What were his words again, beautiful, princess? He offered to take her back to Moscow. She smiled inwardly, then looked at her glass. She hadn't taken a sip yet.

Chelsea was never a drinker, nor did she think alcohol should be had at work, but this was a momentous occasion that needed celebrating. She would just take a sip. She closed her eyes and twirled the liquid in her mouth and swallowed, then tossed the rest in the flute down her throat.

The champagne cooled and burned its way down to her stomach. She opened her eyes, smacked her lips, then her eyes widened. She looked at the empty glass in her hand and at the door to the boardroom again. Like Michelangelo's statue of David, ready and confident, stood Police Chief Rip Chord, his gaze directed at her.

40

Chelsea

s she walked towards him, Chelsea became aware of her own heartbeat and the warmth flooded through her. Her body did a 360. Now she had a strong desire to be touched, held by Rip. Was it the bubbly golden liquid? She smiled as she met him by the door.

Rip swallowed and smiled. "You look beautiful in that suit."

Chelsea's smile widened. "Oh, thank you."

"Did I interrupt an office get together?"

"No interruptions! You came at the right time. Just the conclusion of a meeting that went very well. We got a new investor!" She did a little dance.

"From the happy faces," said Rip. "It must have been a great deal of money."

"An obscene amount! It will help us get in better shape to go all in and find a solution for this virus and others out there." Chelsea let out a 'phew' and fanned herself with both hands. "I need fresh air. You mind if we step outside? Oh, sorry my mistake. You came to see me, right?"

"Yes, I came to see you, and not at all. I don't mind stepping out. It's nice out with a light jacket."

Chelsea led the way. People shot worried glances at them. Chelsea knew it was simply because she was walking with a man in uniform. But, seeing the smile on her face ought to make them relax. She hadn't committed any crime.

Landscaping was an essential part of XRCure, with several benches situated at intervals on the grounds, the type you would see in a public park. The pavement became a pedestrian trail that wound around the property and led into the woods to a little pond. Employees walked this trail for brainstorming sessions outside the confines of the office. Chelsea took Rip along this part.

"So XRCure is a research lab? I mean...I Googled it. I didn't know you were at the forefront of tackling this virus that is right now ravaging the rest of the world."

"Yes, we're doing our best, and I convinced them that bringing on board a technology component to the medical aspect would speed up our process."

"Technology?"

"Yeah, like computers, coding, and artificial intelligence."

Rip nodded, and they walked side by side along the path in comfortable silence until Rip spoke. "I'm sure you're wondering why I came."

Chelsea jerked her head to look at him. "To see me, of course." She immediately let out a weird sounding laugh and shook her head. "Sorry, must be the champagne. I'm not normally that presumptuous. It just felt like old times again... with you beside me when I was happy." They walked on. "So, why did you come?"

"Well, to see you for sure-"

Chelsea pointed a finger at him and laughed. "And…"

"You remember the old man I rescued from a car accident last week?"

"With post-traumatic amnesia?"

Rip nodded.

"Yes. How's he doing?"

"Still the same." Rip stopped and turned to look at Chelsea. "I'm wondering if you could spare the time to come by and see him. Or rather for him to see you. You've already seen his picture." Rip stuttered. "I mean, I can show him a picture of you too."

"At the police station?"

"No, he's still at the hospital. Hendonville Medical Center, third floor."

"You know a psychiatrist would be a better fit."

"Oh, yes, I know," said Rip. "He's already been evaluated by them." Rip exhaled. "Remember, I told you about a piece of paper in his pocket that had Chelsea Piers on it?"

Chelsea nodded. "Yeah."

"Apart from the Chelsea Piers in New York, you are the only other person with that name around here. I just want to explore all leads. I've already been to New York, and it wasn't promising. I'm sure it means nothing, but…" Rips voice trailed off.

Chelsea started to walk again, rubbing her hands together. "Could he be dangerous?"

"There's no indication for that, but I'll be there too. You saw his picture. The man is in his sixties, looks fragile. I feel sorry for him. Better still, I can come and pick you up and escort you myself."

They were now at the end of the trail. The small pond glistened with the sun sparkling off its surface. Chelsea sat on a park bench and Rip sat beside her. She looked at him and felt the familiar rush she felt back then. It was still there, waiting.

"You don't have to. I just thought I'd ask." Rip's lips were pursed. He glanced everywhere but at her face.

Chelsea knew that move. He was processing rejection, trying to show that he understood her refusal. It was okay for her to say no. "Rip." Her voice was soft and quiet.

Rip froze. "Yes." Their eyes met.

Chelsea's eyes pierced into his. "I'll come and see him." Her eyes clouded with tears. "I'm so sorry." She leaned closer and kissed Rip on the lips. Just like that. She felt Rip's body go tense, he didn't respond. Chelsea pulled back, looked at him, then leaned in, and kissed him again. This time Rip kissed her back.

Chelsea felt like someone had lit a fire inside her, and she was right where she should be, in his arms. She wished she could go back in time and change things. Happiness and sadness clashed inside her. "I'm so sorry...so sorry." She said repeatedly.

Rip kissed her back, his tongue finding hers. Then he pulled back.

"I'm so sorry," repeated Chelsea.

"Shush, it's okay." Rip kissed her forehead. "That's water under the bridge."

She started to sob and laid her head on his chest while he brushed her hair with his fingers. They sat like that for a moment until they both heard a sound and turned.

Bob stood there, clapping. "Bravo. Wow." He cocked his head. "Fancy finding your fiancée kissing someone else." He gestured wildly with his hands. His voice getting higher the more he spoke. "You blew off the billionaire and almost lost us eleven million dollars in investments." He laughed without humor. "And here you are, making out with a policeman."

Her head jerked up. "What?" she hissed.

Bob cracked his neck from side to side and came towards them.

41

Feodor Konstantin
Latvia 1988

As if he knew that Feodor needed privacy, Dimitri left the next day for Moscow, citing that they always needed his counsel in Moscow. Even though Dimitri had studied law at the university, Feodor was sure the advice they needed from him was changing a person's state from living to non-living.

"If it's not this crisis, it's another one!" said Dimitri, his forehead furrowed like ridges left behind by a farm tractor. Keep up what you're doing. Don't leave any stone unturned; I'll be back soon."

And that's what Feodor did. He left no stone unturned. He attended other gatherings and rallys that were anti-USSR and pro-Latvian, taking note of who was there and what role they played, All the same time, getting closer to Anna's family.

Feodor told Anna about his boss. "My boss was called back to Moscow and I have the house all to myself."

Anna had smiled. "We shall see about that."

He continued to attend Anna's father's rallies, and in most cases, as the talk got underway, he and Anna would sneak away to a dark corner where they took and gave each other pleasure. Sometimes she would come back to the rented house with him and they would continue where they left off. But Anna always slept at her home.

Feodor met her twin sisters, whose interests in him didn't get beyond who was better looking, him or their boyfriends. Anna's mother was very protective of her daughter, at one time wanting to know his intentions for Anna.

"Mother!" Anna had yelled at her mother when she asked Feodor of his intentions at a rally. "Always trying to marry me off to someone."

"At least you like this...someone." Her mother had replied.

The question of where he was from never came up.

After every rally Feodor attended, he would make a note of one or two people that seemed to be part of the planning, close associates of Anna's father. Their names he kept in a folder in his room.

By his second month in Riga, Feodor had enough information to put away Anna's father and his associates, if that was Dimitri's intentions. He knew everybody in Anna's father's inner circle. But the surprising thing was none of them was larger than life. They all had the same motivation. The passion for seeing their country freed from the shackles of Soviet leadership. They were teachers, doctors, bakers, engineers, bus drivers, lawyers—people from all walks of life. Regular men and women with extraordinary determination.

By the third month, Feodor had gotten into a rhythm. Visit the office, hang out with Anna, and attend rallies. Dimitri had yet to come back, even though he kept in constant contact by phone and fax. That was how Feodor expected things to continue, until one afternoon, Dimitri returned.

On the evening of the day Dimitri came back, Feodor heard a knock at his door. *Dimitri must be done with his nap*, thought Feodor, *and ready to catch up on what he'd missed all the while he was gone.*

"Yes, come in," said Feodor.

Dimitri peeped in. "You remember the briefcase I gave you a while ago with money in it?"

Feodor nodded. He felt like the carpet had been yanked from underneath him. Feodor swallowed. He had put Anna's travel documents in it.

Dimitri stepped into the room. "Can I have it, please?"

42

Rip

Rip walked back to the parking lot, upset with himself for getting carried away and kissing Chelsea. Then Bob showed up to complicate things further. What about that fiancée denial part? It wasn't his business. He had only gotten worried when Bob flexed his neck and started to approach. Rip wasn't the bragging type, but becoming a member of Special Ops in the Army had taught him a thousand and one ways to kill a man, and he had tried a good number of them to completion. The only way Bob could take him out was if he, Rip, was sedated, and Bob was the operating surgeon. He had risen to his feet slowly and spoken to Bob.

"I'm Rip Chord, Chief of Police, Hendonville. I'm here in an official capacity, and what you witnessed wasn't what it really was."

"Really?" said Bob. "It's like telling me," he looked up,

"the sky is red, not the blue, I see." Eyes wide, he continued to approach.

Chelsea stood between the men and placed her hand on Bob's chest. "Bob, I don't owe you an explanation, but I don't want to create a scene. Rip…Rip, and I go back a long time. You know that already and you saw him here a few days ago. Like he said, he needs my help in identifying a man they rescued from an accident with post-traumatic amnesia." Her eyes darted from Rip to Bob and settled on Bob. "I…I got emotional, and that was it. And…and I'm not your fiancée. Where did you get that from?"

Rip saw the fire leave Bob's eyes and knew he might not get a better chance to extricate himself. "Dr. Piers, you can visit the HMC directly, or call the station at any time and we'll make arrangements for you to come to see the patient. Enjoy the rest of the day."

The ringing of his phone brought him back to the present. Rip ignored it. He banged his hand on the steering wheel. "You don't need this, Ripken." She's bad news, and now you've gone and complicated things. The phone stopped ringing. He pushed the start button, and the cruiser roared to life. He backed out and drove out of the parking lot. The phone started to ring again, and this time he looked, It was Cathy.

"Good work Chief," said Cathy breathless. "According to the DMV, based on the numbers indented into the wallet, there were only a few possible driver's license numbers that matched, and only one person who fit the description of this guy. Looks like we have a match."

Rip let out a deep breath.

"His name is Feodor Konstantin, sixty-three, lives in Dover, and works at Swift Gas Station on 14th Street. No criminal record. Clean driving history. It seems like he just showed up in 2008. Must have immigrated from somewhere."

"Russia," said Rip.

"Maybe, I'll check that with immigration and ICE."

"All right. I just left XRCure Labs and spoke with Dr. Piers. She agreed to come and see, sorry, Feodor." Perhaps it wasn't necessary anymore since they now had a positive ID. Maybe he'd call Chelsea to cancel. Rip wondered if he should head back to the hospital and present Feodor with the new facts and see if that would jog his memory. What about if his name didn't ring any bells? He decided to travel to Dover and get more insight into the man.

"Chief? Are you there?"

"Yes…I'll drive down to the gas station in Dover and see what I can find out. We still haven't ID'd the dead man."

The traffic into Dover wasn't bad. People tend to make way for any police cruiser on the highway. Something about seeing a cop car makes everyone feel guilty, even when they're not. Rip took advantage of that and got to Dover in record time. He punched the gas station's address into the GPS and soon was on his way to 14th Street.

It was a small station with four pumps and a convenience store. Rip parked and got out of the car. He wore his friendly cop face, his lips set as if he were about to smile.

The door beeped when he pulled it open. The guy behind the counter looked up and gave a subtle nod. Rip returned it and scanned the store for the refrigerator. It was located on the wall to his right. He didn't want to spook the store guy by coming on directly with questions. He walked towards the fridge, his eyes scanning the convex mirror on the ceiling of the store. One customer was in front of the counter, another walked up the aisle.

Rip wasn't thirsty, but he picked up a bottle of water from the fridge. On his way to the front, he grabbed two bars of chocolate. He stood behind a middle-aged woman at the counter and waited for his turn.

The lady dropped a pack of gum on the counter. "Marlboro lights, please." Her voice was deep and hoarse.

"Sure." The store clerk was a chubby white man dressed in a brown polo shirt branded with the station's logo. He wore a nose ring, two rings in each ear and was probably in his early twenties. He spun around, his fingers going to the shelf, and grabbed the right brand.

He moves like he's been doing this for a while, thought Rip. The woman paid and left.

Rip placed his drink and bars on the counter, cocked his head and squinted at the guy's name tag. "Roy? Busy day today?"

Roy shrugged. "Not bad. Slowed down now after the morning rush."

"Hey, is Feodor in today?"

Roy raised his eyebrows and shook his head slowly. "I don't think anyone by that name works here."

"Perhaps he's one of the guys that pumps gas."

"Maybe, I only work during the day. He might work at night too."

"Can I show you a picture?" Rip unlocked his screen and started to scroll through looking for the picture. Rip felt a presence behind him and turned. Another customer with a cup of coffee was behind him. He found the picture and showed it to Roy. "Recognize him?"

Roy looked, then pursed his lips and shook his head. "Six fifty, please."

Rip stared at him. "Oh, sorry, I forgot." He brought out his wallet and paid with a ten. "Is there a manager I can talk to?"

"He's in the toilet right now," said the cashier as the

register automatically dumped the correct change into the coin well. "He's been going in and out. Caught a bug or something." He glanced to his left and put Rip's stuff in a bag. "I'm sure he'll be out soon."

"Okay." Rip stepped aside and the cashier attended to the next customer. He looked at the toilet door, checked the time on his phone and wondered if he should go and leave his business card with the cashier. Just then, the door to the toilet opened and a guy wearing the same uniform as the cashier came out. He looked tired, his forehead dotted with sweat. Rip locked eyes with him.

"That's the manager," said Roy.

The manager approached with confident steps. He stopped abruptly. "Oh God. SHIT!" He hissed. He turned around and shuffled back towards the bathroom.

Rip followed and found the man on tippy-toes, his mouth hung open, his fingers stabbed furiously at the door's keypad combination lock. The door beeped, he pushed it open and slammed it shut behind him.

Rip didn't think the man was running from him, but he went to the door and listened. He heard a flurry of movements, then a groan and a sigh. The man had to go.

Rip knocked on the door.

"Occupied," said the manager in a shaky voice.

"Mr Manager, I'm the policeman in the store. I'm looking for Feodor?"

"Who?"

"Feodor Konstantin. He pumps gas here."

Silence. "Oh, Tintin. He's on vacation." The voice sounded more alive now.

"Tintin? The comic character?"

"Yep! Nobody can pronounce his name, so we just call him Tintin. Short for Konstantin. Is he okay?"

"Do you have a minute?" asked Rip.

"Once my stomach calms down."

"Take your time. I'll wait."

By the time the manager came out, Rip had finished his two chocolate bars, and his bottled water was down to half. He was glad the manager didn't offer to shake hands. He introduced himself and said why he was there. The manager said he needed some fresh air, so they walked out to the parking lot.

"He's as reliable as a cell phone clock. Does his job, keeps to himself and smokes a lot." The manager looked at Rip. "You mean he doesn't know who he is? Fuck, that must suck."

"Did he ever talk about where he was going on vacation? What he does after work?"

"No, I thought he just needed the rest. Sometimes when I take a break to smoke, he would join me and make idle chatter. Once he said that one day he would like to travel across the country sightseeing, starting with Lady Liberty." The manager shrugged. "Like I said, he was always here apart from Wednesdays, once a month, he goes to the doctor."

"Was he sick?" asked Rip.

"Hmm, now that you mentioned it. Could be. Has lost a lot of weight."

"Do you, by any chance, know his doctor?"

The manager looked like he was about to say no, then stopped. "He normally... I'm not sure, but he strolls up the road. There's a doctor's office at the end of 14th Street."

The manager placed his hands on his stomach, then glanced at the cashier who was looking thier way, not looking happy.

"One more question before I let you go." Rip took out his card from his wallet. "Does he have any family? Friends?"

"None that I know of."

Rip handed him the card. "Thanks so much. If you remember anything you think might help, please call me. I hope your stomach gets better."

As Rip walked away, he called out to the manager. "Which country did he immigrate from?"

He threw his hands in the air. "I don't know. Germany, Ukraine, Latvia, maybe Russia. One of those countries."

"Thank you."

Rip walked back to his car. A loner. Everything about Tintin gave him chills.

43

Feodor Konstantin
Latvia 1988

F eodor watched Dimitri trying to keep calm. If he handed the briefcase over, Dimitri would see Anna's documents, and then what would become of his plan.

Dimitri raised an eyebrow. "Anything wrong? You look like I said I wanted to sleep with your mother."

Feodor managed to chuckle. "No, not at all." His heart beating so loud he feared Dimitri might hear it, he walked to the closet and retrieved the briefcase.

Dimitri took it and turned around. "I need money for the night. We'll have dinner together."

Feodor stood in his room staring at the door, his insides tied up in knots. This was it. Stupid you. You went and fell in love, stupid you, he admonished himself. He tried to come up with a cock and bull story for Dimitri, but his thoughts ran like a cat with its tail on fire.

"Feodor! What the fuck!" thundered Dimitri.

Feodor felt like the rug had been yanked out of underneath him. One on one, he could kill Dimitri, but fear did not even let him entertain that thought. His knees shook as angry footsteps approached his room. The door burst open, and a red-faced Dimitri walked in.

Dimitri shoved the case at Feodor. "I have to go shower. Open it and bring out some money. I've forgotten the combination." He turned, walked away, and slammed the door shut.

Feodor's knees gave way, and he collapsed to the floor. He blew air out of his mouth. He would have laid there for a while, but he realized he'd just dodged a bullet and wouldn't get a chance like this again. He jumped to his feet, put in the right combination, removed the passport, and brought out a bundle of money. That night, they just had dinner and came back to the house. No drinking, no women.

"I'm still tired," said Dimitri after dinner. "Tomorrow, we'll go out for brunch, okay?"

Something was off, and Feodor couldn't put his finger on it. It made him uneasy. Dimitri asking for money, going out at night and then just coming back, not spending as usual. What about the amount of time he spent in Moscow? Something was not right. Or Dimitri was keeping things close to his chest.

Old Riga had charming open-air cafés and restaurants dotted around the city. Feodor and Dimitri sat in one of them having lunch. It was not the usual one Feodor frequented.

Dimitri was hunched over his second plate of pasta with meatballs in tomato sauce, his jaws working overtime. While next to him sat Feodor, enjoying potato pancakes with sour cream and speck sauce. Suddenly Dimitri raised his head, and his eyes widened. He looked like he had a heart attack as his mouth, smeared with tomato sauce, stopped moving and dropped open.

Feodor turned around and felt like he had been kicked in the balls. Coming towards them was Anna Karena, glowing like the afternoon sun, with a big smile on her face.

Dimitri quickly wiped his mouth. "My goodness, she's coming this way," he said under his breath.

Feodor got up, smiled, and spread his hands wide for a hug, and Anna embraced him. He gestured at Dimitri. "My boss Mr. Chicherin." And then at Anna. "My good friend Ms. Karena.

Dimitri extended his hand. "Call me Dimitri."

Anna lowered her eyes. "Please call me Anna."

Feodor saw the look on Dimitri's face and knew he was treading on dangerous grounds.

"Why don't you join us," said Dimitri. "Sit down and have some meatballs."

Anna gave an apologetic smile. "Maybe next time. I'm coming from the market. My mother's expecting me at home." She turned to Feodor. "See you later, okay."

Feodor nodded.

Dimitri's eyes remained on Anna until she rounded a corner and was out of sight. "Wow. That's a pretty piece of ass." He threw himself into his chair, then smiled at Feodor. "You dog, you've been busy, eh? Have you…?" He rolled up the cuff of his shirt to expose his right arm, made a fist, and mimicked punching while whistling. Then burst into a deep belly laugh.

A bitter taste flooded Feodor's mouth. He wished he were somewhere else. Deep down, he knew that was the beginning of friction between him and his boss.

"Karena, Karena," said Dimitri. Rolling the name on his tongue as if it were a fine wine. "It sounds familiar."

Later that evening, Dimitri said he was going to bed early again.

"No dinner?" asked Feodor.

Dimitri ran his hand over his stomach. "Not tonight. I almost forgot, could you give me the dossier you prepared for the university lecturer?"

Alarm bells went off in Feodor's head. "I still have some to type in. Let me put it all together and give you a comprehensive folder." It was a lie, only the last entries hadn't been typed in.

Dimitri shrugged. "Give me what you have. It's not like I'll go through the whole thing tonight."

Back in his room, Feodor opened the folder and brought out just the first few months he'd typed in. His reports were not sugar-coated. It described Anna's father's activities. To him, this day wasn't supposed to come, but here it was. He would have to alert Anna and let her tell her father too.

"I'll step out later," said Feodor to Dimitri when he handed him the file. "Go for a walk, get dinner."

Dimitri slapped his hands on the folder. "Ah, you're going to see the girl with the cute ass. Enjoy, I hope this will send me to sleep sooner than later; enjoy your walk and dinner."

As soon as Dimitri retired to his room, Feodor dressed up. Black jeans, a grey shirt, and a jacket. He was ready to go and pulled his pistol from the holster and checked the magazine. He didn't want any surprises.

Feodor checked the two public parks first before he saw Anna's father's entourage at another park. He looked for her in the crowd. he saw the sisters with their boyfriends, but no Anna. He asked one of the twins and was told she was home, not feeling well.

"But I saw her earlier in the afternoon," said Feodor.

The sister shrugged. "Now, she's not feeling well."

Feodor thanked her and headed for their home. He would have walked all the way but luckily got a taxi. He paid the driver and left the change as a tip. The cab drove off, and he walked to the door. Feodor banged on the door, knowing that Anna would be alone since her parents and sisters were at the park.

The curtain hanging on a window close to the door moved, and Anna's face appeared. Her eyes widened. "Feodor!" She disappeared from the window, and moments later, she unlocked the door with a click, and it swung open.

Inside, the house was warm and smelled of apple pie. To the left was their living room, and right behind Anna was the staircase. Feodor guessed the kitchen or dining must be to the right because he could hear the humming of the refrigerator.

Feodor took her hands in his. They were soft and smooth. He looked into her eyes and saw the uncertainty in it. "I came as soon as I heard. I saw your family in town. Are you alright?"

Anna lowered her head.

Feodor looked around. "Can I come in?"

Anna stepped aside and he went in. They stood in the foyer, and he took her in his arms and kissed her. "I'm sorry about this afternoon, my boss is too crude."

He didn't know how to deliver the information, so he just laid it out. "Anna…I…I think your father's in danger. You know I'm with government intelligence. You must talk to your father; he must stop his activities. I think the KGB is on to him."

"Father will never stop," said Anna. "But there's something I want to tell you."

He placed the back of his hand against her cheeks, neck, and forehead as if checking her temperature. "What's the problem?"

"Just headaches, body pain. Sometimes fever. They come and go."

"Okay, I'll take you to the doctor."

Anna raised her head and looked into his eyes. "Feodor, I'm pregnant with your child."

44

Chelsea

Luckily, nobody saw the argument. Or rather, no one had asked yet about it when she came into the building. Chelsea would probably hear from Lisa if it were in the grapevine. The atmosphere was still jubilant when she walked into the building. The technology firm they were to acquire would remain at their current location, but in the next fiscal year, they would all work out of the same location, probably a new building that could hold them all.

Poor Rip, thought Chelsea. It looked like she was just bad luck whenever she was around him. Why did she even kiss him? She hadn't planned to. It must have been the champagne, the euphoria of being hit on by Nikolai, and the nostalgia for love.

Instead of taking the elevator, Chelsea took the stairs to her office. What was Bob thinking? He was ready to whore her off to Nikolai without a second thought, and in the next breath he was talking marriage? Was that how guys propose to women where he was from? Chelsea shrugged it off as him trying to make a comeback from how he'd handled Nikolai. But it didn't matter. She had told him it wasn't going to work. It wasn't anything he did or didn't do; it was all her. She apologized if she's led him on.

"Don't act hurt," she'd told him, surprised by his reaction. "You'll get over it." As far as she was concerned, all he wanted was to sleep with her. He was all about competition and conquest. If he had to marry her to get between her legs, it was a win-win situation for him. If she didn't have her emotional baggage, she would have let him, just to get him out of her system.

Back at her desk, Chelsea fired on her computer and opened the file with the list she'd made earlier on her course of action to follow. With a team to write codes and crunch data, she could now focus on finding new directions to guide their interests. New viruses to study their cell walls, and hopefully, find ways to penetrate them.

But, Chelsea's mind was going all over. She thought about Rip, Nikolai, and Bob. She felt like a teenager, suddenly finding herself the center of attention, and she was trying desperately to put it behind her. The more she tried to work, the less she was able focus.

Finally, Chelsea threw up her hands in disgust. The best thing would be to go home, rest, and tomorrow get a brand new twenty-four hours to tackle her job, without the debacles of today.

"Calling it a day?" asked Bob, coming out of the elevator as she was about to get in. He was so casual, as if the event on the company grounds an hour ago never happened.

Chelsea took a deep breath before answering. "Thought I'd get an early start on tomorrow."

Bob chuckled. "I like that." He winked at her just as the elevator door closed.

As she drove home, Chelsea thought of how pathetic her life was. She was grasping at straws, trying to hold onto a past that had moved on. She thought of the patient Rip had told her about. His life, once full of experiences, was now empty because he couldn't remember any of it. He must be wallowing in darkness, just like she was. But her memory was intact.

Chelsea entered the house through the garage as usual and met her father in the kitchen, getting a glass of water.

Her dad glanced at the wall clock when Chelsea walked in. "The battery must have died on that clock. I better change it."

"No Dad, I came back early today. The clock is right. It's only 5 pm."

"Right, how did the presentation go?" he beamed. "See, I don't always forget." He waggled his eyebrows.

"We got it!"

"I knew you would. Come give your father a hug."

Chelsea hugged him. "Thanks Dad." Her mother, who had been sitting on the couch in the living room, got up.

"Hello, Mother." Chelsea noticed her mother's lips were drawn thin. Her face, expressionless.

"Hi, Chelsea. I already know you got the investment."

Both Chelsea and her dad did a double-take.

"You do Jenny? How come?" asked dad in his soft voice; his bushy eyebrows with speckles of gray narrowed.

"Dr. Brown, Bob called."

Chelsea's shoulders slumped. "Oh God." She sighed. She'd hoped to leave the office at the office. Now it had come home with her.

"Your coworker?" asked her dad looking at Chelsea. "The one that came for dinner and talked about Portugal?"

"Same one," said Chelsea, surprised by her dad's recall, which was overshadowed by the tension of the moment.

Her mother's cane tapped on the wood floor as she shuffled towards them. "He said a Russian invested millions into the company."

"What, Chelsea? Russian? Where's your American pride?" said her dad.

Chelsea wondered if she would have been better off staying at work. Now her dad, too, was attacking her. "No Dad, anybody was free to invest. We would have taken anyone's money…I think." For a second, Chelsea wasn't sure anymore. Was there something else? She decided to change the subject. "Why don't we have dinner?

"But Russia?" repeated her dad. "What if the cold war started again? A major American research lab would be in Russian hands."

She yanked the fridge open and rummaged through it. "Maybe Mother should have asked Bob that. He's in charge of the business decisions. We can eat grilled chicken, with mixed vegetables and fried sweet potatoes." She called the items out as she found them. "What do you think?"

"I asked him something else," said her mother. "He said to talk to you."

Chelsea was pulling the chicken out of the freezer compartment and froze."

Her mother continued. "He said some police officer, an officer Chord showed up, and you stopped reasoning."

Chelsea rose slowly and tried to meet her mother's gaze, she couldn't. Her eyes found the floor. In an instant, she felt like a little girl, a teenager once again, her mother deciding her every move, and angry she played with kids that didn't measure up in her eyes. Riff raffs, she called them.

"Don't tell me it's that Ripken kid again," spat her mother. "I thought I took care of him for good the last time!"

Chelsea stared at her mother. "Which last time?" Her words sounded like a mumble. The buzzing of a bee heard in slow motion. She had a sudden urge to sit down. Lay down and curl into a ball. She held the door to the fridge as her whole body shook. In the background, she heard her phone ring. The events of the past flashed through her mind. Chelsea saw it as if it were yesterday. Rip had invited her to a dance.

45

Rip

Before Rip left the gas station, he brought out his smartphone and tapped Google maps. He believed Google maps were more up to date than the GPS that came with the cruiser. He typed in 'clinic' and chose the option 'closest to me'. Like the gas station manager had said, there was one clinic down the road.

Rip made a right out of the gas station and headed for the doctor's clinic down the road. It was about two blocks away. When he arrived, he immediately knew he was in trouble. It was one of those medical buildings that housed multiple doctors' offices.

"Jesus Christ," he muttered. He got out of the car and entered the building. Two glass doors and a short corridor separated him from the receptionist in the lobby. He needed a plan. His uniform might get him some leeway, but once he started asking probing questions, he knew that without a court order no one would give him any real information due to privacy policies.

Rip held the door open for an elderly woman to pass and then proceeded slowly, looking at the framed credentials of the different physicians on the wall. What type of doctor would a sixty-year-old man see regularly?

He ruled out the doctors as he read their qualifications. Pediatrician, OBGYN, psychiatrist, cardiologist, oncologist, orthopedic surgeon, and dentist. Rip scratched his head. It could be any of these except for the first two. Now he was in the reception area. Behind the counter sat a middle-aged man in a tie and light blue suit. He looked up from the monitor.

The man smiled. "Hi, how can I help you?"

"Hello," said Rip and leaned against the counter. "I'm Chief Chord from Hendonville, I need your help. I'm following a lead, and I'm looking for a white Caucasian male, gray hair, probably in his sixties that comes in at least once a month. Feodor Konstantin is his name."

The receptionist chuckled. "The name doesn't ring a bell, but the description—that would be seventy percent of the people that come into this building. Does he have anything I could work with…do you know his doctor's name."

"He's probably about five feet nine, speaks with a faint Russian accent."

"We're getting warm, but he's easily in the five percent of patients that come here. I need something more concrete."

Rip pursed his lips and nodded. "I understand."

"Sorry, I couldn't be of assistance. But, if you had a name, God forbid, a picture just might help. Do you have any of those?"

Rip smacked himself on the forehead. How did he forget? He pulled out his smartphone and pulled up Feodor's picture.

The receptionist smiled. "Oh, Tintin! Yea, I know him.

Nice guy, quiet. Loves to read." The smile quickly faded. "I hope he's okay?"

"He's fine." The look on the man's face told Rip he didn't buy what he was selling. "Who does he see?"

"Ortho. Something to do with his knees."

Rip let out a breath he didn't even know he was holding.

"I told him all that walking, to and from wasn't helping him."

"Thanks so much. I guess I'll come back on Wednesday when the doctor's here."

"They're here," said the receptionist. "Business is booming." He laughed. "Hip replacements, knee replacements. All those older folks need to get around without pain."

"Which floor is he on?"

"She. Second floor." He ran a finger on his monitor. "Unit 203. Make a right once you step out of the elevator."

Rip nodded. "Thank you, I owe you."

The receptionist waved him off. Rip was surprised he had given him any information at all. But he wasn't going to mention this breach of privacy.

Rip got off the elevator on the second floor. He found room 203 easily. Dr. S. Nelson, Orthopedic Surgeon, was written on a plaque on the wall beside the door. He knocked, turned the handle, and stepped in.

The reception area looked like someone's living room. Rip was always surprised by how big the inside of these offices looked. A flat-screen TV hung on the wall. Below it was a table with magazines spread out on it.

An older couple sat in a corner with a walker stationed in front of the woman. Rip walked over to the receptionist's window.

"Hello, are you a new patient?" asked the pretty brunette,

probably in her twenties. A sliding glass panel separated her from the reception area.

"No, actually, I was hoping I could speak to Dr. Nelson about one of her patients."

"She's in surgery today at Denville. I could take a message."

"Where exactly in Denville?" Rip looked at his phone. "I could go there. I have time."

"She has several surgeries booked for the day. It might turn into a long wait for you. Dr. Nelson is good at returning calls, especially to law enforcement. Just give me your name and number and the patient's name." She passed Rip a piece of paper and a pen.

Rip scribbled his name and cell phone number and the other information she requested and gave her the paper.

She looked at the paper and looked up sharply. "Rip Chord?"

Rip nodded.

She batted her eyes at him. "Interesting name. She'll call you."

By the time Rip got back on the highway heading back to Hendonville, it was early in the evening and he was trapped in the evening rush. He could put on his siren and make a dash for it. In fact, once the cars in front realized a police cruiser was behind them, they would give way. When they did that, he took advantage.

The ringing of his phone coming through the car's speakers jolted him.

"Chief Chord."

"Hi, Rip." Dr. Aggarwal's voice boomed through the speakers.

Rip flinched and turned the volume down. "Yes!" He was alert.

"The X-rays came back, and there might have been some hanky panky."

46

Feodor Konstantin
Latvia 1988

F eodor had come to Anna's house straight from the park, and she'd just told him she was expecting his baby. At first, Feodor looked confused. As if he'd been standing in front of a group, blinked, and one of them assaulted him. Confused, he looked at each one intently, trying to figure out who slapped him. Then his lips stretched in a smile as warmth radiated through his chest. He reached out and hugged her. "That's great news!"

Anna's lips wobbled, not sure whether to smile, laugh, or cry.

Feodor cradled her face in his palms and kissed her lips. "I love you with all my heart."

Anna let out a strangled sob. "I love you too."

He stroked her cheeks and wiped a tear that streaked down with his thumb, then he remembered why he was there.

"Listen, my love. Your father is in danger. In fact, your whole family is in danger."

Her forehead furrowed. "What are you talking about?"

"I think something is about to happen. The KGB has been watching your father for some time because of his rallies."

"But he's not the only person bringing people together."

Feodor gripped her tighter. "I know, but Dimitri has been acting funny since he came back. I need to get you out of here. Will your parents agree to come away?"

Anna gripped his hands. "You're scaring me...you're hurting me."

Feodor relaxed his hands at once. "Sorry...but we have to leave Latvia."

"We? Leave? It's my home. My family is here."

"My queen, I know, but things are happening so fast. We don't have to sit and wait." Feodor looked around. "Come, let's sit down. I'll tell you everything." He led her to a couch in the living room. Pictures of Anna and her sisters adorned one wall. A chronology of their lives from birth to elementary school to university. On the other wall were photos of her parents, their wedding, as young parents of two, to a bit older parent of three. Pictures of vacations, birthday parties. Things that were not part of Feodor's childhood. He grew up in the orphanage, the pictures on his 'family walls' were graffiti and swear words.

Tears rolled down Anna's face. "I was so scared. Every week I'd say, 'I'll tell him next week, next week.' It was always next week."

Feodor stared at her stomach. There was no bump. "How far in are you?"

"This is the beginning of the fourth month."

"Fourth month!"

"I didn't mean to hide it from you. I thought you would notice and ask me."

Feodor held her. "Everything will be all right." He ran his finger through her long blond hair, his head rested on her shoulder. She smelled of wildflowers, vanilla, and musk. He could close his eyes and recount every contour of her face. Now they were going to have a baby. They would have to move fast, with or without her family. He never had a normal life, but the least he could do was provide one for his child.

"Anna, listen to me. We must leave at once. I think Dimitri wants to have his way with you. I cannot let that happen. Tomorrow we will leave for the West."

"What about my parents? My sisters?"

"Talk to them tonight. I'll come and get you tomorrow afternoon."

47

Chelsea

Her mother had always ruled her life. Even when she was in elementary school, and they lived in Lake Placid, New York, her mother would not let her play with the neighborhood kids. Right now, Chelsea could see her mother calling out to her as a kid.

"Chelsea! Haven't I told you several times not to play with those kids? You should not be associating with them."

"But mother, they are my friends from school."

"Don't speak back to me," said her mother. "Now go to your room and stay there.

Father would always object, but he wasn't always there. He had to be at the hospital at odd hours; most often, babies came into the world at a time of their own choosing. He worked at the community hospital while her mother worked as a psychiatrist at the correctional facility, now turned prison.

"Jenny, there's nothing wrong with those kids," said her father as Chelsea walked into the house to her room. "I delivered most of those children with my own hands. Let her play with them and have fun."

"David! Chelsea should not associate with low-lifes, and that's that!"

Her father had always been mild-mannered, and her mother would overrule him.

So Chelsea grew up with no friends, losing herself in books and schoolwork until Ripken Chord came into her life in high school. He had come to live with his grandparents after he lost his parents in a boating accident. They both enjoyed science and would meet in the library after school.

Rip was bold. Despite the aloofness Chelsea's mother had cultivated in her, Rip, unlike the other boys, was not deterred. He would still talk to her when he saw her out and about with her mother. He was captain of the football team, and many girls admired him, including Chelsea. Then came a school dance. Rip asked her, and she accepted.

Chelsea's mother would have come with her if she could, but even she knew that would be ridiculous. But, after Rip brought her home and they shared a kiss at the door, Chelsea didn't think she was asking for trouble.

She entered the house, went up to her room and changed into her stay at home jeans and a tee shirt. When she came back downstairs, her mother, who apparently had spied on Rip and her, went off on her.

"He lives with his grandparents and is not at the same... the same social class as you!" Her mother had screamed at the top of her lungs. "I forbid you to have anything to do with him again."

Her father, watching television in the living room, heard

the commotion and came into the kitchen to intervene. "Jenny, she's not a dog. You can't control her life. She-"

"Yes, I can," snapped her mother. "I have to guide her to make the right choices!"

That was when Chelsea, who couldn't take it anymore, got up and sprinted out of the house, straight into the woods. Her father called after her, rushed out, and gave chase. But driven by anger and being twenty years younger, she was a lot faster. She ran and ran.

Chelsea was not scared of the woods around the house. She'd gone on hikes so many times, but tonight she went further than she'd ever gone until she could run no more. She doubled over, hands on her knees, sucking in air. Despite the cold night, sweat poured down her body. Her heart thundered so fast she thought it would burst out of her chest.

As she caught her breath, she thought of her mother. Why was she so controlling? Deep inside her, Chelsea wished she had the choice to choose both her friends and mother too. The sound of pounding blood in her ears subsided, replaced by the sound of the night. Chelsea straightened up and looked around. She had no idea where she was, but she knew it would only take her time to find her way back. Did she want to go back to her mean mother?

A twig snapped, and Chelsea whirled, but it was too late. A strong hand, rough like sandpaper and smelling of stale sweat, grabbed her from behind, covered her mouth, and pulled her tight against his body. There was no doubt it was a man. The odor that enveloped her, like the inside of a forgotten gym bag with days-old sweaty clothes, was suffocating. She struggled to free herself, and the man's hands tightened around her like steel.

"If you know what's good for you," said the hoarse and deep voice of a man, "You better stop struggling."

Chelsea froze. But her heart kept on pounding as if she was still running. His foul breath was hot against the back of her neck, his body odor stifling.

"If you do as I say, and be a good girl, no harm will come to you."

Cold, clammy skin rubbed against Chelsea's neck, and the man made sniffing sounds behind her. She wanted to jump out of her skin.

"God, you smell good. I hope you taste even better." He pressed himself hard against her. His breathing got faster and faster. Suddenly the man stopped and listened.

Chelsea's whole body was shaking. Her knees could barely hold her. Despite the pounding of blood in her ears, she heard it too—barking dogs. Someone was out there.

The man released her, cupped his ear, and listened. Chelsea wanted to dash away, but the legs that sprinted and brought her here were not the same. They were now jelly. Then she noticed the man was wearing a uniform, an orange outfit with ACF printed on it. Chelsea realized he must have escaped from the Adirondack Correctional Facility. Was he one of her mother's patients? Iron, like fists, grabbed Chelsea's wrist again.

"We have to get out of here before the dog's pick up my scent."

The man dragged her along with him through the woods until she could walk no more. Chelsea was limp and cold to the bone and was sure he would kill her. The sound of barking would fade out for long periods and then resurface again, depending on the breeze. Each time they heard the dogs, the man would yank her forward and increase his pace. At one point, Chelsea could not move anymore, and she collapsed on the ground.

"Get up! Get up!" hissed the man. He looked like a caged

animal, now talking a lot to himself. He glanced around, not sure which direction to go, then his eyes settled on her as if he just saw something in her he hadn't seen before.

Chelsea felt the man's rough hands on her. Every living fiber in her agreed she was in danger, but she froze with terror.

"They'll catch us," said the man. "I might as well enjoy you before they do. This time they'll throw away the key."

His hands roamed over her body, pressing and squeezing. He groped her chest, his fingers fumbled with her belt, trying to get it undone. Chelsea screamed, and with the last of her energy, kicked out.

It was a well-placed kick, and the prisoner doubled over in pain. But her win was short-lived.

The convict was infuriated. "Bitch," he screamed and grabbed her again, and his hands tightened around her neck.

Chelsea couldn't breathe.

Without warning, blinding pain exploded in her legs as the crazed man grabbed her thighs, one after the other, delivering devastating punches. Darkness with flashes of light dotted her peripheral view. Chelsea's thighs felt heavy like they were encased in concrete. She couldn't move them, couldn't resist as her jeans came off. At that point, she knew she was fucked.

The prisoner's hands were going to places she considered private. The thought of what was to come and the weight of the man on her was suffocating. She struggled to inhale, to exhale, to move, but she was pinned down. The sound of barking dogs got louder and louder, then darkness.

48

Rip

R ip shook his head and braced himself for the news that was coming. The medical examiner loved those words.

Aggrawal continued. "It showed the passenger had a broken neck."

Rip's whole body went tense. "Was it broken before, during, or after the accident?"

"We've already determined that your passenger died before the fire because there was no soot in the upper airway. Remember the India dowry murders?"

"Yes," said Rip.

"Okay, in this case," continued Aggrawal, "with the skin changes after the fire, it's difficult to say if the broken neck happened before or after."

"He was murdered?"

Aggrawal exhaled. "His neck is broken for a fact. It could

have happened before or after the accident. You had enough time to drag the driver out of the car before the car went up in flames, meaning he could have died from the impact of the accident before the fire started. The victim was wearing a seat belt and wasn't thrown during the rollover, I think there was some…some hanky panky. His neck was probably broken before the accident, possible homicide." There was a pause. "My office will send over the formal report. Remember, don't be a stranger. Drop by when you can."

The line went dead as Rip thanked him for the call. "My goodness."

The drivers of cars passing Rip were staring at his car, making Rip realize he had almost slowed to a crawl while the medical examiner was on the phone. He increased speed just as his phone started to ring again. The name on the screen was Sara Nelson. Rip was about to let it go to voice mail when he realized it could be the orthopedic surgeon. He pulled over to the shoulder of the road and took the call.

"Hello, Chief Chord?" said a tired girly voice.

"Yes, Dr. Nelson, thanks so much for calling me back."

"The pleasure is mine. What do you want to know about Mr. Konstantin?"

"He's one of your patients, right?"

"Yes, but not until four weeks ago. He'd come to me because of knee pain. He spends about eight hours on his feet daily, so he kind of was asking for it. I advised him to spend less time on his feet. In the future, it's likely he'll need a new knee. He didn't receive the news very well."

"Can you explain it further?"

Dr. Nelson laughed. "He would rather meet his ancestors intact…without any new appendages. He also was having difficulty sleeping, which he attributed to his old job."

Rip tensed. "What was his old job?"

"He didn't elaborate, but I'm guessing some type of military or paramilitary job. According to him, he saw a lot of deaths. I felt he had post-traumatic stress syndrome and referred him to a psychiatrist on the second floor of our building."

Rip felt the hairs on the back of his neck rise. Was the man depressed? Maybe the terrorism theory wasn't farfetched after all. Rip thanked her for calling and wrote the psychiatrist's name and number down.

Rip sat in his car and tried to make sense of all the information he had gathered so far. The man's identity had been confirmed. He is an immigrant from Russia, worked at a gas station, and lived in Dover. Thus, the primary problem they had of identifying him had been solved.

Next would be identifying his passenger, then the questions of what caused the accident? Was the passenger's death an accident or homicide? Why did he want to get rid of his fingerprints? What happened to his fingers? Even though he'd ruled the Piers out, was he mistaken? Like the manager at the gas station said, maybe he was on his planned trip to see the US. And that should account for having the name Chelsea Piers on a piece of paper in his pocket.

Rip made up his mind. He, too, would drive straight to the hospital. *Tintin has some questions to answer.* Rip remembered they still had the issue of memory loss to deal with. He sighed and looked at the rear-view mirror, looking for a chance to get back into traffic. He found an opening and eased in.

Ahead he saw the golden arches sign and a Dunkin' sign and wondered if he should get some coffee. He decided to go through the drive-thru. He grabbed a cup of coffee and a donut and continued to the hospital. The cars in front of him slowed, and traffic went down to a crawl.

On the other side of the highway, cars were also slowing down. It could only mean one thing, an accident. For a second, Rip thought of putting on his lights and driving on to the hospital. Any mishap on the road would slow him down. But, it was his duty to attend to accidents. He turned his light on, let the siren do a single whop-whop to get people's attention, and eased into the shoulder of the road. He hoped whatever was ahead would be easy to dispense with, and not take up too much of his time.

49

Feodor Konstantin
Latvia 1988

That night, Feodor lay on his bed listening to the orchestra down the hall. Dimitri's inhales and exhales as he slept made sucking sounds like a kid with a straw trying to get the last drop of soda from the bottom of his cup. More than once, Feodor got off his bed to check up on Dimitri when the sound suddenly stopped. Dimitri would splutter and cough, then the rhythm resumed.

Feodor spent the whole night second-guessing himself. What would Anna's parents say? They would treat her as a child and wonder what she's gotten herself into. Maybe he would have to talk to them himself, but who knows how they would react? Secrecy was particularly important.

Feodor only convinced himself that he was doing the right thing when he thought of their unborn child. He thought of the nights at the orphanage. The beatings. The nights without food. Being tossed from one older boy to another, and the night it was his turn to sleep in the dorm master's quarters. No child of his would go through what he went through.

Feodor's plan was simple. Pick up Anna and any member of her family that would come. Fly to Berlin, smuggle Anna and her family across the Berlin Wall into West Germany and defect as a KGB officer, with the rank of major and a close associate to the youngest and most ambitious colonel in the KGB. Feodor had no specialized knowledge he was bringing but he hoped his connection to Dimitri would be enticing for the Western consulate he surrenders to.

Sleep still eluded him until the early hours of the morning. He only drifted off as the sunrays drifted in through his window, and birds that wanted the early worm were chirping in the garden.

Feodor woke with a start and looked at the clock on his nightstand. He was surprised it was 11:30 in the morning; he had overslept. He rushed into the bathroom, showered, and rushed out. He wondered where Dimitri was. He would have to get Anna and find out if she told her parents.

Feodor retrieved Dimitri's briefcase from the closet, opened it, and took out a bundle of rubles and Anna's passport. He then retrieved his own travel documents. Once he put the money in his pocket, he knew he had crossed the point of no return.

Feodor headed for the kitchen to get a drink of water before stepping out to get Anna. He heard movement in the living room and went to check. Dimitri was pacing back and forth with a drink in his hand. Sitting on the couch was a junior KGB officer Feodor had seen in the Riga office. But what made Feodor's blood run cold was what Dimitri had on. He was dressed in his full KGB officer uniform. This was an all-out assault.

Dimitri raised a glass of straw-colored drink in his hand. "Finally, Major, you've woken up. I was beginning to wonder if you expired in your sleep."

The official salutation was not lost on Feodor. He had to learn more. Was he in trouble, or had he indeed missed something trivial? Feodor decided to try a joke. If Dimitri laughed with him, then he could infer that all was well.

"If you were not snoring like a locomotive, sleep would have taken me sooner than later."

Dimitri roared with laughter. "Not only are you competent, you always speak your mind. That's why I like you."

Feodor smiled and exhaled; it was a false alarm, and he felt the tension lift from his shoulders. Whatever got Dimitri into his uniform must have been an activity that didn't involve what he was working on.

"You missed the action, but no worries."

Alarm bells went off in Feodor's head. "What action?"

"We took your recommendation, they're all in custody, the whole family." Dimitri raised a finger. "But the sexy girl from yesterday afternoon. I want her."

50

Chelsea

The tap-tap sound of her mother's cane on the wooden floor penetrated Chelsea's ruminating.

"Chelsea! Chelsea!" yelled her mother.

Chelsea shuddered, stared at her mother, and wrapped her hands around herself. The police hounds had shown up just at the right moment and pushed the prisoner off her. He didn't violate her, but her mind was ripped apart. Human touch could never be seen as friendly again. The prisoner was taken back to the prison, and Chelsea later learned he was serving life for three rapes and killing two women.

"Chelsea!" barked her mother.

She jerked, and refocused on her mother, back to the present.

Her mother exhaled. "I can't always come to your rescue. You must for once do what you're told, so you won't need to be rescued.

Chelsea rolled her eyes. "Here we go again," said Chelsea, wondering why she had frozen vegetables in her hand.

Her mother walked closer to her. "Bob is good for you." Then she shook her head. "That Ripken kid. I had to keep the two of you apart to stop you from making a mistake. I told the police that the last person you were with was Ripken Chord, and we believe he lured you into the woods that night. I told them you would corroborate the story."

Her father waved his hand in the air in an arc. "All this shouting reminds me of that night Chelsea ran into the woods and got lost."

Chelsea nodded. That was true. It reminded her of the same event sixteen years ago, in another small town, in another kitchen. But this time around, she was not running.

"Then after we found her," continued her father. "Jenny convinced us that the boarding school in Massachusetts was the best thing for her. And Ripken, you convinced to join the Army. Chelsea's father shook his head. "I always told you, Jenny, it's not good to impose your wish on people. That was why Chelsea rebelled then and refused to go on vacation to Portugal anymore."

Chelsea looked at her father. "Dad...?" She was worried he had finally tipped over into dementia.

"Your mother loved vacationing in Portugal," he said. He glanced at Chelsea. "Someone is going to The Algarve, right? That Bob guy." He shook his head. "I don't like him. Too forceful. Too in your face." He paused and looked around. "Where was I? Right The Algarve. You know, it was in the news a few days ago. Some girl was kidnapped, and her parents were considered suspects. You know her parents are physicians too. Just like your mom and me."

Chelsea remembered the story. Her dad was mixing up

the dates. It was May 2007, three-year-old Madeline, her two siblings, and their parents were vacationing in The Algarve region of Portugal. One night their parents left them alone in the room and went to a bar inside the resort complex they were in. When they came back, Madeline was gone. The *British Daily Telegraph* had described the disappearance as 'the most heavily reported missing-person case in modern history.' Chelsea could never forget it. Her heart had gone out to those parents.

"A Russian was questioned and later released," continued her father. "I hope it wasn't the same Russian I met when you were born."

Somewhat amused, Chelsea gave her mother a side glance to see if she also noticed that her father seemed to be deteriorating. But her mother had turned pale. "Mother, are you okay?"

"Rus...Russian? What...what Russian?" she stammered.

Father scrunched up his nose. "You know, in the hotel. I never told you. But you were there! You must have forgotten. Chelsea, if it wasn't the day you were born, it would be a night I'd prefer to forget."

"I was there," her mother said. "But my abdomen felt like I had eaten all the black-eyed peas in Portugal." She sat down. "Why don't you tell us what happened.

51

Feodor Konstantin
Latvia 1988

F eodor felt like a fish at the display table in the fish market. On the outside, he looked whole, but his insides had been gutted out.

"The whole Karena family is in custody," said Dimitri. "We picked them all up from the university like flies, except for the cute one. They said she stayed home, sick. I don't want her damaged in any way. She trusts you, she would come without a fight if you're with us. We'll go bring her. I have plans for her. Maybe when I'm done with her, you can have her."

Feodor bit his cheek to control the rage building inside him.

"The others we had to rough up a bit in public. Slapped them around as an example to others. To let people know that holding rallies and talking trash about the Soviet leadership is unpatriotic." Dimitri walked closer to Feodor, patted him on the back, and looked at the uniformed soldier. "Look at him, he's too modest. He won't even gloat over the role he had to play here."

Feodor swallowed and forced a smile. "I'm only doing my job." His mind was pulled in a million directions on what to do next. Run for it. Confess what he'd been up to? Or when the accusation comes, deny, deny. But he couldn't help but wonder if Dimitri had found out his plan. The more Feodor thought, the more he felt like a cornered rat. There was no way out. He would have to lead them to the house and pick up Anna.

"Should I put on my uniform?" asked Feodor.

"We don't have much time," said Dimitri. "Maybe for the next round of arrests we make."

Dimitri should have picked another family for his first round of arrests instead of the Karena's, thought Feodor as they got ready to visit the Karena's residence. Less than thirty minutes later, they were there. Feodor wished that word had gotten to Anna about what happened, and she would have vanished. He knocked on the door and waited. His stomach tightened when he saw Anna come to the window. The bitter taste of bile flooded his mouth. He pushed it down.

Anna saw Feodor and smiled. She disappeared from the window, and he heard the door being unlocked. Her eyes almost bulged out of their sockets when she swung the door and saw Dimitri and a uniformed KGB soldier standing with Feodor.

"Hello Anna," said Feodor with a smile. "Can we come in?" He did not dare wink or make any sign that could alert Dimitri.

Anna hesitated. "Sure."

Dimitri beamed at her. "Anna, how are you?" He took her

hand and kissed it. "Feodor said you would love to have lunch with us today."

Anna's turned to Feodor, a questioning look on her face. "He did?"

"I'm sorry, I should have sent a message to warn you we were coming," said Feodor.

Anna looked at herself. She was wearing stay at home slacks and a tee-shirt. "That's okay, I'll get ready. Why don't you wait in the living room?" She disappeared up the stairs.

The next ten minutes were tense. Feodor was still looking for a way out.

Dimitri stood up and paced the room, leaning in to look at the picture frames on the wall. "Nice family. What a shame," he said in a low voice, as if he were talking to himself. He glanced at his watch and exhaled.

Feodor got up. "Let me see what's holding her up."

Dimitri nodded, clasped his hands behind him, and continued to pace around.

Feodor walked up the stairs. At the top, he called out to Anna.

"Over here," came Anna's muffled voice.

He walked down the corridor, similar to the one below, with doors on the left side. Anna ran into Feodor's arms as soon as he came into the room she was in.

Feodor kissed her lips, then her forehead. "I have to get you out of here," he whispered. "Your parents and sisters were arrested at the university."

Anna deflated like a balloon and started to sob. "Oh God. It's all my fault." She fell apart, her voice, a mixture of sobs and cries. "I didn't warn them this morning."

"Shh, don't blame yourself." Feodor's voice was low. "I won't let them have you too. Put on your shoes. We're getting out of here."

His heart pounding, Feodor watched her pick up her canvas shoes. He tapped his hands against his jacket and let his hand rest on his gun.

Anna was dressed in jeans and a long sleeve shirt. Feodor pointed at her jacket and motioned for her to put it on. Once she was ready, he motioned for her to follow him and headed towards the staircase. Feodor reached into his jacket, once they came at him, he would start shooting.

Anna grabbed his hand and shook her head.

Feodor eyebrows shut up.

She pointed backward and whispered. "Another staircase in the back."

He nodded and followed. It was a spiral staircase.

Anna went first. It creaked and groaned, and she stopped.

Feodor waved her on. "Continue going," he whispered. He followed right behind Anna. The staircase terminated in a long corridor that led straight to the living room. On the right were the doors to the laundry and kitchen, and an opening to the staircase. On the left was the main entrance into the house. Behind them was a door that led outside.

"What's keeping them?" said Dimitri's voice. "You, go upstairs and hurry them up."

"Yes sir!" replied the driver.

Feodor heard and knew the driver would appear on the corridor soon and see them. He placed Anna behind him and held his breath.

The driver bounded to the staircase, climbed up one step, then stopped. He stepped back, and his head jerked to the right.

Feodor flashed him a smile and waved him over. When he was halfway down the corridor, Feodor spoke. "Come, help me. The bitch is trying to run away."

The driver walked towards Feodor. "What?" He tilted his

head, first to the right, then to the left, trying to see behind Feodor.

Feodor stepped behind Anna and grabbed her. "She's a wild cat. Tried to sneak away. Grab her legs. We'll have to carry her to Dimitri."

Anna whirled to look at Feodor. She didn't need to act her part. Confusion and sheer terror was written all over her face.

The driver chuckled, muttered something vulgar, then bent down to grab Anna's leg.

Feodor leaped out from behind Anna, gave the soldier a judo chop behind his exposed neck. The soldier went down. Feodor heard footsteps coming in the living room and knew Dimitri would appear soon. He fell on his knees, grabbed the moaning driver by the jaw, and in two swift moves, broke his neck.

"Feodor! Feodor!" barked Dimitri. "What's going on?"

Hunched down on the floor, he was an easy target. Feodor leaped to his feet. Behind him, he heard whimpering and crying. For a seasoned agent like Dimitri, the only advantage he had was a surprise. It was a kill or be killed moment. In one fluid movement, Feodor pulled his pistol from the holster and pointed at Dimitri, who was still pulling his gun out. Feodor Konstantin pulled the trigger twice.

52

Rip

With his lights on and occasionally hitting the siren to sound a whoop-whoop to deter motorists from getting on the shoulder of the road and running into him, Rip drove towards the source of the traffic jam. He was relieved when he found out it was a five-car fender bender with moderate damage, but with plenty of anxiety.

One of the women in the cars was a tall, blue-eyed, athletic blond who looked just like Chelsea. His mind drifted to what transpired in the parking lot earlier that day. He thought of what made them go their separate ways sixteen years ago. He knew Chelsea's mother had been a bee in her bonnet and was the driving force behind keeping them apart. He had wanted to fight the absurd notion that he had tried to take advantage of Chelsea in any way or had anything to do with the escaped convict, but his grandparents, God bless their souls, in their infinite wisdom had cautioned against it. He remembered his grandfather's words, in his hoarse gravelly voice.

"Rip, some people have opinions and assumptions that have been passed down for so many generations that it has become fact to them, the way things should be. There's an African proverb that says 'what a man can see standing up, a child cannot see even if he climbs the tallest trees.' We want you alive Rip." He'd squeezed Rip's shoulder and continued. "You've always wanted to join the Army anyway. Think of it as accepting an early decision."

But something inside of him had died. Or so he'd thought, until he met Chelsea a few days ago, and then today. She said she wasn't involved with anybody and demolished the Bob guy today.

The woman he had been staring at smiled at him, jarring him out of his reminiscing. Rip smiled back, rubbed the back of his head, glanced around, and pointed as if he just found what he was looking for and walked away.

Eventually, the traffic situation was settled, and Rip walked back to his car. He looked at the time on his cruiser dash and cursed. He had spent almost an hour at the accident scene. He had just picked up his phone to call the hospital when it started to ring. He took one look at his screen, and his mood changed for the better. Max Brandon. Rip was looking forward to telling him that he didn't need his help anymore.

"Hi, Max. I was just about to call you."

"Really?"

"Yes, we finally cracked it. The amnesia guy's name is Feodor Konstantin, a gas pump attendant here in New Jersey." Rip paused and waited for Max to applaud him.

"Phantom 13, congratulations."

Rips stomach tightened. That was his Special Ops team code name.

"That's just one half of it. We must meet. It's one thing to get a request from a civilian for help, and another to share sensitive information."

"Jesus," muttered Rip.

"Where're you? Any landing strip, local airports, open space, football field around you?"

Rip thought fast, he knew he had passed an airstrip, in fact, there were several in this area, a fact that had surprised him.

"Come on, Phantom. I don't have all night," growled Max.

Rip winced at the use of his code name again. This must be serious. "There's one on Route 639 in Wantage, New Jersey," he blurted.

"Sussex Airstrip?" said Max

"Yeah."

Max exhaled. "I'll arrive at 2010 hours. Be there."

The line went dead.

53

Feodor Konstantin
Latvia 1988

F eodor's ears rang from the blast of his gun. Dimitri was hauled back into the living room by the impact of the bullets. To Feodor, there was no turning back. Feodor turned to Anna. "We have to go."

She didn't move. Her lips were wide open, but words deserted her. Feodor grabbed her shoulder and shook her, removing any remaining vestige of confusion from her eyes.

Anna was crying. "Are…are they dead?"

Feodor was utterly running on instinct. "We have to go now, or we'll end up like them." He bent down and reached for the soldier's pocket. He found what he was looking for, the keys to the car.

They stepped out of the house. Outside, the sky was getting dark, and Feodor welcomed the cold air on his skin. A cat scurried across the street, the only sign of activity.

Feodor led Anna to the car and opened the passenger side for her. Her hands wrapped around herself, her lips quivering, eyes wide. She got in, and he ran to the other side and got in. He started the car, and despite his intentions to drive off slowly, he took off with s screech of tires.

"Where are we going?" asked Anna in a shaky voice.

"We must get out of Latvia. The sooner, the better. We should be long gone before they start looking for us. I'm sorry, Anna, we can't do much for them. They lapsed into silence again as Feodor drove back to his house. He must retrieve the briefcase. Money wasn't everything, but when you have it, it could grease a lot of stuck gears and get them moving, their key to a new life.

"Wait in the car," said Feodor and dashed into the house he shared with Dimitri. He went straight to his room and removed the suitcase from the closet. He stuffed as much cash as he could into his coat pockets and threw the rest into a canvas bag. He had already retrieved Anna's passport and his own travel documents earlier, before Dimitri surprised him with the shock of apprehending Anna's family. He dashed down the stairs. The street was completely dark now.

"Where are we going?" asked Anna again.

Feodor was already speeding along the road. "To the airport. We're going to East Germany."

Anna gasped and started to cry. "My parents...my sisters..." Her voice trailed off.

A painful lump formed in Feodor's throat, and he felt her despair. "Let's be safe first. They're already in custody." He didn't want to tell her what Dimitri had said, that they were beaten up. "Once they miss Dimitri and put two and two together, they'll come after us."

Anna looked away, not asking any more questions. The reality of the situation must have become apparent to her.

As they drove to the airport parking lot, Feodor wondered if they could be walking into a trap. He shook that off. Dimitri should still be on the floor of Anna's living room with rigor mortis setting in.

Dimitri had kept him out of the loop, but by tomorrow morning, when neither of them showed up, the Riga KGB office would start looking for them. At least to know what to do with the people Dimitri had in custody. By then, he and Anna should be far away.

Their main concern would be buying their plane tickets. After Feodor parked the car, he contemplated leaving the key in the ignition. Someone might steal it, and investigators would focus on the theft. He left the key. They needed any advantage they could get. He got out of the vehicle and went to the other side to help Anna out.

Anna looked up as a jet engine roared overhead. She lowered her head, her gaze fixed on Feodor. "I…I don't have a passport."

"Remember the photos we took at the park, I used one of them to have a passport made for you." He wanted to say more but decided any celebration should wait until they were in the air. "Come."

As they approached the ticket kiosk, Feodor knew something was not right. There were no passengers lined up. "Two return tickets to Berlin."

"Sure. We have flights leaving at 9 am, 12 noon and 6 pm tomorrow."

Feodor shook his head. "No, for tonight."

"The last one took off a few minutes ago."

Feodor had picked Berlin on purpose, to ease their way into the West. After World War II, Germany was split into two, the Western part occupied by the allied forces made up of the United States, France, and the United Kingdom. In contrast, the Eastern part was occupied by Soviet forces. The Eastern part would later become known officially as the German Democratic Republic (GDR). It was a satellite state of the Soviet Union until a complete transfer of administrative responsibility to the GDR was completed in 1949. The Soviet Union still maintained a sizable military force and influence in the state, and that was what Feodor had counted on. To arrive and depart swiftly before the news of Dimitri's demise got to East Berlin. But, when he made his plan, murder was not part of it, and now he could be stuck in Riga.

"Sir?" asked the ticket, man.

"Okay, two tickets for tomorrow morning."

Feodor and Anna left the airport and drove to the center of town. Feodor had already changed his mind on how they must travel. They must leave tonight, tomorrow would be too late. They walked to the nearby bus terminal and got on a night bus going to Vilnius, Lithuania. At Vilnius, they stayed in a hotel to get some rest. The next morning, they headed for the train station.

"Feodor…look," said Anna. She'd stopped at a newspaper stand and pointed.

Feodor saw the headline. 'Outspoken Latvian Prof Dead'. He bought the newspaper. He felt like he had been punched in the stomach. Dimitri had lied to him. Did Dimitri know about his plans beforehand? Feodor had felt remorse about killing Dimitri, but based on what he now saw in the headlines, he was glad.

"Oh God, oh God," mumbled Anna.

He wrapped his arm around her. "Come on, let's go."

Once seated on the train, he found what he was looking for on the second page. In the foreign news section, the article mentioned the death of a Dr. Janice Karena and his family in Riga in a tragic fire at their home. No mention was made of

Dimitri or the soldier. The article said the fire was so intense they're were still going through the wreckage. It was very possible that the Karenas were not actually brought back to their home after they were killed. KGB would not want to be seen bringing four bodies into a house in a residential neighborhood. The 'intense' fire was a good cover for the fact that the bodies would not be available for burial. If that were indeed the case, it was good news for Feodor. It meant they would not have found Dimitri and the soldier yet, if they thought to look there at all. Dimitri may not have mentioned Anna, wanting her all to himself. If they didn't know about her, they would have no reason to suspect he'd gone to the Karena home.

Anna sniffed and wiped her eyes. "I want to read it." She read it. "All lies. They killed them.

From Vilnius, they boarded a train for Warsaw, Poland. An hour into the journey, Anna was overcome by grief. Feodor was so distraught he felt he wished he had the power to turn back time. But what was done was done.

They eventually got to Berlin, and that was when things took a turn for the worse. He couldn't just contact the KGB assets he knew to facilitate his travel. Most of the Soviet Eastern bloc countries were agitating for one thing or the other and trust had become a limited quantity. With his added condition of being a rogue agent, contacting anyone now would be like eating his gun. Feodor thought hard, he hadn't come all this way just to give up or be apprehended.

Their only saving grace was the cash Feodor brought with him. They stayed in a hotel and passed themselves off as tourists. He sold some of the currency he had with him for marks using the hotel manager as a go-between. When the manager tried to get wise and came up with a cock and bull story about rising exchange rates, Feodor introduced him to his persona as an officer of the KGB. The manager said it was all a mistake.

Crossing the Berlin border into the West was now out of the question. He made new plans. Their safest bet would be by sea. They found their way to the harbor town of Rostock and started searching for a vessel willing to take the risk and smuggle them.

Eventually, he found a ship sailing for Portugal, whose captain didn't mind smuggling people for some cash. He and Anna joined it. Now, they had been on the run for three months, and the ship to Portugal was the toughest yet. It hugged the coastline and stopped at every port. The captain had made papers for Feodor, passing him off as a sailor whose wife forgot to disembark after she came to say goodbye.

Once in Portugal, Feodor would meet up with a contact he got from East Germany to make travel documents for him and Anna to travel to South Africa or South America. He hoped they could leave at once, before the baby came. Anna had refused prenatal care in East Germany.

"We've come this far," Anna had said. "We don't want to visit a doctor and blow our cover." She took Feodor's hand and placed it on her stomach. "See, good baby."

They were exhausted by the time they got to Portugal. Anna was mostly quiet as if resigned to her fate. A life, Feodor believed, she never imagined in her worst nightmare. Deep down, Feodor believed that if her family had survived, she would have wanted to go back to Riga. He too, wondered if he did the right thing. The one thing he was sure of was that he would die first before he let anything happen to Anna or their unborn child.

54

Chelsea

Chelsea's mother had asked her dad to tell them what happened in Portugal. Chelsea knew they only had a small window. Her father seemed to drift in and out of recalling past events.

"Come on Dad, tell us," said Chelsea.

Her father laughed. "We were on vacation, and we had roughly six weeks before you were due to come. I'd advised against it, but you know your mother once her mind is set. Anyway, it was a stormy night, your mother woke up with abdominal cramps. I examined her and knew something was wrong. I called the receptionist. We needed to get her to a delivery room fast. He recommended we come down to the resort's clinic. The clinic was more suited for first aid, nothing more. They had stethoscopes, gloves, iodine, some pain killers, and some scalpels and sutures to close wounds. I examined Jenny and found her uncomfortable but stable.

Anyway, the nurse called for an ambulance, and we waited. I could hear the storm raging outside."

"When did the ambulance come?" asked Chelsea.

"Ambulance? A man brought his wife to the clinic. She was in bad shape and needed to get to the hospital too. And was also pregnant."

"The Russian?" asked Chelsea.

Her father nodded. "But I didn't know that then. The nurse pulled a curtain that separated her bed from your mother's. Then she mumbled something about the ambulance delayed because of the rain and vanished. I could hear the man on the other side. He was in anguish, trying to calm his wife in Russian. Your mother was stable, so I went over to the foot of her bed to see if I could help. The man saw me, looked up to the ceiling, hands raised, and jumped to his feet. He struggled to find the words but dragged me towards his wife."

Chelsea walked toward her father. "He presumed you were a doctor?"

Dad smiled. "Good question."

Chelsea felt her dad was returning to his former self.

"I still had the steths around my neck from examining your mother. I told him I was a doctor from America on vacation. He hesitated, then spoke in accented English. He said his wife had complained of the mother of all headaches, blurry vision, fainting, shaking, nausea, and vomiting. I asked if I could examine her." Dr. Piers chuckled. "The man looked at me as if I'd asked a stupid question. "By all means, the man had said. By then, I was getting apprehensive, ruling out alternative diagnoses in my head, and trying to keep a neutral face. I knew we would need a hospital soon and, remember, your mother was on the other side of the curtain. I could tell the woman's face was swollen, so were her hands. I asked him when she peed last. He didn't know."

Chelsea's mother tapped her cane once on the floor. "How was the woman?"

Her dad looked at his wife. "Moaning softly."

Her mother had both hands on the head of her cane, shoulders hunched, rocking slightly. "You checked her blood pressure?"

"Eclampsia, right?" said Chelsea in a low voice.

Her father nodded, went to the cupboard, took a glass, then walked to the fridge and poured himself a glass of orange juice.

Chelsea and her mother watched him fill his glass with the bright yellow liquid.

The faint smell of the fruit, which Chelsea knew was due to limonene, abundant in the orange peel, reached her nostrils, making her want to pour a glass for herself. She licked her lips and swallowed.

Her mother's eyes were fixed on her father, impatient. "Continue David. What happened next?"

Chelsea looked at her father and wondered if the window of opportunity had passed. Then his lips moved.

55

Feodor Konstantin
Portugal 1988

Feodor and Anna arrived in Lisbon, Portugal, three months and two weeks after leaving Riga. Even though Feodor had paid handsomely for their passage on the cargo ship, every night, he'd slept with a knife he picked up from Rostock under his pillow and one eye open. He considered it lucky that neither he nor Anna had seasickness, only discomfort from the new experience and confined spaces.

Once in Lisbon, they checked into a hotel, and for the next two days and nights, just ate and slept. Feodor suggested they go see a doctor now they were relatively safe.

"Maybe later," said Anna. "Apart from a little headache now and then, I'm fine. I think it was all that rolling about in the sea."

The same underworld contact that connected Feodor to

the ship captain also gave him the information for someone to meet in Lisbon. The once bulging bag of money was now almost empty. Feodor had no idea what to do. Maybe he should walk over to the American embassy in Lisbon.

On the third day after their arrival, Feodor left Anna at the hotel and went to meet the man using the address he was given. He was surprised when it turned out to be a legit travel agency.

"I have a better plan for you," said the man who identified himself as Lisbon.

"Like the city we are in?" asked Feodor.

"Yes, yes!" said the chubby man dressed in a white linen shirt and pants. He looked like he was of Middle Eastern heritage and spoke in accented English. "Berlin told me about your special skills."

"Berlin?"

"Yes, the contact that made this meeting possible." It comes with an annual salary of one hundred thousand dollars, plus travel allowance and housing."

Feodor thought he didn't hear right. He kept a straight face, not to betray his desperation. Inside, his heart did a backflip. He knew he would accept it, but he acted along. "What's the job, and where?"

"Security consultant for a Nigerian senator. You'll also have trainees attached to you." Lisbon smiled. "The job is located in Lagos, Nigeria."

"Nigeria?" Feodor made a mental note to stop repeating everything Lisbon said. "How can an elected official afford such salaries?"

Lisbon scoffed. "That's none of your business, but a Nigerian senator" monthly entitlements and salary alone are comparable to that of a Wall Street investment bank managing director. Then add perks and lobbying monies, and it easily doubles or triples."

Feodor nodded slowly as he did calculations in his head. He could take the job, save up for three years, and then quit. "Okay, I'll take it."

Lisbon sat up and rubbed his hands together. A big smile on his face. "We'll prepare documents for you and your wife."

"Emmm…we…we-"

Lisbon's eyebrows shot up. "Any problem?"

"We're not yet married."

"Ah," Lisbon laughed. "No problem. I can arrange that. A Las Vegas type wedding. Today, okay?"

"Sure," said Feodor, not sure what a Las Vegas type wedding meant.

"After that, you can have your honeymoon at The Algarve," said Lisbon. "Quiet, beautiful white beaches. Take one week, or two, and relax. When you come back, the papers are ready, and you travel to your job."

Feodor watched amazed as Lisbon made a few phone calls, and the wedding was arranged. All he needed to do was bring Anna to the address in three hours, he told him.

"How do I pay for all this?"

"Your employer pays me a finder's fee," said Lisbon. "The wedding and vacation are on me. You do a good job, your employer refers more clients to me."

Feodor bought the wedding bands at a store Lisbon recommended, then went back to the hotel and collected Anna, and they went to the location. It was just the wedding official, a witness, and the exchange of vows. Feodor braced himself that Anna would breakdown because her family wasn't there, but she pulled through with just misty eyes.

Soon they were on the train to The Algarve as husband and wife. Feodor told Anna about the change in plans.

"As long as you're fine with it, I'm okay with it, too," Anna had said.

At The Algarve, they relaxed and forgot the problems of the past three months. He and Anna would go for walks along the beach, enjoying the sea breeze and warm weather. Anna gathered shells, and one morning giggled with delight when she found an enormous starfish. It was one of the happiest times of their lives, then things took another a turn for the worse.

Early in the evening on the seventh day, just after dinner, Anna complained of a headache after a walk on the beach.

Feodor felt her head. "You have a fever. I'll call the receptionist, there must be a doctor here."

"No, I'll take an aspirin and sleep it off. Anna rubbed her stomach. "Probably overdid this time."

"But, Anna, you have to see a doctor and make sure you and our baby are doing great."

"Okay, when we get back to Lisbon. Maybe your friend there knows someone. Come lay down with me."

"I'll get the aspirin." Feodor called room service and they sent a messenger up with aspirin.

Anna swallowed the medicine. "Just hold me. I'm sure the medicine and a nap will take care of it."

Feodor joined her on the bed after he put the glass of water away. Within a minute, she drifted off to sleep. He lay there awake, thinking. Should they have waited until the next day and taken the second flight out of Riga? They would have been in Berlin within hours. Or should he have ignored her, left her alone the first time he saw her? Or he could abandon her right now. Just walk away. He wrapped his arm around her and pulled her closer. Soon he drifted off to sleep.

56

Rip

R ip was worried. A thousand thoughts flashed through his mind. This time he knew speed was of the essence. He turned on his lights and siren and stepped on the gas. It was like approaching an automatic door at the airport or grocery store, it always opened.

Rip wondered if he should call the Mayor and tell him what was going on. Mark Ortenberg had appointed Rip Chief of Police after the last chief retired and moved to Florida. The old chief had joked that unlike teachers who got their reward in heaven, he wanted his on earth.

Rip knew someone at the agency had played a role in him getting the job as Chief of Police,

But before then, he had been offered his old job back, which he turned down. Then a spot at the CIA was dangled. Most of his Special Ops buddies were there. He declined that also but maintained a good rapport with Max. He'd roamed the country trying to find himself after leaving special ops and encountered quite a few injustices which he righted the only way he knew how. Someone had been busy cleaning up behind him. In the back of his mind, he knew it was the man he would be meeting at the airstrip.

The sign for Route 639 came up, and beside it was another sign about when the town was founded and its population. Rip turned in and decided he would let the mayor know once he got a tangible lead.

That stretch of road was picturesque, night or day, with homes and farms on each side. Usually, Rip enjoyed looking at the old abandoned barns, newer barns, horses, cattle, and sheep that roamed the farms. Most of the farms he believed were now shadows of their former glory, but they provided a storybook escape for city dwellers. Tonight, he didn't see all that beauty. His mind was preoccupied. He wanted to know what Maxwell Brandon was doing in Sussex County.

With traffic scanty along the single road, Rip turned the strobe lights and the siren off. A few minutes later, the sign for the airport came up. He slowed, turned off, and drove into the airport's parking lot. He got out of the car and drew in a deep breath while looking around.

A few small propeller planes were parked on the airstrip. It looked and felt peaceful. Rip loved the feel of small-town airfields. They reminded him of the times he was in a small airstrip like this, alone or with his team, in hostile territory waiting for a bird to literally drop out of the sky and whisk them away to safety.

Just like those nights, and because he was expecting it, Rip saw the helo approaching before he heard it. Like a fully fed hawk, it swooped down and landed. A door opened, and

one passenger disembarked. Dressed in a suit and wearing a
tie, Max Brandon could pass as the CEO of a Fortune 500
company. He stooped low and ran towards Rip.

57

Feodor Konstantin
The Algarve, Portugal 1988

Somewhere in his slumber, Feodor heard a phone ring. It sounded like a dentist's drill working on his tooth without the benefit of anesthesia. With each ring, the drill got louder and the pain worse. The smell of the drill's motor burned his nostrils. He tasted blood, as the drill cut through enamel and tissue, ripping apart everything in its path, just like his life in the past three months—ripped apart.

Feodor jerked awake. He felt around his mouth with his tongue, there was no drill. The phone rang again, and he jerked to look at it. It was an outside call, not the single ring like when the receptionist called. Who could it be? He thought of Lisbon and exhaled. He disentangled himself from Anna, walked over to the phone and picked it up. He didn't speak, he just waited.

"I know you're there," said a familiar voice.

Feodor stiffened. His inside churned.

"I always have my Kevlar vest on."

Feodor's stomach churned. His dinner, or what was left of it, headed north. He swallowed hard. A cold sweat broke out on his forehead. How did this happen? Lisbon betrayed him. Berlin?

"Feodor Konstantin, you had potential. You are ruthless, ambitious, smart, and with no family ties. With that combination and some guidance from me, you would have risen high in the bureau. Then you went and fell in love and gave it all up for a little pussy."

Feodor's knees turned to jelly. He wanted to speak, but words deserted him.

"You lost your mind because she was pregnant? You didn't want your child to go through what happened to you? I get that. We don't choose who we fall in love with, but never fall in love with a pretty girl."

Feodor shut his eyes tight. Dimitri was speaking to his inner soul. *We can't choose who we fall in love with.* He drifted back to the conversation.

"You totally fucked up. You deserve to be shot for putting a pregnant woman through hell. You spent months on the run for nothing."

Feodor clenched and unclenched his fist.

"If you've been following the news, you should know a lot is happening, and that's why your phone is ringing instead of a bullet flying towards your head. You are young and highly skilled. I can overlook this one transgression and bring you back to the KGB as if you never went AWOL and tried to kill me."

Feodor's pulse raced as adrenalin pumped through his veins. This might be the only chance he would ever get. But there must be a catch. "What…what would it cost me?"

"Ah, you found your voice. It's simple. It will cost you something you love to secure my trust. Terminate Anna by morning and set yourself free. Only then will I forgive and forget." There was a pause. "If you see that through, my men will have you on the next plane to Moscow. Yeltsin needs men like me, and I need men like you. It's your call. 9 am. Freedom or a bullet to the head."

The line went dead. But Feodor still held on to the receiver. Soon his ear ached from pressing the phone against it. The tone of the phone reminded him of the flat line of an ECG when death occurs. His hand shook as he lowered the phone and put it back into the cradle. Someone betrayed him. Berlin, Lisbon. He would find whoever it was and kill them. He thought of his escape; it was impeccable, except he didn't know Dimitri had on a bulletproof vest. He had been in such a hurry to leave that he didn't add a headshot. Feodor hoped it wasn't Lisbon, because, in his present situation, he would need his connections.

Feodor looked at Anna, and something wasn't right. He walked back to the bed-she was drenched in sweat. Feodor touched her forehead, and it felt like she was being heated up from inside like water in a saucepan on a stove.

"Anna, wake up." He tapped her on the shoulder. "Anna?"

She opened her eyes lazily, her lips started to part in a yawn when she clasped her head with both hands, her hands shaking. That was when Feodor realized that was not a yawn, but a silent scream.

"My love, what is it?"

"I have a terrible headache."

Feodor realized why she looked different. "Anna, your face…it's puffy."

"My head, my head…" Her voice was barely audible.

Feodor grabbed a towel and mopped sweat from her brow. "I'll go get help." He looked out of the window. It was dark. A tropical storm was brewing. Its ferocious winds shook electric wires causing the hotel lights to flicker. He heard the faraway rumble of thunder and knew soon they'd be listening to a symphony made by raindrops as they clattered on the roof and windows. The air already smelled and tasted of rain.

Anna's eyes were wide. "Everything is cloudy." She moved her head from side to side. "I'm scared. Don't leave me alone."

He felt her forehead and her body. Feodor didn't know people could get that hot. Anna's night tee shirt was soaked in sweat and looked like a wet sack of corn placed on her abdomen. Feodor saw movement. The baby was moving. Fear trickled down his spine like an ant crawling down his shirt.

"*Дорогая*, Sweetie. I must get help." He didn't wait for her reply. He dashed to the door and ran to the reception area. There was nobody there. He was about to knock on the nearest door when he saw the receptionist come out from a door and shut it quietly.

"I need help! My wife is ill," said Feodor in Russian.

The man raised an eyebrow and shook his head.

Feodor remembered the Portuguese word for sick. "*Doente!Doente!*"

The man nodded. "*Vamos!* Let's go!"

Feodor grabbed him by the hand and took him to his room.

The man took one look at Anna, and in a *potpourri* of languages-Portuguese, English, Spanish, and French, pantomimed they would have to move her. They helped Anna up and led her to the hotel's clinic. A man was already attending to another woman. Feodor let out a sigh of relief. Finally, a doctor to look at Anna.

Six hours later, Feodor stood beside Anna's lifeless body. On her side lay an infant showing no sign of life. In the distance, he heard the wail of a siren. He had to go. "I'm so sorry," he whispered. "So sorry."

58

Rip

Rip noticed that the pilot did not power down, so this would be brief. He waved Max towards the cruiser. At least this would reduce the roar of the helo's engine.

Max looked Rip up and down. "So, this is what the mighty Phantom 13 has become. A real ghost of his former self!"

Despite being inside the car, the bird was still loud.

Rip clicked the ringer of his personal phone off. "Good to see you too! What's the story?"

Max cocked his head. "Moscow is missing two people. One old geezer in your backyard, and a younger one who flew in to see him. The old guy, your gas attendant, was old school KGB. Sent over to the states to furlough. We never knew he was here. He must have been exceptionally good at keeping low."

Rip said nothing. The good stuff was yet to come.

"The second agent flew in through Newark Liberty. Our contact in Moscow said they confirmed their man landed, made contact with Konstantin, and then they both disappeared. He couldn't find out what the mission was."

"Couldn't? Or wouldn't?" asked Rip.

Max nodded. "We dug deeper, and the only thing we got was more info about the character with amnesia. Three decades ago, he fell out of favor with Moscow after a debacle in Latvia. He was on the run but became compromised. His handler had made him an offer, murder your family, and he would forgive and forget the Latvia fiasco, and reinstate him."

Rips head jerked up.

Max shook his head. "Don't ask me. I don't know their beef. Some heavy shit must have gone down between those two."

"Konstantin was in Portugal with Lebanese travel documents to immigrate to Nigeria, when one night, he kept his own part of the bargain he made with his handler. He strangled his pregnant wife while she slept, cut her open her, and brought out his unborn child."

"Jesus."

"You haven't heard anything yet. His boss demanded proof. He took pictures and sent them to him. He was reinstated and became one of the most brutal and ruthless assassins the KGB ever had. Active in Dagestan, Chechnya, Moscow, London, Doha, Yekaterinburg-throughout the nineties and early 2000s. One out of every three assassinations has been attributed to him."

Rip whistled. But something was still missing. He exhaled through his nose. "So, Ivan the Terrible is in retirement, and chose my backyard as his Florida, why?"

"Well yeah," said Max looking around as if he could see the countryside in the darkness. "I don't blame him. It's nice out here."

Rip faced Max. "So what…he's been sleeping peacefully and suddenly he ran out of pension money and decided to come out of retirement?" Rip looked Max in the eye. "Why are you here?"

Max chuckled. "You got me. The FSB has already dispatched a two-man cleanup crew. They should be touching down any moment."

"Langley is going to let them take someone out on US soil?"

"As long as they're taking care of their business, we won't interfere. We're not taking proactive action. Our contact in Moscow has his head so high up the FSB director's ass that if they think we got a warning, it would mean they have a motor mouth at the highest level and would restructure. Our guy could be moved, or, if found out, disappeared. We don't want that. Basically, my team is here to babysit from afar."

Rip knew he was telling the truth, and he was also adequately attired, all in black. Max Brandon never liked surprises. Rip contemplated telling him about the piece of paper found in Konstantin's pocket and the medical examiner's suspicions that the man from Moscow— the dead guy in the car fire--was murdered.

"But something doesn't add up," said Rip. "Why did he remove his fingerprints? He must have been up to something."

"Did you check his apartment?"

Rip shut his eyes tight. How did he forget that?

"I guess that's a no. Phantom, you're getting soft. Tell you what, we'll check it out for you."

"I appreciate it. I'll get you the address," said Rip and reached for his phone to call the station.

Max opened the door of the cruiser. The whoosh-whoosh of the helo rushed in. "No need. We have his name. Remember, we are the CIA?" He got out of the car and ran towards the bird.

The helo took off as soon as Max got on board. Rip got into his car and headed towards Hendonville.

59
___

David Piers

avid Piers knew he could not tell the rest of the
story. He had guarded his mind since that day so
many years ago. Now that he was losing the battle
to Alzheimer's, he would never intentionally divulge it. He
took a drink from his cup; his mind was so clear that he felt
he was in that stuffy clinic room in Portugal many years ago,
confronted with two medical emergencies that made his
nightmares look like child's play.

The other woman who her husband called Anna was a
classic case of eclampsia. Sky-high blood pressure, convul-
sions, headaches, and by the time David Piers did a quick
examination, she was unresponsive. She'd slipped into a
coma. That day, for a brief moment, Dr. Piers had forgotten
he was on vacation in Portugal and wanted to tell his chief
resident to call all the junior doctors to see for themselves, a

textbook case of clampsia. A teaching moment that doesn't happen every day because of modern medicine.

The howling of the wind outside, and the sweat trickling down his forehead reminded him where he was. A blood-curdling scream from the other side of the curtain drew his attention.

"David!" screamed his wife.

David Piers whirled around. "Oh no. Jenny!" He turned to the man. "My wife! She too is about to deliver. I'll be right back."

"Dave, it hurts," said Jenny making a hand motion over her stomach as soon as David came through the curtain.

David touched her stomach-it was as hard as wood. He listened again for a fetal heart sound. There was none. Since he'd picked up the stethoscope about an hour ago, he had been trying to find the baby's heartbeat and hadn't been successful.

David took off the gloves from examining the other woman and pulled on a fresh pair. He examined Jenny, her cervix was only slightly dilated, and his finger came out bloody. She was panting for air, her heart rate was too fast, but her pulse was weak.

Jesus, thought David, she's hemorrhaging internally. Jenny screamed in pain; the roar of the wind and the clatter of rain on the zinc roof, like an out of sync orchestra, drowned out her screams. David opened the surgical tray, found the syringe, and filled it with morphine. He raised the syringe to the light and flicked the plastic tube repeatedly with his finger to gather air bubbles to the top. He pushed the syringe plunger expelling the bubbles. Air embolism would compli-cate an already dire situation.

David picked up an alcohol swab sachet, ripped it open,

and wiped Jenny's left cubital fossa. All he saw were shadows on her ghostly skin left by the previously full veins. He didn't have a lot of options. He picked one shadowy line and plunged in the needle. David pulled back, and a red cloud shot into the syringe. He exhaled. He was in a vein. He pushed down on the plunger with his thumb and shot the morphine into her vein, emptying the syringe.

The drug worked fast, relieving her discomfort. Jenny was already exhausted and fell asleep. Her abdomen continued to ripple as if trying to expel the fetus. David placed the surgical kit closer to the bed. He pushed the thought of infections away from his mind, hoping the nurse would return with the ambulance. The truth was he had no options. He knew it could be *abruptio placentae*, the placenta coming off the walls of the uterus causing bleeding. David went in with his hand, surprised to find the placenta blocking the cervix.

Slowly, he maneuvered the tissue out of Jenny's vagina, reached in, pierced the amniotic sac, and waited for the gush of fluid to subside. He then guided the baby out, and swiftly, clipped and cut the umbilical cord.

David noticed the bi-lobed after-birth had been compromised. A part of it was still trapped inside the uterus, and blood continued to flow out of Jenny. He eased his hand into her again, swept around with his finger, and found the torn piece. He brought the bloody tissue out and observed her. Slowly, the bleeding stopped. Relieved, he turned to the baby. He already knew, but still, he tried to resuscitate. It was no use. He looked at Jenny, and now knew what she'd been trying to hide. The secret that made her put her life in danger and made them travel to Portugal where no one knew them. If only she'd told him. Grief overtook him, and tears clouded his vision.

"Doctor! My Anna-"

David spun around. The Russian had pushed the curtain aside.

"She's…she's not moving. Just staring…not blinking."

David moved the curtain and rushed to the woman. He felt for her pulse; there was none. David removed the pillow from under her head, positioned her neck, and started CPR.

After a concerted effort, he felt her pulse, then turned to the Russian and shook his head. "I'm sorry-"

"Why did you stop?" The Russian pointed at her stomach. "She's still alive. Her belly is moving!"

David looked, saw the movement, and gasped. "The child. We can still save the child!" He rushed back to Jenny's bed, grabbed the surgical kit, and took out a scalpel.

Eyes wide, the Russian shouted. "What are you doing?"

David was blunt. "Your wife is dead! But the baby is alive…we don't have time. We can still save the baby. Turn around and close your eyes."

The Russian stood with slumped shoulders. Then slowly, ever so slowly with shuffling footsteps, he turned.

David exposed the woman's abdomen. It looked like a huge melon. He palpated the abdomen and determined the baby's position. It was head down in the uterus. Good. He would go with a low transverse incision. For a brief second, he wondered if he would still have a medical license when this day was over. The baby moved again, prompting him to take action. He picked up the scalpel.

Quickly he cut through to the uterus, and soon he had the baby. David clamped and cut the cord. A quick slap to the baby's buttock and its cry filled the room. David blew out a shaky breath and turned to the Russian. "Congratulations, you have a daughter," said David in a shaky breath.

The Russian seemed to stare through him.

"You have a daughter," repeated David.

The Russian swallowed, his eyes fixed on the dead woman on the bed. He shook his head, his lips trembling. "She was my life." He muttered.

David was not a religious man, but he said it anyway. "This is divine intervention. You have a beautiful daughter."

The man inhaled and let it out throw his mouth. "Your wife? Your child?"

David shook his head. "Jenny's sleeping. The baby…" His voice trailed off.

The man looked at David and cocked his head. "It was meant to happen." A maniac laugh escaped his lips, then sorrow overtook him. His shoulders shook as he sobbed. Then his head jerked up. "Doctor, she was my life, and now she's gone. We were going to Nigeria to start a new life. That dream is gone." He looked at his daughter for the first time. "If it weren't for you, that baby would have died with her mother. You are more her father than I am."

David blinked. He could sense where the man was going. "No!"

"Doctor, my name is Feodor Konstantin. I'm a KGB agent, but I became *persona non grata* after I fell in love and messed up an operation in Latvia. It's only a matter of time before they find me. I have no other family." He looked at his daughter, and a tear trickled down his cheek. "With me, the miracle of today will have no meaning. With you, she would have a chance," said Feodor in a low voice.

That was when David noticed the rain had stopped. In the distance, he could hear the wailing of a siren. He thought of Jenny, what her complication could lead to. No more children. He made a decision. "Come with me."

Quickly, they swapped the babies as the siren got louder

and louder. The man stood still and watched the dead woman. His eyes filled with tears.

"I'm so sorry," said Feodor in a whisper. "I'm so sorry."

"You have to name her," said David. "It's your right."

"I…I don't know."

"Give me a name!" Dr. Piers said in a hushed whisper.

He took his wife's hand in his, his face a mask of pain. Running footsteps came towards them.

"We don't have time! Tell me something." David glanced at the dead woman. "What did she like?"

Finally, the man smiled. She loved the sea…picking shells as she walked on the beach."

"Good," said David as his lips spread in a smile. "Chelsea," he said aloud.

"Dad! Are you okay!"

David Piers jerked and looked at his daughter coming towards him, her eyebrows drawn together, lips pursed.

"Dad, you were staring into space, then you called out my name. Are you alright?"

"David! David!" said Jenny. "What's so funny?"

"What?" David's eyes darted from Chelsea to Jenny.

"David, you're always losing your mind!"

Chelsea faced Jenny. "Mother! That's cruel."

Jenny exhaled. "Finish the story. What about the Russian and his wife, what happened to them?"

David just stared, then took another sip of his orange juice. "What…what? Are you talking to me?"

Jenny let go of her cane, and it crashed to the floor with a clank. She made a fist and shook both hands in the air. "What about the Russians. What became of them?"

David lazily glanced at Chelsea, then back to Jenny. "Why are you yelling? I don't know about any Russians. I'm going back to the living room."

He turned and walked away. If he had turned around, he would have seen the darkness in Chelsea's eyes that seemed to say they had lost him again.

60

Chelsea

C helsea went back to her room and sat on the bed. It had been one heck of a day, a day of reminiscing. Not that she knew for sure it would have worked out between Rip and her, but it was her life to experience and make changes as she deemed fit. Chelsea looked up. Someone had knocked on her door.

"Yes, come in."

The door opened with a creak, like in an old western movie. Her mother peeped in. "Can I come in?"

"Of course." Chelsea half expected to see tumbleweeds and dust trailing in behind her. "Are you okay?"

She didn't answer but walked in, leading with her cane. She lowered herself beside Chelsea on the bed.

Chelsea looked at her. "Is Father okay?"

She nodded. "He's fine, enjoying his orange juice and listening to the news."

Chelsea kept quiet. She wondered what brought her mother into her room. They sat in silence; not the type of silence Chelsea would enjoy with a person like her dad, but the type when you're wondering what someone is thinking, and what you might say that would tick them off. It was that type of love-hate relationship teenagers have with their parents, except that she wasn't a teenager.

"Chelsea, a long time ago, before I met your father, I was in love with another man. My family would have disowned me if they'd found out."

Chelsea was tired and wanted to sleep. She had her own issues to work out and knew that if she asked questions, it would only prolong how long her mother stayed, so she kept quiet. Hoping it would be fast.

"He was tall, handsome, broad-shouldered, all the works. I tried as much as possible to keep away from him, but I couldn't. Finally, I let him know I was interested. Dave was in the same hospital as us then, but he was a nerd. I knew he was head over hills in love with me, and one day he summoned the nerve and asked me out. I shot him down."

"You did?" asked Chelsea, feigning surprise. She already knew the outcome. Dad must have made a comeback.

Her mother smiled and looked down at her hands.

Chelsea wondered where this was going.

"I started dating that guy, and somewhere along the way, I got pregnant. He wanted to marry me. I didn't have the courage to face my parents, and I was scared out of my mind. I can't remember exactly what happened, but I must have come across Dave somewhere, and he asked me out again. Not only did I say yes, but we also went out that night, and after dinner, I invited him back to my apartment and slept with him."

Suddenly I was wide awake. "What are-"

Her mother held up her hand. "I'm not done yet." She drew in a deep breath and exhaled. "I pressured Dave, and within weeks, we were married. Four weeks after we first slept together, I announced I was pregnant." Her mother stared at her hands again. "My immediate problems were solved for the next eight months, assuming everything went well. I mean, my pregnancy."

Chelsea felt a lump in her throat. Her heart went out to her father. "Okay."

"Dave was a hardworking doctor," she continued. "He's the kind of doctor you want on your team when there's a complication. Even fellow doctors wanted him to deliver their kids. There was no excuse not to have him as my obstetrician, but I said no, citing that a non-relative would be more objective in his management." She paused and looked Chelsea in the eye. "Then the other issue was that when I delivered, my secret would be out there. It would be more affordable to have the baby in a hospital David or I was affiliated with. You know, employee perks."

Mother stopped speaking. Chelsea looked at her and saw tears streaming down her face. She knew it took a lot for her mother to come into her room and lay herself bare.

Chelsea remembered a physician in her former practice who refused to be examined for an enlarged prostate. He said he would rather die than have anyone stick their finger up his rear end. Her mother was of such caliber. Chelsea reached out and touched her shoulder. Her mother nestled her chin on it. She inhaled and exhaled, wiped her eyes with the back of her hand, and continued.

"Remember, my expected date of delivery was one month ahead of what David knew?"

Chelsea nodded.

"So, I said to David, let's go on vacation before the baby

comes. He said no, too close. But...but I argued, and he relented."

Not much has changed since then, thought Chelsea.

"He agreed," said Mother. "Because...because, he loved me so much and wanted to make me happy."

Now she cried like she was heartbroken. "Over the years, I've grown to love him, but I never told him, and I don't think his mind can now process it if I told him how sorry I am and how much I love him."

A nervous laugh burst out of me. "But Dad has always been Dad. He's the only father I've ever known."

"No, no no, Chelsea, you don't understand. I've always thought maybe I made a mistake with my EDD, and David is really your biological father. He never explained what happened the night you were born. He'd always known. I think he did something that night to hide my shame—with that or he is your biological father."

"What shame?"

Mother let out a shaky breath. "It would have been embarrassing, especially to David, explaining to people why our child was mixed. I grew up in the South, and my parents were from a different time with different views which their own parents had instilled in them, and they passed onto me. But it didn't stick in me. I fell in love with a black man and didn't have the courage to fight for him."

"So, I'm of mixed heritage, and just look white?" asked Chelsea. "But again, the phenotype is not always congruent with the genotype."

Her mother nodded. "That's why I dragged you to Portugal every vacation, hoping that one day we'd find answers to questions I couldn't ask." With a shaking of her head, she continued. "I'm really sorry for interfering in your love life. We can't pick and choose who we love. After so many years of being apart, you and Rip have met once again."

Heat rushed to Chelsea's cheeks. "Yes, but we drifted apart."

"No Chelsea. It was my doing. I forced you guys apart. I was going to press charges against him for statutory rape saying that you had agreed to corroborate my story."

Chelsea's eyebrow narrowed. "I wasn't going to do that."

"Yes, you were. You won't remember now, but after the ordeal with the prisoner, you were so shaken up, and I took advantage of that. You were agreeable to whatever I suggested. The local police at Lake Placid did the rest. I was already familiar with them from working at the correctional facility, and they were happy to talk to Rip, give him 'career advice'. They convinced him to join the Navy and see the world rather than risk being drawn into a nasty case of statutory rape. His grandparents helped persuade him too. We shipped you off to the secondary school in Andover, Massachusetts. Eventually, you two drifted apart."

Chelsea sat beside her mother. Tonight had been a fire hose of revelations.

"I did what I did because I thought it was the right thing, but I was wrong. Love always finds us. Yours has found you again after all these years. Please forgive me. I hope it's not too late for you and Rip."

61

Kill Team

Two first-class passengers got off the Aeroflot flight 121 from Moscow. They both had no hand luggage, nor did they check in any suitcases. The first one was blond, crew cut, and about six feet tall. His broad shoulders filled out the black tailored suit he wore. He kept his head high and straight and followed other passengers as they headed towards immigration. A few feet behind him was his colleague with a similar physique and style of dress, brown hair, no luggage.

By the time they approached the overhead sign for baggage pick up, they were walking side by side as if marching to a band. The two men followed the sign for the exit while their fellow passengers from Aeroflot walked towards the carousels.

Outside they stood by the curb side. A black Mercedes

Sprinter van pulled up and stopped in front of them. The passenger window came down.

"добро пожаловать, welcome," said the driver.

Both men nodded. The blond got in the front passenger seat and the other behind.

The soft click-click of the left signal filled the car as the driver studied the traffic behind in the rearview mirror. He found a break in traffic and eased in, then followed the sign to the airport exit.

"Your tools are in the glove compartment," said the driver in accented English. "There's a Faraday messenger bag in the back. The chloroform balls are there too."

"The whole bag is Faraday?" asked the blonde.

The driver nodded. "Complete Radio Frequency Identification—RFID blockade. No signal goes in, and nothing comes out."

The man in front opened the glove compartment and brought out a package. Inside the package were an icebox and two Glock 19 Gen5s with suppressors. He handed one to his mate. He reached again into the glove compartment. "Hmm, stun gun." He looked at the driver, shrugged, then pocketed the gun in his jacket pocket.

Each of the men checked the magazine and inserted it into the chamber.

The driver merged onto I-678 N. "Hendonville Medical Center, here we come."

62

Chelsea

C helsea watched her mother leave her room and shut the door behind her, then lowered herself onto her bed, thinking of all that she had learned in one night. Her mother had made sure she and Rip broke up way back then in high school, and her dad might not be her biological father.

She could do an ancestry DNA test, but Chelsea had read numerous newspaper stories about people's surprises after receiving their ancestry report, and their lives completely upended. She would leave that as a backup plan. She wasn't that curious yet.

Chelsea thought about Rip and why he came to see her at her office the first time. A chill traveled down her spine and she sat up straight. Was there a connection? Rip said they found a piece of paper with her name in the man's pocket, could the man with amnesia be the same Russian man her father met in Portugal? Could he be her father? Where was her mother?

But she looked like her parents. Everyone said she had her father's eyes and looked like her mother when she was upset.

Chelsea smiled. She remembered reading an article that said older married couples tend to look alike because they've stayed together so long that they mimic each other's expressions. Was she mimicking her mother's expressions? She hoped not.

Mimicking or not, she had to talk to this man. Rip said he was at HMC. She got off the bed, changed into a pair of khaki pants, blouse and sweater. She stopped briefly in front of the mirror, brushed her hair, and put on lipstick. She picked up her purse, then clipped the retractable key-holder with her office ID to her belt.

Chelsea knew her mom would be worried if she told her where she was going, so she decided to lie. "Mom, I need to pick up a file at the office. I'll be right back."

"At this time of the night? Don't you think you should stay home and keep your parents company?"

"It's important. I'll be back in no time."

"Chelsea?"

"Yes, Mother."

"Better show me that file when you get back."

Chelsea smiled. Her mother had quickly reverted to her usual selfish, mean, and sulking personality. "Okay, Mother." Once inside the car, she called Rip, but it rang through and went to voice mail. She redialed, and it went to voice mail again. This time she left a message.

pushed the first button and worked his way down. Different voices distorted by static came through the speaker. The bald man ignored them and continued to push buttons. He was almost to the bottom when there was a buzz, and the door lock was disengaged. Someone is always expecting something.

They took the elevator to the third floor. The elevator door opened ushering in the faint smell of old kitchen garbage and fried food.

The bald man pointed at a sign that said '300–310' with an arrow that indicated they should go to the right. He nodded and led the way. They walked down the corridor, lit up by a dusty yellow bulb. Conversations, music, and the sound of TVs drifted along the corridor from other apartments. They stopped in front of apartment 310.

The man with the beard knocked on the door. "Mr. Konstantin? CIA. Open the door." They knew the man was in the hospital, but they had to follow procedure.

Silence. He knocked again and repeated the request. They got the same response. He looked around to make sure the corridor was clear, then he nodded at the bald man.

The bald man pulled out a lockpick gun and crouched down to insert the tension wrench and thin steel rod. He pulled the trigger four times, and turned the tension wrench. The door clicked open.

Head glistening with sweat, he put away the device and pulled out his Glock. He eased the door open and signaled his colleague to go in.

The room was dark with the exception of some illumination from the streetlight below that cast long shadows on the walls. They fanned out. Within seconds they'd secured the tiny one-room apartment. The man lived simply. One couch, an L-shaped table in the dining space with a laptop on one arm of the L, and some paperback novels on the other. The kitchen was clean, a few plates and cups were stored on a rack close to the sink.

In the bedroom, the bed was made, pulled tight with military precision. An orange, heavy, winter jacket with yellow stripes, the type seen in construction sights, hung in the closet with three pairs of pants and some shirts. Both men stared at the right wall in the room.

"Shit," said the bald man and took out his smartphone and started to take pictures. "What the heck?" He stopped and switched to video and recorded the whole wall. Then he sent the video to a number. Moments later, his phone rang. He put it on speaker.

"This is Max. This better be good. I thought you were in Dover. Why are you sending me a video of all the nooks and crannies of Chelsea Piers?"

The bald guy cleared his throat. "That was the whole wall in Mr. Konstantin's bedroom. I think an attack at Chelsea is imminent."

"Fuck!" said Max. "Head straight to the hospital and take Konstantin into custody. I'll get there as soon as the Piers are secured."

64

Chelsea

C helsea had been to Hendonville Medical center a few times for one conference or the other to earn Continuing Medical Education credits. Visiting time was probably over, so in her mind, she was working out a scenario on how to bluff her way through. Rip hadn't returned her call.

She entered the hospital lobby and looked at the wood-paneled reception area. There was nobody behind the counter. *Probably on break*, thought Chelsea. Typical. At this time of the night, most hospital foyers were mostly empty.

A flat-screen TV hanging on the wall like an unframed photo with no visible wires was on a medical channel. In one of the four aggregations of couchs and tables like a living room setup was a man in scrubs sleeping. Most big medical center entrances looked more and more like a five-star hotel lobby. Chelsea headed for the elevators. Rip did mention the man was on the third floor. She rode to the third floor, got off the elevator, and looked around. She saw a nurse in the nurse's station and walked slowly towards her, trying to figure out what to tell her.

The nurse smiled at her. "How can I help you?"

"Hi, I'm here to see the patient with amnesia, Rip asked me to drop by."

The nurse frowned. "Rip?"

"Oh, I'm sorry. Chief Ripken Chord, Chief of Police, Hendonville. He was at my office earlier today and asked me to see the patient."

The nurse smiled. "It's past visiting hours, and who are you?"

"Piers, Dr. Piers."

The nurse nodded. "One second."

The nurse looked down, and Chelsea thought maybe she was consulting a logbook or a computer screen.

"What's your name again?"

Chelsea didn't want to get mad. "Dr. Piers." She pursed her lips. "You know you can call the police station, and I'm sure it can be straightened out when you speak with him.

"Chelsea!"

Chelsea whirled to the deep voice at the same time as the nurse. A gray-haired older man wearing a hospital gown over a pair of pants stood by the entrance to a room.

The nurse then looked at Chelsea. "There he is."

Chelsea raised her head to do a quick nod, then changed her mind.

The nurse did a double-take. "Isn't he supposed to have amnesia?"

"Emmm…" Chelsea raised her eyebrows. "I'll just go and see him."

"Chelsea," repeated the old man and waved her over.

She walked towards him. As she passed the door adjacent to where Feodor stood, it swung open, and another old man in a hospital gown jumped out.

"Boo!"

Chelsea shrieked.

"Got you!" yelled the man and started laughing.

"Mr. Pippin!" said the nurse. "Stop scaring visitors. Halloween is still far away."

"Oh my God," gasped Chelsea. Her hand pressed against her chest, breathing hard.

"I see everything. I hear everything," said the man. He went back into his room and shut the door.

Chelsea looked back at the nurse who shrugged apologetically, then continued with what she was doing. Chelsea continued down the hall and stopped at the man's door.

The man's face and neck were flushed with color, his eyes twinkled. A broad proud smile stretched his lips. "You look just like your mother." He placed his hand on his chest and pressed down as if brushing off lint.

Chelsea scrunched up her face and spoke in a low voice so the nurse wouldn't hear. "Have we met before?"

"Yes, perhaps you don't remember. Come in." The old man walked into his room.

Chelsea followed.

He pointed to a chair and sat on the bed. A faint unrestrained smile on his face threatened to break out into happy laughter. The moment passed, and they scrutinized each other. He looked a lot like Kevin Costner, and Chelsea wondered if he was the Russian her father was talking about. Finally, she broke the silence.

"I heard you were in an accident; how do you feel?" asked Chelsea.

He waved a hand in dismissal. "A lot better."

Didn't he lose somebody in the crash? Or maybe he hasn't recovered that part of his memory, wondered Chelsea.

"A mountain lion of all things got caught in my headlight, and I lost control."

Chelsea cocked her head. "Did you say, mountain lion?" She vaguely remembered some animal crossing the road in front of her car not too long ago. She shrugged it off.

There was another awkward silence.

"My plan was never to brake-" They'd both said it at the same time.

"You go ahead," said the man.

Chelsea laughed. "Never to brake when an animal runs into the road in front of me." She liked the old man. "So, where did we meet?"

"Yes, you drive a red BMW, right?"

Chelsea nodded.

"I pumped gas for you once. When I looked up the expiration date from your credit card, I noticed your last name. I remember pumping gas for a man with a similar last name, who I presume was your father."

Chelsea's pulse quickened. "Where?"

The man opened his mouth to speak, then shut it. "Right now, I work out of a station in Dover. But I've pumped gas all over the state of New Jersey. Probably served him in one of those places. He must have left a big tip, and I guess your mother had been in the car." He rubbed his hand on his pants.

Chelsea nodded. She knew it was possible, she'd read the history behind it. Nobody pumped their own gas in New Jersey. In 1949 self-service fuel filling was banned in New Jersey. Today, New Jersey is the only state in the United States of America where it is illegal to pump your own gas. An attendant must do that for you. Every year there are arguments for and against the law. So far, supporters of the law have always won, sighting the loss of tens of thousands of jobs and the emotional burden it would put on elderly motorists if the law were abandoned.

"So why did you come to see me?" asked the old man.

"The police chief came to my office and said they had a man with amnesia, and he had in his pocket a piece of paper with Chelsea Piers written on it. You know, that's my name."

The man smiled. He tried to say something, but it looked like he changed his mind.

"He showed me a picture of you, and I didn't recognize you. He said maybe I should come around, and let's see if you would recognize me. And he was right!" Chelsea spread out her hand. "Your memory seems to be back. I should call Rip and let him know you recognized me. So, what's your name?"

"Feodor Konstantin. Like Theodore for you Americans, but with an F."

"Feodor," repeated Chelsea. You...are Russian?"

"Well, I was born in Moscow, and worked for the Soviet Union; from 1991, after the collapse, I worked for Russia. I retired, moved to Canada, and then migrated to the US."

"You seem to have traveled a lot." asked Chelsea.

"I was an interpreter. I have a gift for languages and went wherever the government needed me." He laughed. "Now, Google translate has taken that job."

Chelsea made eye contact and looked away. She wrung her hands, exhaled loudly, then looked at Feodor. "Emmm, you mentioned my parents."

Feodor nodded. "Yes."

"I was talking to them a few hours ago and they, my father, mentioned meeting a Russian, many years ago in Europe. Were you ever in The Algarve, Portugal-"

Feodor's eyes widened, and a nervous laugh escaped his lips. "I've been all over Europe. When?"

"Some time in 19-" Chelsea stopped and cocked her head. There seemed to be a scuffle out there in the corridor.

"You can't go in-!" It was the nurse's voice.

A phew phew sound, like a nail gun shooting out compressed air reached them, cutting off the nurse's voice.

"What was that?" asked Chelsea.

Feodor was on his feet, his eyes on hers. He pressed a finger to his lips. "I need your chair," he said in a whisper.

"Why? What is it?"

Feodor made the shape of a gun with his hand and pointed towards the corridor. Chelsea flew out of her chair. He took it, shut the door gently, and as he was about to jam the backrest under the doorknob, the door flew open, knocking him to the floor.

Chelsea gasped. Two men dressed in black suits stormed in and crouched low. One pointed a gun at her and the other at Feodor. She remained where she was, frozen, her eyes on the weapon. It was like she was in a movie.

"Colonel Konstantin," said the blonde in accented English. There was awe in his voice.

Chelsea's heart thundered in her chest. Her eyes were on Feodor, who was on one knee, hands raised. She saw the subtle acknowledgment in Feodor's eyes.

The blonde smiled and nodded his head in deference to Feodor. "Your reputation precedes you, sir. It's an honor to meet you. We learned a lot about your methods and tactics at camp. It was a required class."

Chelsea watched, not sure what was going on. Was this like training of some sort?

"Colonel," said the other man with a nod. His gun still on Chelsea.

"We're only following orders," continued the blonde. "Deputy Director Chicherin extends his regards."

Chelsea's eyes darted from the men to Feodor. Do they know each other? Has she unwittingly walked into something that doesn't concern her?

Feodor slowly got to his feet. "Yurik told me the plan. We disagreed. I'm here, and he's not. The plan will not only hurt America but the whole world. If you follow the plan, both of you will not leave this country alive. Russia is my priority, and it should be yours. We are not in the business of fulfilling personal vendettas." He raised his hands higher, and the men gripped their guns tighter.

Chelsea gasped.

Feodor pointed at Chelsea. "Dr. Piers here is at the wrong place at the wrong time. Let her go. I'm the one you came for."

The blonde looked at Chelsea, then at his colleague. "Dr. Piers?"

Chelsea repeatedly nodded, hoping they would ask her to leave, and bring an end to this nightmare.

"Actually, she's part of the plan," said the blonde. "We were to fetch you first, and then her."

"What?" asked Chelsea in a whisper. "No, I'm not part of anything-"

"Enough small talk," said the second man.

Chelsea's heart thundered like a battering ram and threatened to crash through her rib cage. What was going on? She watched in horror as the blonde transferred his gun to his left hand, reached into his jacket pocket and pulled out another gun and pointed it at Feodor. Her whole body started shaking.

"Please! No!" Chelsea screamed as he pulled the trigger.

65

Rip

Max's name appeared on Rip's smartphone screen, seconds before it rang. He answered and put it through the car's speakers via Bluetooth.

"What's up Max?"

"Phantom, we have a problem. It looks like the bird in your cage was actually planning a terror act. My boys found a whole wall covered with pictures of Chelsea Piers in his apartment."

Rip felt like he'd been punched in the stomach. "What's his MO? Kidnap? Rape? Torture?"

"Rape? Are you smoking something? He has on his freaking wall detailed pictures of Piers 59, 60 and 61, along the Hudson River. And even 54 and 55! Jesus, how many people is he going to rape? Probably has plans for mass casualty!"

Rip exhaled, the tension in his stomach relaxing. "So, your boys are coming to pick him up?"

"I wish it were that simple. We're coming all right. But so are the Russians. Facial recognition software picked up two of their assassins at JFK airport roughly an hour and twenty minutes ago. Boris Polivanov, blonde, also known as 'Ice'. And Stanislov 'Stan' Smirnov. Black hair, aka, Hawk. Both have Tom Brady-like physiques but in better shape. No, more like Dolph Lundgren in *Rocky IV*. They report directly to the deputy director of FSB. So, there's some real high-stake shit going on. We haven't got eyes on them yet, but my best guess is their headed your way."

"My way?"

"Well, they still have business with the old man. So, expect some trouble at the medical center. But I'm confident my men will get there before them and scoop everybody up. If for some reason they all meet up there, things can get out of hand really quickly."

"I'm on my way then."

"Okay, bye." Max hung up.

Rip thought of alerting the hospital's security but felt it might just lead to more confusion. He noticed he had a voice message from Chelsea. A warm feeling spread through his chest. He tapped it, and Chelsea's voice came through the car speakers.

"Hi, Rip. I just learned a few things from my mother for the first time about the events of…what? Sixteen years ago. Anyway, I'm on my way to see the old man at the hospital. I'll drop by my office to pick up a folder on my way back. If I don't see you tonight, we'll talk tomorrow, bye."

"Shit, shit, shit!" The sound of Rip's heartbeat thrashed in his ears. He stepped down on the accelerator, and the cruiser leaped forward. If anything happened to Chelsea, he would never forgive himself. Rip tapped his phone, went back to the message, and tapped on Chelsea's number.

He looked up just in time and swerved to avoid hitting a car that had the right of way. That was when he decided to turn on his lights but not the siren. At least people would pay attention to his cruiser.

66

Chelsea

C helsea froze as the electrodes slammed into Feodor. Feodor's face contorted with pain as if he had been poked with a branding iron. His screams of pain assaulted her eardrums. She'd never seen anything like that before. Wires from the gun must have pierced his top and skin and anchored in because they dangled in the air.

Feodor reached for the wires then jerked away like he changed his mind. Chelsea later learned that grabbing the cable, which would be anyone's instinct, would make the shock worse. His body roiled like someone doing the Macarena in triple fast playback. Feodor dropped to his knees then fell on the floor spasming.

Chelsea's pulse raced. She wanted to run, but her legs wouldn't move. They could barely hold her up. *Was he dead? Are they going to kill me? Oh, God, are they going to rape me? Not again,* she thought to herself. Memories from that night trapped in the woods with the convict flashed through her mind. *Who are they?* Chelsea wanted to yell for help, but she couldn't form words, her saliva dried up by fear.

The blonde looked at Chelsea. "If you give us any trouble, you'll get the same treatment as the Colonel. And, maybe more."

Chelsea swallowed. "Who...who are you?"

"I'm Hawk, he's Ice. We're...how, do you say it, acquaintances of the Colonel," said the man with black hair.

Feodor moaned and tried to sit up.

Ice reached into a messenger back he had slung over his shoulder, brought out a zip lock bag with balled up cotton wool. He walked over to Feodor and shoved it under his nose. Feodor lowered himself back to the floor, his eyes closed, chest rising and falling gently.

Hawk looked into the corridor, then left the room. Moments later he came back pushing a wheelchair with a white coat slung over it

"All right, Dr. Piers, your turn," said Ice. "First, hand over your phone and the keys to your car."

Chelsea slipped out her phone from her back pocket, reached into a small clutch she'd brought with her and retrieved her BMW key, and handed them over to Ice.

"Give me the purse too."

With shaky hands, Chelsea handed the purse over and watched Ice put them all in the messenger bag.

"Good," said Ice. "We will all walk out of here together." He pointed at a corner away from the door behind them. "Sit on the floor. We're going to lift the Colonel onto the wheelchair. Don't give us any reason to get physical with you. We won't hesitate."

Chelsea did as she was told and sat on the floor. Would they let her go? They worked as if they'd done this a thousand times before. Hawk detached the wires from the gun and rolled them up. Once he reached Feodor's skin, he placed a palm on him and expertly removed the taser out. Chelsea was right, she saw the prongs that had hooked into Feodor's skin.

The two men crunched low on each side of Feodor, then lifted him and placed him in the wheelchair. Feodor's hospital issued non-slip socks stuck out when they placed his feet on the chair's stirrups and arranged him as if he were sleeping. Ice then put the cotton wool under his nose again, produced a zip tie handcuff from his messenger bag, and cuffed Feodor. He grabbed a blanket from the bed and draped it over his hands and tucked it in by his sides. Feodor now looked like a patient who was sleeping.

Hawk turned to face Chelsea. "Your turn."

Chelsea's eyes widened. "What…what's that?" She backed away and hit the wall, wishing she could burrow into it.

"It's chloroform. Puts you to sleep fast, but you already know that." He reached for the white coat resting on the wheelchair and tossed it at Chelsea. "Put it on." He put the cotton ball back in the zip lock bag and threw it to the blonde. "You are one of the nicest doctors here. You just discharged our father, and you're helping wheel him to the car."

They walked out of the room with Chelsea pushing the chair and both men on either side of her. They looked like two business executives, who, after a long day at work, had come to bring their father home after he was discharged from the hospital.

Chelsea stared ahead. There was no one at the nurse's station. She remembered the sound she and Feodor heard while they were talking. Did they shoot the nurse that was on duty?

Both men were vigilant. Glancing around, checking, and

rechecking the ward as they walked. As they passed the room adjacent to Feodor's, Chelsea saw a shadow move under the door. She prayed the inquisitive old man would remain where he was. They wouldn't hesitate to kill him. "Where are we going?" asked Chelsea in an attempt to distract them.

"Q," said the blonde.

Chelsea felt a tightness in her chest. Please, God, don't let the man step out of the door.

"XR," said the other one.

They rolled passed the door. It was only when the door to the elevator opened that Chelsea let out her breath. She hoped that someone would figure out something was wrong when they got off the elevator at the reception area. But she also knew that this late at night, hospitals were like a ghost town. There might be nobody in the lobby at all.

The receptionist had not been there when she came in, but she was there now. She looked up and stared at them once they stepped out of the elevator.

The sound of blood rushing through Chelsea's veins throbbed in her head. Chelsea expected something to happen. Her pulse raced. From the corner of her eye, she saw the receptionist, a girl probably in her twenties, was still looking at them. Then she broke out in a smile and waved. Chelsea saw Ice's hand coming down from waving to her.

The automatic doors opened as they approached. A black Mercedes van stood in the carport. That was Chelsea's last hope, she would make eye contact with the driver. Her hope was crushed when the driver got out and directed them to a ramp deployed behind the car for the wheelchair.

"Climb on board," said Hawk.

67

Rip

Cars got out of the way when they saw him coming. He tried Chelsea's phone again, and it rang through to voice mail. Once he exited the main road to enter the hospital's driveway, Rip turned off the strobe lights. Two cars ahead of him drove at a snail's pace. Rip pulled out to overtake them just as a black Mercedes van flew down on the opposite side.

"What the-!" Rip dashed back into his lane and looked in his rear-view mirror. "This is a hospital road!" He tried to locate the registration plate and memorize the number. He found the plate and only made out the first letter of the plate number B before the van disappeared around a curve. He had a mind to turn around and give chase. Calm down Rip. This is no time for road rage. He gunned his cruiser uphill.

Rip wanted to screech to a stop at the hospital's carport and rush in, gun in hand. But his Special Ops training wouldn't let him do that. He found the closest parking spot to the entrance and parked the cruiser. He approached the door, his eyes darted from left to right, and walked into an empty lobby.

A bored-looking receptionist sat behind the counter. At least that's good news, thought Rip. He remained vigilant as he approached the elevator, his hand hanging by his side close to his holster. The elevator dinged, and Rip almost reached for his gun.

"Easy boy," he mumbled to himself. The door opened, and a nurse walked out. Rip let out a breath. He was about to step in when he realized the elevator would announce him too once it got to the third floor. Anyone on the lookout would spot him right away. He headed for the stairs.

Rip eased the door to the third-floor open. The staircase was at one end of the floor, and this time he would be coming in reverse order. He would pass the rooms before he got to the nurses' station. He looked ahead to the nurses' station; there was nobody there. But he could hear the beeping of gadgets and the sound of the TV. He pulled out his Glock 17 and approached.

The room on his left had the door shut, and no light came from underneath it. Rip assumed it was empty. The room on his right had its door open.

"This is CNN," said James Earl Jones' deep rich voice from the TV.

Rip peeped in. The occupant of the room, another old man, lay propped up on his bed, sleeping, his TV remote in his open palm. Rip continued; the next room was Feodor's. The door was open. No sound came from it. Rip inched closer, he took a deep breath and held his gun barrel up in front of him in a two-hand grip. He went in. Empty. A chair lay on the floor. He checked the closet and the bathroom, both were empty. Rip lowered his gun, the Russians must have beat him to it. Apart from the chair on the floor, there was no other tell-tale sign of a struggle.

He left the room and approached the nurses' station, and saw the foot on the floor. He raised his gun and looked around. Satisfied he was alone, Rip crouched down. It was the nurse from the first day he came. Two red dots stained her blue scrubs on the left side of her chest. With his left hand, he checked her pulse; there was none.

"I saw it all," said a shaky voice behind him.

Rip's body tightened. He whirled, expecting to take a bullet and was a hair's breadth from putting enough pressure on the Glock trigger to discharge. It was the man from the first day he came to visit, Mr. Pippin.

Rip blew out air through his mouth, gun pointed down, but still alert. "Who else is here?" Rip's voice was a whisper, but urgent.

"It's just me. They left already."

"Okay, Mr. Pippin, what did you see?"

68

Feodor

Feodor had a terrible headache, his chest hurt, and he knew why. The curved prongs of the laser gun had penetrated his skin, and he was sure the boys had just ripped them out. Feodor's chin rested on his chest. His mouth was dry and tasted bitter. Worst of all, the ground underneath him was moving.

He opened his eyes. He was in a dim tunnel heading towards a glass door. On either side of him was a man in a dark suit. Immediately he knew where he was, and since he was being pushed, they must have enlisted Chelsea to do the pushing. They couldn't leave her there. If they had and she wasn't doing the pushing, she was likely dead. He felt cold. The events that had happened earlier, flashed through his mind. What would have been the best moment of his life had turned into a nightmare.

On the opposite side of the glass door stood a black man

in the blue shirt and black pants of a guard's uniform watching, his eyes bulging as we approached. He raised both hands in the air as if signaling us to halt, saying what's going on.

"Dr. Piers, could you please do the honors," said Ice. "We know your key will get us into any part of the building."

Feodor raised his head and looked over his shoulder. The movement seemed to launch a missile into his head in the form of an excruciating headache. He ducked down and reached for his head with his hands and was reminded they were handcuffed.

"Ah, the colonel is awake," said Hawk smiling. "Should I put the colonel back to sleep?"

"No, we need everyone thinking," said Ice through gritted teeth, trying to maintain a smile on his face.

Feodor knew the smile was for the benefit of the guard. A Pan Am smile, fake smile in which only the zygomatic muscle is used. They needed to get into the building, but for what?

"And moreover," said Ice. "The boss wants to speak with the colonel."

If it was a ploy to distract him, it worked. Feodor now focused on what Dimitri would want to talk to him about instead of thinking of taking advantage of the situation. He still was not in any shape to do anything. Just turning to look over his shoulder had made him dizzy.

Chelsea stepped forward with the key card attached to a retractable lanyard on her belt loop and waved it in front of a pad. A small green light flashed, and the door unlocked with a click. She stepped back behind Feodor, and his head jerked forward as she started to push the chair into the building.

"Dr. Piers!" said the guard in a loud voice, both his thumbs resting on his belt. "You brought company."

Feodor thought it was more of a statement than a question. He tried to place the man's accent, probably West African.

He licked his lips and smiled. "Emmm...I've never had this many visitors at this time of the night. Is-"

There was a phew phew sound.

"No!" screamed Chelsea.

The guard glanced at his chest then back at us, a look of utter surprise on his face. Two red dots appeared on his chest, expanding as he fell backward. Even though Feodor had expected the shots, it happened so fast. He watched as all six feet and two hundred pounds of the man fell to the floor.

Chelsea whimpered. "Oh God...oh God. You didn't need to do that." She started to sob.

Ice cleared his throat. "All right, Dr. Piers, please take us to the boardroom."

"To the boardroom?" said Chelsea, her voice unsteady.

Ice stepped forward beside the wheelchair. "Yes," he said with a flourish of his left hand, the murder weapon still in his right.

Hawk held the door open, and Feodor rocked forward as Chelsea pushed the wheelchair into the lobby and past the fallen guard. Feodor stared at the guard and shook his head. His eyes were open in death. Feodor heard Chelsea whimper. *She must have known him.* All the innocent deaths he had caused this night, what a shame. And there would be millions if their plan is not stopped.

Chelsea pushed Feodor's wheelchair out of the lobby into the corridor and down a few yards to the double doors of the boardroom.

Ice pointed at the door. "Right here?"

Chelsea nodded.

He pulled the door open and held it.

Feodor stared into the darkness as Chelsea pushed him

into the room. He smelled the richness of the fine leather and polished wood. She flicked on a switch, and the room lit up, blinding him for a second. Feodor blinked and looked around; *beautiful*, he thought. Even Chelsea looked a bit surprised, maybe it wasn't like this the last time she saw the place.

Feodor looked at the two men. He could take one, but then the other would shoot him. His sacrifice would only be beneficial if there were someone else to take advantage of the diversion. There was no use trying to break the zip tie handcuff. Once it's clamped on, only a sharp tool can free you from its bondage. He might as well save his energy for something more purposeful. Feodor drew in a deep breath and exhaled. No matter how he sliced and diced it, he was not coming out of this alive.

"Dr. Piers," said Ice. "On which chair was Mr. Nikolai Masterkova sitting when he was here this afternoon?"

69

Rip

Rip called his office and notified them of what he found. With the phone in the nurse's station, he called the receptionist and asked for hospital security. His people arrived in under ten minutes.

'I didn't see anything' now sounded like a mantra amongst the people they'd interviewed so far. Once the crime scene had been secured and everyone had something they were doing, Rip focused on the man who saw everything. Personally, he believed the man was a little off, but he should at least hear him out.

"What's your name, sir?"

"Oh, Lewis Pippen. Call me Mr. Pippen. I like the private rooms and the floor, very quiet. Whenever they admit me, which is often, I ask for a private room."

"I'm Chief Chord, Chief of Police here. So, what did you see?"

"Well, I'd been sleeping and had just opened my eyes. Something must have woken me. My room was dark, and the door slightly open. When the nurse said, 'You can't go in-.' I was listening hard, trying to find out where you couldn't go into. But what I heard were two weird sounds and something heavy falling. I got out of the bed and tiptoed to the door."

The man got out and tiptoed to the door. Rip thought he made an excellent impression of the cat Tom in Tom and Jerry.

"I'd wanted to jump out and surprise them, the way I surprised you."

Rip shook his head. "I'm glad you didn't, then what happened after?"

"Perhaps they were shooting a new *Men in Black* film. You know the movie?"

Rip nodded, thankful that Chelsea hadn't gotten there yet.

"But they were both white. No Will Smith and none of them looked like Tommy Lee Jones."

"So, what happened next?"

"The man in the room must have seen them. He was trying to shut the door when they barged in, and there was all kinds of noise."

"What kind of noise?" asked Rip.

"You know, bzzz, like a fly getting zapped in one of those lights."

Probably a stun gun, thought Rip. *They needed to take Konstantin alive, but why?*

"Go on."

"Relax, don't rush me. I'll get there. They stayed awhile, then one of them came out, walked down the corridor and came back pushing a wheelchair."

"Wheelchair?"

"That's what I said. Now you're not listening. They put the old man in the chair and wheeled him away."

"How long after they left did I show up?"

"Probably less than ten minutes. If I were a betting man, which I'm not—I swore off gambling–" Mr. Pippen leaned in. "I'd say you must have passed them on the way. Perhaps in the lobby or car park."

They could be anywhere by now, thought Rip. He hoped Max and his team knew what they were doing.

"One more question, do you by any chance know where they were going? Did you hear them mention anything?"

Mr. Pippen cocked his head and gave Rip a peculiar look. "Is that a trick question?"

Rip sighed. "No, it's not. Just in case they were talking as they left and said something to each other."

"The girl asked the same question as they left."

Rip felt the hairs on the back of his neck rise. "What girl? There was somebody else with them?"

"Of course!" Mr. Pippen looked at Rip as if he'd asked a stupid question. "Somebody had to push the wheelchair." He looked at Rip and winked.

Rip leaned forward. His heart pounding. "Describe her."

Mr. Pippen shrugged. "Just a girl. Real pretty but looking scared."

"What was she wearing? Eye color, hair color…"

"Blonde hair, tall, blue eyes. Wearing a doctor's coat. They passed right in front of my door. The old man was in the chair sleeping while the two men walked on each side."

"What did they say when she asked where they were going?"

"Something like QSR or QRS,"

"Qrs, srq," murmured Rip. It didn't mean anything to Rip. "How did they say it exactly?"

"Just like that. One of the men in black said Q and the other SR."

Rip repeated the words again. Maybe that was how it sounded, but it wasn't what they meant. "Did they have an accent?"

"Everybody has an accent these days," said Mr. Pippen.

"SR...XR," murmured Rip. He has had cause to repeat similar sounding words in the past few days. He just couldn't put a finger on what context they used it, or what it was. Rip got up. "Thank you so much." He reached into his pocket and fished out his card. "Please, if you remember anything else, give me a call."

"Your office is here in Hendonville?"

"Yes, I work at the police station right on Main Street. You can always drop-." Rip stopped talking. XRCure, Q, cure, SR, XR. Said with their accent, there was no question as to where they were headed. Rip moved quickly towards the elevator hitting his speed dial. "I'm heading out to XRCure in Fargo Falls," he told the desk sergeant. "Get six men over there. No sirens, no lights. Get into security and tell them the situation. Those Russians have got Dr. Piers and our amnesia patient. I need them to review the last two hours of footage on their close circuit TV starting with the most recent moments and heading backwards. I need to know what part of the building these guys are heading to. We're looking for two men in suits with a woman, probably Dr. Piers, pushing a guy in a wheelchair. And their likely armed and very dangerous. Be particularly alert. They'll kill you before they even look at you."

"I'm on it, Chief."

70

Chelsea

C helsea soon realized that whatever was planned for tonight was bigger than her wildest imagination. But if she hadn't been at the hospital, how would they have found her? Would they have come to the house for her? She shivered. They would have come and hurt her parents; it was better they had only her.

"Doctor, we have a plane to catch," said Ice. "Where was Nikolai Masterkova sitting?"

Nervous laughter exploded out of Chelsea. "Nikolai?" The night was unraveling like an onion, each layer revealing something new. "Over...over here." She pointed to the chair where Nikolai had sat and placed both her hands over her mouth. She felt like she was about to have a nervous break- down. Only hours ago, she was trotting her stuff. Selling an idea to a billionaire, who Lisa suspected made his money from the Russian government. "What does he have to do with all this?" she blurted.

They ignored her.

Ice nodded, and Hawk bent down and looked under the table.

Hawk yelped. *"Это здесь.* It's there!" He reached under the table and pulled out a rectangular black case. He tossed the box at Ice.

Ice's eyes widened. "Нет! No!" He caught the box as one would catch a baby falling from a third-floor balcony. "Are you trying to kill us?"

"I forgot," said Hawk.

Ice eyed him. "Don't forget again." He pointed at the boardroom's star-shaped phone at the center of the table. "Get the deputy director on the phone."

Chelsea didn't know what to do. She glanced at Feodor. He still looked groggy. She had no doubt they would shoot her in the back if she tried to run. Laughter bubbled in her stomach. Who cared where she was shot? Being dead was all that mattered to them.

"Dr. Piers?"

Chelsea jerked to attention.

Hawk held out his hand with a piece of paper toward her. "Dial that number." She took the paper and dialed it.

A deep voice picked up at the second ring. "Hello."

"Sir!" said Ice standing at attention. "Colonel Konstantin is here, sir!"

Feodor tried to get up. "Dimitri-"

Ice pushed him back onto the chair.

"Dimitri, this is insane. The cold war is over-"

"It is, but we have to regain control. In 2014 we annexed Crimea. Some argue it was an attempt to return Russia to the glory of its pre-Soviet days; to that I raise my glass in a toast." Dimitri laughed. "They are correct." He laughed some more as if already drunk, then continued.

"In the past few years, China has embarked on global colonization to control both ends of the supply chain. They control the raw material source through huge loan arrangements with African, South America, and other developing countries, with the country's natural resources as collateral. And the finished product is then sold back to the same people or other parts of the world, at a premium of course."

"Okay," said Feodor. "Perhaps, they've found a better way than Russia ever did to make communism and capitalism work. What has this got to do with a virus and killing millions of people? I assume that's why we're here, at XCure."

Chelsea's blood went cold. She was all ears waiting to hear the explanation. That was her territory. She couldn't believe that all that happened tonight has now turned full circle to viruses. She saw the man called Ice place a syringe and a vial on the table along with two canisters on the table.

Dimitri laughed. "Feodor, you never see the forest for the trees." His voice boomed from the speakers. "That has always been your problem. It's all about the phrase, 'The empire on which the sun never sets.' It was a term first used to describe the European and American domains of King Charles V. Followed by the Spanish Empire of Philip II and his successors in the 16th, 17th, and 18th centuries. Then the British Empire in the 19th and early 20th centuries. The United States' global reach of power has also been described with that term. But, since the late twentieth century and into the twenty-first century, China has been quietly inching towards its goal of world dominance through whatever means they can."

Chelsea noticed the alarm on Feodor's face. He seemed to

be forming a question in his mind. She had her own questions. What was in the syringe? Her pulse started to race. She had her doubts. Ice and Hawk couldn't have come to the US just to give themselves an injection. It was either she or Feodor, or both who would be injected.

Feodor sat up in the wheelchair. "How does the plan Yurik brought fit into all of this?"

"As you already know, our friends in China isolated a new virus-Wuhan virus, COVID-19, Chinese Virus–I don't know why there's an uproar about the name. Most viruses are named after where they were first isolated. Lyme disease, Ebola, Lassa, Marburg-they're all named after where they were found. It is novel, already an epidemic, and presently has the potential to become a pandemic." Dimitri let out a breath.

"Honestly, we don't know their intentions with the virus. Maybe it was manufactured or escaped their level four labs in Wuhan. Or jumped hosts. We don't know! But what we do know is that China wants to become an empire on which the sun never sets."

"An empire on which sun never sets?" repeated Feodor. "What is that?"

Let me explain. The United States and all developed countries have either diverted their manufacturing to China or have closed their factories and shifted what's left of it to China, and then they import finished goods back from China. Additionally, developing countries have mortgaged their raw materials to Beijing. Now China holds the world by the яйца, balls. And in the next few years, it will control everything. We cannot let that happen. I cannot let that happen."

"Isn't that capitalism?" asked Feodor.

"Its free enterprise," said Chelsea. Her voice was shaky and low.

"Their own version of free enterprise," said Dimitri with a tinge of annoyance to his voice. "When a communist regime is practicing capitalism, they are not playing by the rules. It is like doping in sports. We agree nobody should dope. Then you dope, hide it well, and run a mile in one minute. And the world says, 'it's not fair', and you say 'prove it'."

Chelsea snorted. "Impossible. The best is a mile in just under four minutes."

"Точно! Exactly!" said Dimitri.

Chelsea heard the excitement in his voice. She imagined him, fat with a large head, a bulging stomach, and eyebrows that linked together.

"The virus so far has shown countries how dependent they are on China. Chinese factories are shuttered to curtail the spread of the virus within China, and countries affected or unaffected, are trying to limit spread by halting importation from China. Some people understand the situation, and some like you do not. But my job is to let everyone understand the threat China poses. If they succeed in controlling the world's supply chains, from raw materials to finished goods and services, checks and balances will be gone, and the dawn of a new empire would be upon us. We…I cannot let one country, other than Russia, be the only superpower. So, Ice and Hawk have a new product that will help people make up their minds."

Chelsea glanced at the men busy with their vials, and then back to the phone as if she could see the man whose accent-laden voice was spewing out destruction on a genocidal level.

"We have a mutation of the virus," said Dimitri. "More aggressive than the original Wuhan version. We hope to create a situation that would give the whole world pause." Dimitri chuckled. "Some people need a shocker to wake them up from slumber. America knows how to get shit done, once they see with the same lens the dangers they face. Go ask the British Empire, Nazi Germany, and the Empire of Japan. Earth was not designed for empires. They rise, and then they fall."

Chelsea had seen videos of Hitler on *National Geographic* making speeches before the Second World War, and that was what came to her mind.

"An opportunity for the west and the world to revisit its unintended decision of relegating its manufacturing to China has presented itself. This new virus, which will make its debut in New York, is airborne and as potent as Ebola, will put a demand on the world's resources. Everybody would be on lockdown, and nobody can reorder to replenish low stocks because the country where the virus took off from is the world's manufacturer. Countries like the US would bring back manufacturing to their shores, and developing countries would hold their leaders accountable for a future they are making possible for some luxuries they won't even live long enough to enjoy."

Beads of sweat sprouted on Chelsea's forehead. The man must be mad. "An outbreak in New York is an outbreak everywhere!"

Ice and Hawk stopped what they were doing and looked at her.

"Do…do, you realize the number of flights coming into and leaving New York daily?" said Chelsea in a shaky voice. "The virus will reach every nook and cranny of the world within forty-eight hours. We're still trying to understand the present version of the virus. We don't need another iteration."

Chelsea's heart pounded in her chest. Her eyes darted from the phone to the henchmen, expecting them to lash out at her. But they stood rigid as if waiting for orders. Chelsea took advantage of the little confusion.

"New viruses are like wildfire. Nobody understands them. They burn through everything in their path. We're not talking of forest brush, we're talking of people!"

"Dimitri, this will destroy us all!" said Feodor.

"Nothing can destroy us all. This is an opportunity that we cannot let go to waste. I am a patriot, and my allegiance is to Russia. Like the American statesman, Thomas Jefferson, said, 'The tree of liberty must be refreshed from time to time with the blood of patriots and tyrants. It is its natural manure.' There will be collateral damage, but we will come out stronger. A new world order will come out of this, and I have taken it upon myself to put Russia in the lead position.

Each word he said tightened an imaginary vice around Chelsea's chest. He was indeed a mad man.

There was a moment of silence. Feodor broke it.

"Why involve me? Why involve Dr. Piers?"

Dimitri laughed. "Dr. Piers is a researcher with a keen interest in virology, and is already working on this coron-avirus. If anyone should have access to it, it is her. Easy to deliver a small batch to her lab. As for you, three decades ago, we had an agreement, and you made a fool of me. They say revenge is a dish best served cold. Enjoy your meal, comrade. Bye."

The line went dead. Chelsea stared at the phone, trying to make heads or tails of what the man Feodor called Dimitri had said.

Without warning, Feodor launched himself forward. In two steps, he was upon Hawk.

"Run, Chelsea, run!" Feodor swung his handcuffed hands over Hawk's neck. He pulled the bands tight across his throat and squeezed with all his strength.

Surprised by the attack, Chelsea hesitated, then dashed for the door. Ice went after her. He dove at her, knocked her down, and drove all the air out of her. Chelsea struggled to get on her feet. Ice didn't hesitate, he drove his fist into her temple. Pain exploded in her head as her vision dimmed.

"Don't move," growled Ice. He got up and ran to the struggling men, his pistol drawn.

Chelsea couldn't move even if she wanted to. Her head throbbed with pain. Bubbles of light grew and popped everywhere she looked. Either she was spinning amazingly fast, or the boardroom was rotating like a centrifuge. She felt herself heave and moments later, a bitter taste coated her tongue. Chelsea swallowed hard, gasping. Then she heard the now-familiar sound of suppressed gunshots.

71

Rip

R ip arrived at XRCure. There was only one car in the parking lot, a 1994 Corolla. Maybe they never came here. His men had called as they were going through the footage from the hospital cameras. They'd seen the two men in suits walk from the reception area to the board room, with a woman pushing a wheelchair with an unconscious or sleeping man in it. There were no cameras in the boardroom. They then went from the boardroom to the parking lot. The vehicle they got into was out of camera range.

Still in his car, Rip looked into the all glass-walled reception area. He'd expected to see the guards head jutting out from behind the reception counter, but it was empty. Rip knew that office building security guards did hourly checks around buildings in their care; maybe that's what the guard was doing. He was tired, hungry, and defeated. Where did they take them to then?

"How long ago were they seen leaving," he asked security.

"About 3 minutes ago."

Rip brought out his cell phone and flipped through the pages of apps to a cell phone tracker app for law enforcement. He put in Chelsea's phone number and braced himself for the worst news. There was no reading. Her phone was not emitting any RFID tags. Rip needed answers, and he was running out of time. Chelsea was running out of time.

He got out of the car and opened the door to the suspended long tunnel-like corridor that led into the building. As he approached, he saw the guard lying on the floor in a pool of blood. Rip pulled out his gun and approached, eyes darting about.

He could be walking into an ambush, the only advantage he had was that he could see into the reception area. The only place someone could hide was behind the counter or waiting just outside by the entrance into the rest of the building. If he called for backup, he could alert whoever was there. Rip took a deep breath, crouched low, and pulled the door open, his eyes focused on the reception counter. The smell of death hit him, and for the next few moments, he relived an experience in Iraq. He was trapped in a Humvee that had gone over an improvised explosive device (IED) with the dead, bleeding and burning colleagues all around him. He pushed the thought away.

Rip stood close to the guard, eyes darting around, he got on one knee and reached for the man's neck. There was no pulse. Still crouched, he moved to the counter and looked behind. Nobody was there, just a chair and a desk with a book open showing the human heart, phone, and two security monitors with images from security cameras. Rip watched it as it showed the gym, cafeteria different exits out of the building, all were secured.

Rip heard a sound and ducked low. Was that a grunt? He grabbed a bunch of keys from the guard's table, crawled to the open doorway into the building proper, and tossed the key into the air. It landed with a clatter and slid several feet along the marble floor before stopping. Rip listened. He heard the grunt again and a weak call for help. It could still be an ambush. He approached cautiously. His back against the wall, Glock raised in a double handgrip. He knew where he was, and the sound seemed to come from the boardroom where he met Chelsea.

By the entrance, Rip saw the foot inside the boardroom and recognized the hospital socks. He had to go in.

"Police! Hands up!"

Feodor sat on the floor, he seemed to be clutching something in his hands.

Rip's finger tightened on the trigger, his eyes not leaving Feodor's. "Feodor Konstantin, I need to see those hands up!" Rip noticed the flicker of recognition in Feodor's eyes, and the zip tie handcuff and blood all over Feodor's hospital gown. It seemed like he had been shot in the stomach. "Anybody else here?"

Feodor shook his head slowly. "They've gone."

Rip didn't believe him and continued to search. He checked under the table and a closet in the room.

"They're gone. You are wasting time," repeated Feodor, his voice weak, hands placed over his stomach.

Rip took out a Swiss army knife from his pocket and pulled out the pliers. "Where's Chelsea?" Rip held his breath and leaned closer to snip off the plastic tie.

"They have her. Took her with them to New York."

Rips shoulders tightened. He felt like he'd been kicked in the balls. "The FSB men? I thought it was you they came for?"

"No, they came to finish the job assigned to me."

"What job?"

"Release some biological agents in the heart of New York. Anthrax and an aggressive form of COVID."

"Jesus," murmured Rip. He pulled out his phone and hit a number he had on speed dial.

"Phantom, how can I help you?"

Rip heard the background sound. They were still in the helo. "Max. I need a ride. The FSB folks took one of my people as a hostage. Can you swing by and grab me?"

"I can. Just remember you're now so indebted you might not be able to crawl out of the hole you are digging for yourself. Where are you?"

Rip told him and gave him the address.

"Okay, I can see their parking lot on my GPS. Good thing you parked the cruiser in front of the building. It would have been tight to put down the bird with the car in the parking lot."

"You can see the building?"

"Satellite, baby. We have eyes everywhere. See you soon."

"On Friday morning, Yurik came in from Moscow and told me of my new instructions. I was supposed to be retired. I disagreed with the task and the only way I could reject it was to take out Yurik."

"The dead man in your car?"

Feodor nodded. "Yurik Ivanov."

"He was burned beyond recognition."

"Good."

Rip exhaled.

"Feodor Konstantin. It took a lot of detective work to figure out who you are. The Sleeper. Top FSB asset."

Feodor shook his head. "No, I'm not the sleeper."

"A kill master," continued Rip. "You removed your fingerprints to make it a little harder to find you and, perhaps, buy time in case something went wrong. Just that nobody plans to be in an accident. The CIA was at your place, and we know you're planning a hit in New York. It wasn't very smart of you. Dedicating a whole wall to the target."

A smile parted Feodor's lip. "That was a stand-in image. I look at it and have other thoughts in my mind."

"What do you see?"

Feodor started to smile, then it faded on his lips. "You have to save the girl." He winced with pain.

Rip looked at his stomach. He had seen injuries like that in Iraq and Afghanistan, it was a death sentence and a slow one. Your body's stomach acids attack you. He pulled out his phone and called 911.

"No use calling for help. The blonde one called Ice shot me in the stomach," said Feodor. "The acid will get me."

"Help is coming."

Feodor's eyebrows narrowed. "I did not remove my fingerprints."

"Save that for the jury. Your memory is back, so what happened on Friday night."

"You have to save the girl."

"I will, just waiting for my ride. The FSB kept you as a sleeper like the Russian sleeper agents the FBI busted in June 2010-The Illegals Program they called them. Agents under non-official cover. Like you, they worked in organizations without official ties to Russia, but were supported financially by Moscow."

Feodor shook his head.

Rip continued. "It would have been better to use an asset of your caliber under some official cover with a position in the government like at the embassy, which provides you with diplomatic immunity in cases like this. When your espionage activities are discovered."

Feodor laughed, then started to cough. "You have it wrong Chief Chord, I was retired. I was trying to do the right thing. I couldn't do what was asked of me. I was looking for a place to dispose of Yurik's body and then head to Canada when suddenly an animal appeared in the middle of the road." Feodor laughed again. "I expected a deer, but it looked like a massive one-eyed cat. I was so confused that I hit the brakes and lost control of the car."

Rip stared at him with clarity coming to him. He remembered the little boy Jude and why he, Rip, was on Route 181 in the first place that night. So, there was a mountain lion.

"I took that route because there had been a reported sighting, and that was how I found you in the burning car."

"The cat must have been starving. It took a few bites off Yurik, and maybe decided I was fresher and attacked me. The fuel catching fire must have driven it away."

Rip could hear the faint sound of an ambulance and a helicopter. He stood up. "I have to go. I found the piece of paper with Chelsea Piers in your pocket. If you're not the sleeper, who is?"

Feodor sighed. Life was draining out of him. "My code name was the sleeper, but I was retired. I only found out that Chelsea Piers had always been a mole, my mole."

"Don't be ridiculous!" barked Rip. He felt a knot tighten in his stomach. It wasn't possible. "I grew up with her. I think I know her. I know her parents. We-"

"Dimitri must have known all along," said Feodor

ignoring Rip. "He said to me, revenge is a dish best served cold."

Rip cocked his head. "FSB Deputy Director Dimitri Chicherin? One of the most powerful men in Russia."

Feodor was fading. "Chelsea…she didn't even know. You have to go and save her."

"The ambulance will soon be here."

"What is she to you?" asked Feodor.

"A lost love from high school, I found her again while investigating your case."

Feodor shut his eyes. "They have an aggressive version of COVID-19 and Anthrax. They'll have Chelsea release it at Times Square."

"Times Square? How?"

"They drugged her with some hallucinogenic agent. The newspaper headlines tomorrow would say, 'Brilliant researcher kills herself, overwhelmed by the pressure to find a cure for the virus'." Feodor winced. "Hurry, they mentioned they have a plane to catch." He provided Rip information about their vehicle, how long ago they left, and the type of weapons they had.

Rip headed for the exit and met the EMT guys in the lobby. He pointed them to where Feodor was. He passed another emergency personnel bent over the guard as he ran to the parking lot just as his ride touched down.

72

Rip

"You're sure of this?" asked Max. "We don't have the luxury of an error right now."

"That's what the old man said. I don't think he would be telling a lie. He murdered the agent Yurik so the plan wouldn't be carried out. He kept insisting we save Dr. Piers."

"Isn't he the sleeper?" said Max. "This was supposed to be his *opus magnum*."

Rip was about to tell him about Chelsea being a mole when he remembered Feodor's words. *That was a stand-in image. I look at it and have other thoughts in my mind.* Was he infatuated with Chelsea for some reason?

"Rip! Where's your mind?" bellowed Max.

"Sorry, I was just trying to process the situation so far."

"I know," said Max. "It still doesn't make sense. Why would Russia want to do such a thing? An airborne virus would get back to Russia too. I'll have my people move into the area and alert the local PD. It's all hands on deck now."

"No! They see uniforms running up and down and they'll detonate it wherever they are. They have a plan. Let's get to Times Square. We know what they look like, they don't know what we look like or that we have our sights on them.

Max reluctantly agreed.

Rip thought they would land on a skyscraper in Manhattan, as close as possible to Times Square. But Max quickly informed him that since 1977 helicopters no longer landed on skyscrapers in New York City, only on designated heliports in the city periphery.

"I'll arrange for an Uber to pick us up," said Rip and started tapping the app on his phone.

Max passed Rip a black jacket. "You don't want to draw attention to yourself."

They came down at the East 34th Street Heliport and quickly got into a waiting Uber. It took them exactly fifteen minutes to get to Times Square, which was surprisingly good time to go eight blocks uptown.

Rip looked around, and there were a lot of people.

"It's like looking for a needle in a haystack," said Max. "I'm looking for two men in dark suits with a blonde woman."

"Let's use that staircase," said Rip pointing towards the Times Square 42nd Street sign over the subway station entrance. "We'll split up inside." Rip kept his eyes peeled. There were people everywhere. He commended the Russians for choosing this site as the ground zero to release the virus. Once the microbe is released into the atmosphere, virus-laden air would rise and disperse through the tunnel to other stations for maximum spread. Within minutes, a significant number of people would be exposed.

Rip saw the turnstiles and wondered what they should do. Jump over it, and a cop would appear from nowhere and draw attention to them. And worst of all, delay them before all this is sorted out.

"I'll get us tickets," said Max as if reading Rip's mind.

Max bought day passes for them. They crossed the turnstile and a few feet away was a policeman, so Rip was glad they had tickets. They walked deeper down a tunnel with people coming forward on one side and people going the other direction on the other side. Rip's eyes darted around, looking as they descended a staircase and got onto the platform proper. On each side of the raised platform was a tunnel that disappeared into the darkness with occasional flashes of light.

A gust of warm air and a distant rumbling like a dragon bellowing came from one of the tunnels. It was followed by an announcement that a train was approaching, and everyone should stand back. There was a rumbling sound as a train shot out through the tunnel at full speed. It did not stop but rattled past at top speed. What if their plan was to push her into the tracks as a train approached and detonate the bomb? Rip felt a tightness in his chest. A speeding train would do a lot of damage to the human body.

Just as swiftly as it appeared, the fast train disappeared, leaving in its wake floating pieces of paper, food wrappers, and an electric odor. More people came down the stairs onto the platforms. Rip felt that familiar sensation of another train approaching. It too burst out from the tunnel with a roar, then the air was filled with screeching as the conductor applied its brakes. Finally, it stopped. The doors slid open, and passengers poured out in a wave. Moments later, others stepped in, the doors shut, and the train took off.

The platform seemed to have lost half the people, and Rip

noticed that something was drawing everyone's attention. All had heads turned in one direction.

"Rip, over there," said Max. "They are going into the tracks."

Rip looked. "A man in a suit was already in the track pit, while the second man was helping Chelsea down. Rip's heart started to pound in his chest as he and Max raced towards them.

73

Chelsea

Chelsea felt like a picture of her should be next to the definition of the word turmoil in the dictionary. Circular bright lights, blinking and changing colors like a Christmas tree garland had been her constant companions since she opened her eyes and got out of the vehicle. Her ears had been assaulted with gurgling sounds like she'd dunked her head underwater in a swimming pool.

People with big bulging eyes stared at her, then backed away. If it weren't for the two fine men propping her up, letting her lean on them and providing support, God knows what would have happened to her by now. She relied on the two men like they were crutches. Sometimes her feet would almost give way underneath her, and they would hold her up and guide her. Right now, she was tired. The roaring sound in her head was giving her a headache.

"Mind the stairs," one of the men had said.

He had an accent. Where was she? This must be a dream, thought Chelsea. They had gone down an insane number of steps, then down a tunnel. The air rushed towards them, cool for a second, and then warm the next, bringing with it a constant wave of people, their facial features coming in and out of focus. Every few minutes there would be a rattling roar as if they were inside a blender with the blades working on a piece of metal.

Chelsea felt like throwing up, and the people around her were spinning. As if they could read minds, the men with her stopped at the end of the platform, and one of the men jumped into a dark hole.

The man stretched out his hand. "Let go, Dr. Piers. I'll catch you."

She did as she was told, and he caught her. In the background, Chelsea heard loud voices, but before she could make out what they were saying, the man tugged at her arm.

"This way," said the man.

They walked down on a rough surface, exchanging the bright lights for darkness. The screeching sound had stopped for now.

They walked for some time in the dark. Eventually, they stopped in a large, wide, dark room. At least the people with their strange faces on the platform didn't follow them. Suddenly the screeching and rumbling started again, but this time louder. Chelsea felt the vibration travel up her legs and up her whole body. She held her head between her hands.

74

Rip

"Those people are crazy dude!" said a young man sitting next to another on a wooden bench as Rip and Max passed. "They are going to make out in the tunnel. The tunnel of love."

"Is that what it's called?" said his companion. "That's wild!"

By the time Rip and Max reached the platform end, the Russians and Chelsea had disappeared into the darkness.

With the spectacle gone, people turned away to tend to their business as if it never happened. Rip wondered what happened to the slogan 'If you see something, say something'.

A slight warm breeze caressed Rips face, the telltale sign that a train was moving fast somewhere in the tunnels. That wasn't going to stop him. As long as those guys took Chelsea down there, he too was going. He took a deep breath and jumped down without hesitation. Anyone watching would think that was what he did every day in his job. Max followed.

"Do these rail lines carry a charge?" asked Max.

Rip turned around to see Max looking down, picking where he placed his feet as if in a minefield. He thought of the screeching the few times he rode the subway, and the sparks that were thrown off, and nodded.

"I should think so. I've heard about the third rail. It carries about 660 volts of electricity, enough to turn a person into barbecue."

Max looked down. "I can only see two rails."

"For now, we'll avoid touching any of the rails," said Rip. "Wow, the great Max Brandon, scared of some static shock. The trains get juice somehow."

"Shut up Phantom. You just talked about human barbecue."

Rip continued into the tunnel, engulfed by a strong electrical fire-like smell in the tunnel. Probably generated by all the friction between the rail and the wheels of the train. Even when a train was moving, it sometimes screeched, as if the driver had one foot on the accelerator and the other slightly on the breaks. Ahead of them, Rip saw a beacon of light, he removed his Glock from the holster.

"Just like old times," said Max in a low voice.

Rip turned, and in the momentary flash of light from the beacon, he saw Max's face, his eyes were alert and ready, his SIG Sauer P365 in his hand.

In addition to the risk posed by the Russians, Rip also felt in the back of his mind the constant reminder that a train could be coming from the back or maybe the front and run them over, keeping his senses very alert. They had been there only a few minutes, but it felt like an eternity.

Moments later, he felt the familiar signals that a train was on its way. In the conical tunnel, there was no place to hide. He walked faster. Cold sweat trickled down his back. There definitely was a train coming behind them. The roar got louder and louder. Would the driver stop if he saw them? They better find cover instead of betting on that.

Ahead of them was a widening of the tunnel, some type of junction with tracks going off in different directions into two more tunnels. Again Rip realized the genius of releasing an airborne pathogen in a New York City subway. The pathogens will always be floating up.

Rip knew they needed to make a decision on which tunnel to follow. Maybe they should split up.

The sound of the approaching train got louder, and now Rip could tell which tunnel the train was coming from.

Rip, and Max stepped into the shadows and stayed there as the train roared past; the men and women in the train cars were either sleeping or reading or staring blindly at them.

Once the train passed, Rip cocked his head and listened. He heard voices. The Russians must have been talking loud to be heard over the noise. Rip pointed in that direction and made the sign of people talking.

Max nodded. "Cover me." He overtook Rip, went flush against the wall, and inched ahead slowly.

Then they were upon them. One seemed to steady Chelsea while the other was a few feet away and had a flashlight which he was pointing at something. If it had been a Special Ops clandestine operation, Rip would have picked them off one by one. But, now, his focus was to try to arrest. As he pondered what to do, Max beat him to it.

"CIA! Hands where I can see them!" thundered Max. His SIG pointed at them.

The men turned around. There was only a moment's hesitation on their part. The flashlight went dead, and bullets started to fly.

Rip dropped to the ground and rolled away. He heard bullets hit where he'd been a few seconds ago. He hoped Max did the same. He didn't return fire because he didn't want to shoot Chelsea.

Max's Sig Saur roared three times.

Rip heard a cry, then something fall with a thud. He was now close enough to see Chelsea in the dimness, cowering and covering her ears. He wanted to yell for her to get down but that would only give away his position. The other shooter was unaccounted for. Feodor's words that Chelsea had been drugged flashed through Rip's mind. She didn't have it all together. He dragged himself forward on his elbows, the little noise he made camouflaged by the sound of an approaching train. He had to get to Chelsea, pull her to the ground, and keep her safe.

A figure stepped out from the dark, grabbed Chelsea from behind, and held her close. He used her as a human shield. He walked backward and, at the same time, took the messenger bag from his shoulder and put the strap over Chelsea's. Then he reached inside the bag.

Rip could guess what was in the bag. Probably the vials Feodor talked about, and explosives. Just enough to cause minimum damage and crack the vials. They wouldn't want to incinerate the contents of the tubes. With their plan uncovered, the man was probably trying to blow them up. No, he would probably have a timer, buy himself enough time to dash away. Rip reckoned five minutes.

The man started to talk just as a train approached. Rip couldn't hear him. Then the man pushed Chelsea forward and dashed back. She stumbled forward. Rip took a step toward her and froze when three shots rang out. He gasped, expecting a bullet to slam into him. Instead, he saw the running man stop as if someone had called his name.

The train roared past, and Rip heard a faint voice. It was from Max.

"Grab the girl and get out of here," said Max. "Raise the alarm so they can seal off the tunnels. The bastard got me in the leg."

Rip ran to Max and helped him up. "Can you walk?"

"With help."

"Good, you take the girl and walk out," said Rip. "That track seems to be abandoned. I'll go in as far as I can and neutralize the explosive."

Max snorted. "You're now an engineer?"

Rip didn't answer. He reached Chelsea and knew she was drugged. He took the bag off Chelsea's shoulder and strung it over his own and walked back.

"Phantom, no!" said Max.

"Go, Max! We don't have time." Rip searched the ground for the flashlight the man had dropped. He shined it towards Max and was relieved to see him and Chelsea helping each other out down the tunnel.

Rip turned around, behind him was the entrance to the tunnel with cobwebs stretched across it, broken in one area indicating that this was where the other man had entered. He brushed them away with the flashlight and started to jog further into the tunnel. If he had projected the Russian's thinking right, he'd get about three to four minutes before it went bang. Rip made up his mind. He'd run for one minute and stop and fiddle with the contents after that. He counted as he ran one thousand and one. One thousand and two.

He stopped at one thousand and sixty and flipped open the bag. He took the small black box out. Rip looked around the tunnel; there were wooden crates and empty oil drums strewn around. He placed the box on top of one of the drums. The amount of explosive would be only enough to crack the vials—and kill or maim whoever was looking over it.

Rip took a deep breath and looked at the vials. From what Feodor said, there should be COVID and anthrax in there. One was a white powder while the other was a bluish powder.

Rip had read about the 2001 attacks in the United States when letters containing anthrax were mailed to multiple media outlets, he recalled it being described as a white powder. Based on that alone, he decided the other must be the improved coronavirus.

He pulled at the vials and discovered they'd been glued onto the inner surface of the box. But where was the explosive device? Between the two vials, Rip noticed a flap of velvet on the surface. He raised it and caught his breath. The whole bottom of the box was the miniature bomb. An LCD display showed he had thirty seconds left. There must be a way to reach the components and rip all the wires out. Rip flipped the box over and found nothing. The clock was ticking.

"Knife," murmured Rip. Cold sweat dripped down his forehead. He felt in his pocket for his Swiss knife and cursed out loud. He'd left it with Feodor. But, he'd felt a bunch of keys and dug them out. He selected the key to his house door and pushed it under the vial with the blue powder.

Rip scraped the bottom of the bluish vial furiously. The glue started to separate. Adrenaline pumped through his veins as he got the COVID vial out. He didn't dare raise the flap and look at the time again. He knew he was out of time, running on fumes. He put the vial in the messenger bag, pushed it away, and focused on the tube with the white powder.

He looked at the drum. If only the opening was wide

enough, he would have just dropped the box in. Rip placed the black box with the white vial on the floor, covered it with the wooden crate, picked up the drum, and placed it on top of the container to hold back a small explosion.

Rip heard a peep, then an eruption, and was thrown backward.

75

Rip

Rip sat in his living room watching TV. He had read books he'd wanted to read for a long time and binged on TV shows and movies. Today was day fourteen of his quarantine, but even at that, New Jersey was on lockdown too.

NEWSCASTER

"The states of New York and New Jersey now have the highest number of cases and deaths from COVID-19 in the United States, the novel coronavirus that presents with flu-like symptoms. A lot of people believe the president should have closed the border with China earlier."

RIP POINTED THE REMOTE AT THE TV AND CHANGED THE

channel. He sighed. Each network seemed to have an agenda. Deciphering the news now was like listening to a debate, the same information provided from different points of view. You listened first, then decide on where the truth lay. He wished networks could go back to when the news was straight forward. They told the story as it happened and kept their opinions to themselves.

NEWSCASTER

"And in another development. The scare at Times Square two weeks ago involved the attempted release of a white powder suspected to me Anthrax by a deranged man. A man and woman had been noticed by commuters as they jumped into the tunnel. When the woman was confronted by reporters, this was her reply.

"'I went into the tunnel to fulfill a fantasy of mine before the world ended,' said the woman who asked to remain anonymous.

"They'd come upon the man who was trying to flush the powder into the subways uptake vent that empties into grates on the streets above. Remember the iconic Marilyn Monroe shot? The wardrobe malfunction when she walked over a grated vent on the sidewalk? Well, the couple talked to the man and convinced him New York City already had enough problems, and adding that to the chaos of COVID would put the city that never sleeps into a slumber it might never recover from. The man agreed with them, and on the way out of the tunnel was so remorseful that he shot himself and ended his own life. The white powder turned out to be regular talc. Over to you John."

"Thanks, Cindy." The commenter spoke in a low somber

voice. *"Such a waste of life. The couple must have powerful persuasive powers. Watch out Dr. Phil!"*

John, the newscaster, cleared his voice. The video cameras caught him from another angle.

"In another development, the drug Hyroxy...chlo...chlo... Hydroxychloroquine. The word is so hard on the tongue. No wonder mosquitoes don't like it either. The drug used to treat Malaria has-"

Rip shut off the TV. He knew the State Department could spin a yarn, but what he just heard blew his mind. He remembered that night in the tunnel, he opened the box and saw the two vials, and knew he had only enough time to get the glue out from one vial before the explosive went off. He thought of 2001, just after 9-11. Democratic Senators Tom Daschle and Patrick Leahy and some news media had received white powder in the mail. Potent spores of Bacillus anthracis, the bacteria that caused pulmonary Anthrax, a deadly disease.

In Special Ops, he had received the Anthrax Vaccine Adsorbed—AVA. Anthrax was a known quantity and could be cleaned up and treated. So, he removed the blue powder. The white powder, Anthrax, could be handled. When the bomb finally went off, he was covered in white powder, and had a mild concussion from the explosion.

Max's people had come in. Sealed up Times Square and shut down the subway system. The blue vial was retrieved, and the white powder cleaned up. Lab testing confirmed that the white powder was indeed Anthrax and the bluish one an airborne, highly contagious form of COVID-19.

Rip's phone rang. It was Max. He was also recovering from a bullet wound to the thigh. The bullet went in and out, and according to him, he would be better than new in no time. He too was on quarantine.

"Hey, just got news out of Moscow. Dimitri Chicherin is fighting for his life from a sudden and strange illness that started after consuming tea about a week ago. His hair has all fallen off, and his immune system is wiped out."

Rip chuckled. "Tea?"

"I heard the man Ukrainians fondly call *khuilo,* dick head, nearly blew a fuse when he became aware of FSB's deputy director's personal vendetta using the state resources and taking matters into his own hands. Especially putting Nikolai, one of his asset manager's, in danger, and nearly creating a rift in his friendship with the White House. After that Chicherin was invited for breakfast with another official. As they sipped tea waiting for their food, he became violently ill. His prognosis is not good."

"I won't lose any sleep over him," said Rip. "However, I did lose sleep over Konstantin. He was a gentleman to the end."

"Hearing that from you reminds us that there is still honor among thieves. I was still puzzled about his fingerprints that were removed, so I reached out to his doctor. It turned out Konstantin had terminal cancer and was being treated with a medication called Capecitabine, which causes what the doctor called chemotherapy-induced acral erythema."

Rip frowned. "Acral, what?"

"To you and me, it means pain, swelling, and peeling of the soles of the feet and palms of the hands with loss of fingerprints."

"Peeling, I can understand," said Rip.

"He must have really taken a liking to Dr. Piers. A healthy infatuation, or is there more than meets the eye? How is she doing?"

"I don't know if there's more to it. She's still holed up at her parents' apartment in Manhattan. Self-isolating, just in case. No need exposing her old folks to COVID."

"Phantom, remember our agreement, once this COVID shit is over, you have a date with destiny at Langley. Or maybe before then."

"We shall see," said Rip and hung up. They really had him cornered.

Rip put the phone down and went to the bathroom. As he washed his hands, his phone started to ring. He walked back to the living room, and his pulse began to race.

76

Chelsea

Dressed in jeans and white tee-shirt, Chelsea sat on the window ledge at her parents' apartment in Manhattan's Upper East Side. She had a good view of Central Park, which today was a shadow of its former self.

The apartment had been her parents' refuge when they got caught up in a hospital emergency or late meeting while working in the city hospitals. After they retired, her parents decided to keep it. She urged them to get rid of it, but her dad refused, saying it was a good investment. And he'd been right. It had appreciated a lot in value over the years.

Today, the apartment served as a quarantine refuge to keep her away from others for two weeks in case she had contacted COVID-19 from her ordeal. Chelsea was also tested for anthrax. It came out negative, but she still received prophylactic treatment just in case.

Chelsea's gaze returned to Central Park. Apart from the trucks and soldiers dressed in military fatigues offloading crates from trucks, there was not a single soul in the park. Not even a solitary person walking a dog. New York City was indeed on total lockdown.

While watching New York's governor's daily briefings about the pandemic on TV, she read that the government was setting up a temporary tent hospital to care for the rising incident of COVID-19 patients; hospitals were getting overwhelmed. The disease was now a pandemic, and the military had been called in to engage an enemy, albeit an invisible one, unlike any war the world has ever known. It was a war against humanity, perpetrated by humanity. It was not a war about land acquisition, pride of country, or self-defense. It was a war of dominance over humankind that could never be won.

Chelsea knew that it was President Franklin D. Roosevelt's now-famous speech that had signaled the beginning of World War II. All she could remember of it was the word infamy. She opened her smartphone and asked Siri to find FDR's speech about infamy. She listened.

"YESTERDAY, DECEMBER 7, 1941, A DATE WHICH WILL LIVE in infamy, the United States of America was suddenly and deliberately attacked by naval and air forces of the Empire of Japan."

CHELSEA HIT THE HOME BUTTON AND CUT OFF THE REST OF the speech. Would that night, two weeks ago, live in infamy for her too?

The day had started on a good note with their company

getting the funding they needed, her mother's confession and apology for messing up her childhood, and her belief that something happened in The Algarve, Portugal the night she was born. Then there was the Russian who could be her biological father. Looking back at those events earlier that day, those were ominous signs of things to come.

Then she'd gone to see the Russian and everything went downhill from there. She was injected with a hallucinogenic agent that rendered her useless. She didn't even need to close her eyes to relieve the experience of that night. It was just there, vivid. The smells, sights, and sound of the subway. The electric fire-like odor, the screeching of brakes, and the blast of warm air that caressed her skin each time a train rushed past the platform.

Chelsea remembered the old Russian and his words when he saw her the first time: *you look just like your mother*.

Short of doing a DNA ancestry test, Chelsea was convinced that the man Feodor was indeed her biological father. Too many coincidences.

From what Rip had pieced together, Feodor Konstantin was an assassin for the Russian government. After an illustrious career, he asked to be furloughed in New Jersey. Rip told her about what he said when he asked him about the wall in his apartment with the picture of the waterfront piers. It was a stand-in image. To her, it meant looking at one Chelsea Piers and thinking of another.

He had marked himself for death when he eliminated the man they'd sent earlier to have her kidnapped and blown up in Times Square. Who would murder for someone that meant nothing to them? Like the saying goes, there's no smoke without fire. But she would leave it at that. The father that raised her was the best father any girl could have ever wished for. It saddened her that all he had left now were pockets of memory.

Chelsea decided to call Rip. She'd spoken with her parents earlier, and her mother asked after him. She wanted to make amends.

"Hi, Rip."

"Chelsea, what's up?

"Tomorrow is your last day of self-quarantine, right?"

"Right."

"My mom would like to have you over for dinner some-time. She owes you an apology, and I owe you one too and want to apologize face to face. When do you think you can make it to the house?"

There was a pause. "I know tomorrow is your last day too. But what part of social distancing don't you understand? And your parents are in the vulnerable age bracket."

Chelsea giggled. "In that case, we can meet somewhere. Just the two of us, and plan for dinner with Mom and Dad after all this is over. We're both essential workers, you know, so it should be okay for us to meet." Chelsea felt like a teenager again. Maybe they could pick up from where they left off. She wasn't attached, and neither was he.

Rip paused. "What-"

"Just kidding," said Chelsea. But she wasn't kidding. She wanted to see him and start making amends. This time she would not let him get away.

"No, you're not. Anyway, I'll be getting back to work tomorrow too," said Rip. "It's been a while, and they need all the help they can get." Rip laughed. "Looking forward to hearing your apology, sixteen years in the making. Better late than never."

"I'll be back in Sussex County tomorrow," said Chelsea. "I've been working from home. But I'll need to get into the lab. There won't be anyone there. They are all working remotely. The computer team we acquired has been doing great, and I'm positive we'll conquer COVID-19 and come out stronger. You think you can make it to XRCure tomorrow to make sure I got in okay?" She paused. "I'll make it worth your while."

Rip's breath caught. "What time should I be there?"

EPILOGUE

The big cat leaped from the tree and landed on the hiking trail, its execution, flawless. It glanced to its left, then to its right. Its rich reddish-brown short and coarse fur looked burnished under the early morning sun. It looked again, left, then right, made up its mind and, in one hop, landed on a massive boulder overlooking the trail.

The cat raised his head and sniffed the air, its ears twitched; it was not alone. It picked up an array of sounds, birds tweeting, different variations of the *eep, eep, eep* of squirrels and chipmunks. The crushing of leaves and snapping of dry branches under the hooves of deer. The faint rumble as fat groundhogs broke out of their holes and ran on the grass, enjoying the morning sun. What it didn't hear was human voices close to the trail, or the groan of car engines on the highway not too far away.

In recent times, there had been an abundance of game. The mountain lion glanced at these potential food sources, and then looked away uninterested. The animals, too, were aware of the big cat but didn't feel threatened. The environment felt different. The landscape of fear they were used to had vanished overnight.

The animals knew by instinct that the super predator that had consciously and subconsciously dominated their lives had taken a hiatus.

Animals like the mountain lion that hid away most of the day now spent more time out in the open. Those more nocturnal came out during the day.

Animals were aware of their landscape; they knew it had changed, but probably did not know that a pandemic had occurred among humans and promoted their lockdown. With time, the super predator would regain its foothold, and animals that had lost their fear of people would be the most in danger.

Animals that once stayed away from parkways and high-ways would perhaps take time to reverse and resume their avoidance. Some would be put down by speeding cars and trucks.

On the sixth week of the lockdown, as the mountain lion raced across Highway 181 after a small doe, an eighteen-wheeler was also making the rounds. The driver never felt the impact and kept driving.

When Rip drove to work early the next morning, he was drawn to take the long way, up 181. When he came across the dead animal in the road, he stopped, turned on his strobe lights, and got out of the car.

He looked at the small doe for a long time. It reminded him of how fragile and precious every life is. The mountain lion watched, crouched in the brush, more wary now, waiting for his prey.

THE END

ABOUT THE AUTHOR

Ion Esimai is the author of *The Sleeper's Mole.* An intriguing thriller that sets the stage for a head-on collision between the superpowers of Russia, China, and the US. He lives with his wife and children in Northern New Jersey.

www.ingramcontent.com/pod-product-compliance
Lightning Source LLC
Chambersburg PA
CBHW031608100726
47898CB00006B/1698